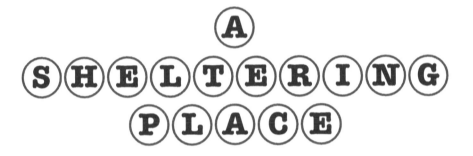

A SHELTERING PLACE

Musings of an Iowa Farm Boy

by

Kēvin Callahan

FLYING KETCHUP PRESS ®
KANSAS CITY, MISSOURI

Acknowledgments

Appreciative acknowledgment to the Lenox Time Table in which all the following stories previously appeared.

Copyright © 2022 Kevin Callahan

Copyright © 2022 Illustrations and photographs are the property of Kēvin Callahan and may not be reproduced.

Flying Ketchup Press® is a trademarked small press in Kansas City, Missouri. Find us at www.flyingketchuppress.com

All rights reserved. Except in the case of brief quotations or reviews, no part of this publication may be reproduced or transmitted in any form or by any means without written permission from the publisher. The events, characters and descriptions depicted in the stories are written from the authors memories.

All inquiries should be addressed to:

Flying Ketchup Press
11608 N. Charlotte Street
Kansas City, MO 64115

Library of Congress Control Number:
2 0 2 2 9 4 4 7 5 9

Callahan, Kevin, A Shelting Place: Musings of an Iowa Farm boy

Softcover ISBN-978-1-970151-44-2
E book ISBN- 978-1-970151-51-0

Other Publications by the Author

Road Map: *Poems, Painting, & Stuff*

Available on Kindle by the Author

Morris' Code
A Day Remembered
Chinese Checkers Run
Shorts Stories

Thank You

Thank you to Polly Alice McCann who believed in me.

A special thank you to JoAnneh Nagler
for the many hours of editing and conversations
designed to set me on the correct path.

Dedication

This book is dedicated to:

My Mom, Ruby

My Dad, Bob

My Grandparents, Fin and Lottie Gray and especially

My Great-Grandparents, William and Mary Gray who had the courage and the fortitude to move half-a-continent away to pioneer a new life on the Iowa prairies.

Also, that little boy growing up and running free on the Iowa prairies, who yet lives inside me.

My Sheltering Place

My hometown is my sheltering place
The place that long-ago invested in me
A place where decade upon decade
I trek to revisit Myself

Returning in October when the land dons new attire
Sharp frosts trigger greens fading to brown
The prairie imbued red, yellow and orange
intermingled with yet-verdant foliage battling transformation

Mother Nature dyes the land,
Her palette of soft yellows and browns, punctuated by slashes and
smears of primary colors
America's heartland becomes a patchwork quilt
spreading over rolling hills and gentle valleys, from Ohio to the Rockies.

The reasons I seek my youthful self are as vast as stars in the sky
Habit scarcely explains clinging to this ritual
Simplest answers: family and friends
My identity native to my pastoral beginning

In life, I have traveled far from the land of my youth
Far in miles/Far intellectually
When I come to reclaim memories of my sheltering place
Welcome awaits, and friends gather 'round

For a few days,
(contrary to the musings of Thomas Wolfe)
I do go home again

So very many years ago, searching for a way to leave
I was forging a pathway to stay
Season after season returning to my origins
I rediscover my sheltering place

Table of Contents

Callahen, Kevin
5235 Walt St
Kansas City   MO   64151-3173

75¢

THE LENOX
TIME TABLE
© 2019 RCL Production Co.
www.thelenostimetable.com

Periodicals Postage Paid at Lenox, Iowa USPS 310-020
E-mail timetable@lenoxia.com

Volume 143

Wednesday, January 09, 2019

Number 02

Fred Haynes recalls early days of Lenox

Steve Hill to Qatar

Local historian Fred Haynes

Forward

I began penning these stories of my youth years ago when my boys were still young. Often there were long gaps before I would be inspired to write the next story. The tales were not, by any means, writen in any particular order. It was up to me, in organizing this book, to provide a chronological telling. Many of the themes I touch on are repeated. Themes of great grand parents, my love of westerns, etc. As each story was meant to stand alone repeated themes serve to ground the reader. When I was invited to gather these stories into one place I made a conscious decision to leave each story as a stand alone piece. It is my contention that many of the important happenings in our lives bear repeating.

—*Kevin Callahan*

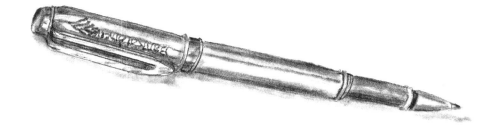

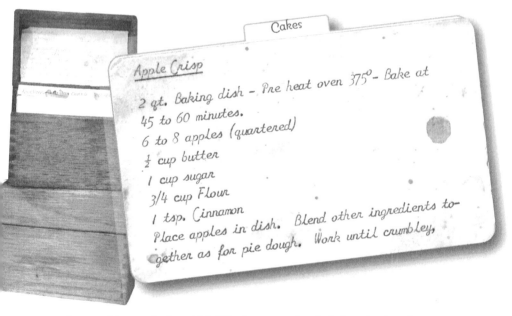

Cakes

Apple Crisp

2 qt. Baking dish - Pre heat oven 375° - Bake at
45 to 60 minutes.
6 to 8 apples (quartered)
½ cup butter
1 cup sugar
3/4 cup Flour
1 tsp. Cinnamon
Place apples in dish. Blend other ingredients together as for pie dough. Work until crumbley.

I wrote this story in the mid-1990s for my son Brad's 3rd-grade class. Parents were invited to write a story and then read it to the class. This tale began many years of storytelling about life on the farm in the 1950-70s.

Life on the Farm

I was born in 1953 in Lenox, Iowa, a small town in the southwest portion of the state. I spent my entire childhood out on a farm. Our first farm was 3 1/2 miles south on a gravel road; it was 80 acres and had a pond and a creek. My father raised hogs, cattle, corn, soybeans, and oats. My mother raised chickens and children.

Our little patch of ground situated on an Indian burial ground, and when the rains would wash out gullies on the hillsides, we would find arrowheads and other stone implements left by the ancient tribes. Our house was a ramshackle affair; it was initially a one-room trapper's shack that had been added onto room by room over the years, and it was a bit creaky. We didn't have indoor plumbing, so our bathroom was an outhouse about thirty yards from the back door.

We did have indoor running water, cold. One of my earliest memories was of my father crawling under the house to install a new water pipe and water heater; then, we had both hot and cold water in the house. Boy, we thought that was something. Before Dad installed hot water, we took baths only on Saturday night. A bath was a tricky affair as we had to heat water on the stove in large pans then pour them into a big round tub that, on bathing-day, sat in the middle of the dining room. When the girls took baths, the boys had to leave the house.

The only heat in the house was an oil heating stove in the dining room. In the winter, when it got frigid, we would hang blankets over the door-ways so that all the heat would stay in that one room and the kitchen. Our bedrooms were unheated, so us kids slept under a pile of homemade quilts, quilts sewn by Mom, Grandma Gray, and Great-grandma Wheatley. Each morning when we got up, we'd would run downstairs to stand by the stove to put our on clothes and get warm.

We also had a storm cellar, just like in the movie *The Wizard of Oz*. In the summer, when tornadoes would come, we would all go outside to hide in the storm cellar in the middle of the backyard. It was dark, wet, cold, and crowd-ed with no place to sit down. But, it was better than being sucked up into a tornado, at least I thought so.

I loved to run all over the farm. I spent most of the time playing Cowboys and Indians. I would climb the windmill or swim in the pond. When I was bigger, about eight years old, I liked to camp out on the creek; sometimes, I would spend two or three days by myself camping and fishing and playing with my dog. We had lots of pets–two dogs, and more cats than we could keep track of. When we would milk cows, the cats would stand and wait to have milk squirted into their mouths.

For a while, I had Rocky a pet raccoon. We got it when it was a kitten, but it grew very fast. It was fun to watch, and when it ate, it always washed its food first. We gave the raccoon bread and milk, and when it washed the bread in the milk, the bread disappeared, and Rocky couldn't figure out what happened. We laughed so hard at that little raccoon, but the bread and milk meals didn't last long. When Rocky grew, the critter would climb on the screen door and rock back until the door swung open and then slip inside and steal food. Mom would get really mad. Finally, Dad said my pet was too big and hard to handle, and he gave it away. I cried and screamed, but it didn't help, the raccoon had to go.

Of course, on the farm, everyone had chores. When I was five, my job was to feed and water our chickens, morning and evening, then after school,

2

"Iowa Barn with broken windmill"

gather up the eggs. Now, my Mom liked chickens. Every spring, she would buy about one thousand baby chicks. By the summer, they would be grown enough to eat. We sold them to other people who didn't want to raise them.

When people bought our chickens, we would butcher ten, twenty, even thirty chickens at a time. Mom would boil large buckets of water, and we had an old stump with two nails driven into the top about two inches apart. I would grab a chicken, put its head between the nails, stretch its neck out, and chop off the head with one blow of a hatchet. The dead chickens were placed into an empty bucket so they wouldn't flop around after they were dead. Then, as quickly as we could, holding them by their lower legs, we would dunk them in the boiling water and pull off all their feathers. We always had snowball fights throwing handfuls of wet feathers at each other until Mom would get mad and make us stop.

With all of these chickens, we also had eggs. As I said, my job was to gather the eggs after school every day. I would have to check in each chicken house and look under the setting hens. I hated this because sometimes the birds would peck me. The chickens didn't just stay in their coops, they would wander all over the farmyard and into other buildings, so I had to look ev-

3

erywhere to find the eggs. I would get a five-gallon bucket full of eggs nearly every day. One day, running back to the house, down I fell, breaking almost all of the eggs in the bucket. Boy, Mom was mad.

I started school when I was five. The school was one and one-half miles up the road with grades kindergarten through eighth grade in one room with one teacher. My brother and I walked to and from school everyday rain–snow, and shine. My older sisters had done the same, but they had already graduated from town school. On really nice days Mike and I would stop and swim on the way home. If Dad caught us, we got whipped; he worried about us drowning.

There were three kids in my kindergarten class, and when we started second grade, everyone had to go to the town school. One of the three children from kindergarten moved to another town, but the other little girl and I went all the way through thirteen years of school together.

It was a lot of fun and a lot of hard work to grow up on a farm. I enjoyed the freedom of the outdoors. But I didn't have many friends, as my closest playmate was a mile away. I still like to go back to the farm and take my boys so they can see where Dad grew up. One time when we visited the barn, the boys saw baby pigs being born. There were a series of three ponds connected by a shallow creek that ran from north to south. The first pond was north of us on our neighbor's farm and was known as the swimming hole. It was maybe a quarter-acre, shallow, and mud-filled.

The swimming hole fed a small pond that lay just north of our fence line. It was called the Crawdad Hole. The small pool and the shallow creek that fed it overflowed with crawdads (crayfish). We would often catch them by the bucketful, using the smallest for bait then we'd let the rest go. Some, a few, were as large as small lobsters with large, fearsome claws that would deliver a painful pinch if you weren't careful when you handled them. We never ate them, but now that I am older and have thoroughly enjoyed eating crawdads in New Orleans, I often regret not partaking as a child.

The third pond was on our farm and was known as the Fishing Hole, and fish it had. We caught Bluegill (sunfish) the size of dinner plates, bullhead, great croaking bullfrogs, and giant snapping turtles. The Fishing Hole teemed with life. It was here that my older siblings and I learned to swim.

In our backyard, a few yards from the door was an old hand pump. We used water from this pump for many things, including getting a drink of cold well water on a hot summer day. One day Mom asked for a bucket of water from the pump, so my brother and I went to the pump and started pumping. Soon the pump gushed cool, clear water, then *plop*! A nice medium-sized frog. I do believe the frog was just as surprised as we were. Just think of it from the frog's standpoint, one minute, Mr. Frog is floating lazily thirty or forty feet down in a deep dark hole when he's sucked up a pipe and quite unceremoniously delivered back into the sunlight, shot into a tin bucket. We looked at each other across the bucket, laughed, then fished out the frog and carried the water to Mom. We never mentioned Mr. Frog.

Mother Could Shoot

My mother, Ruby, was a fiery redhead. She was generous of heart but also had a quick temper. One thing few knew about Mom was that she could shoot. In the front yard of our first farm, there was a row of pine trees growing close together with low hanging branches that brushed the ground. Often, especially on cold winter mornings, we would discover the lower limbs lined with pheasants huddled out of the wind. If Mom were in the mood for a fresh bird, she would merely stick the shotgun out of the door and fire away. Us boys were then directed to clean the birds for dinner.

I was born on that farm and lived there until I was twelve years old. The most memorable feature was the lack of indoor plumbing. One tends to remember this, especially in the winter, when I am most thankful for the multiple bathrooms I have in my current home.

6

I remember every speck of black dirt and every dusty cobweb in the corners of the house and the out buildings. I remember the shrieking of the old windmill that pumped the water up for the cattle. And the house-lot sized garden we kept in the summer. Oh, there is so much I remember.

For several years we had a Hereford bull we named Sammy. Sammy was as gentle as he was massive. When Sammy would lay down in the pasture in his majestic repose, my brother and I would clamber all over him, petting his ears and perching on his tabletop-sized back. He would never move a muscle until we were off his back and safely away. Sammy became a character in another of my stories.

Years ago, 1999, if I remember correctly, I drove out to the old place and was pleased to see the barn was still standing. The original barn burnt in 1948, under mysterious circumstances, before I was born. My father and grandfather rebuilt the one that still stands as I write this. I spent the afternoon recording it in my sketchbook.

I remember milking cows in that old barn and sometimes squirting the milk into the mewing cat's mouths. I remember Old Joe Probasco lining a steer up against the side of the barn where Joe would shoot it from about five feet away with a single shot from a .22 rifle. In my youthful exuberance, I would always shout, "Good shot, Joe!" Then, in the nearby shed, the steer then butchered into steaks, hamburger, and roasts. We had no money, but we ate well.

Mom and me—I was three months old.

7

Quick Coffee Cake
1 3/4 cups sifted flour
2 1/2 tsp. baking powder
1/2 tsp salt
1/3 cup sugar

1 well-beaten egg
1/2 cup sweet milk
1 tsp. vanilla
1/4 cup butter

Sift flour, baking powder, salt and sugar together. Cut in the butter. Add egg and milk and stir vigorously until well blended. Add vanilla. This makes quite a stiff dough. Spread it in greased 9 or 10 inch pan and brush top of dough generously with melted butter. Mix together 1/3 cup sugar, 1 Tbsp.

Counter Checks

You know how, when you look through binoculars backward, everything is smaller and far away? That's how reflecting on your life sometimes seems to me. We all remember our past with a certain gauzy nostalgia. That simpler life we all reflect upon with tales to bore our children. The same as our parents did us. In other words, the good old days.

I grew up on a rural farm, in a rural town, in a rural state. It is somewhat remote, even today. Back in the mid-1900s, it was more so. Lenox located forty-five minutes from any Interstate highway and is two hours from the closest major city. Until the early 1970s, the roads around our part of the world were old, narrow, and winding. Interstate 35 running out of Des Moines and south to Kansas City ended at the Iowa border. There was a twelve-mile gap that connected the interstate via a two-lane highway, which wound through a couple of small towns before it re-connected. I-35 wasn't connected until 1978. All this I write, so you the reader, can begin to understand how many of the inventions and conventions of post-WWII life had not fully caught up with our little town, even as late as 1970.

I was three years old in 1956 when my mother took a job in town. My father was a farmer but not a prosperous one. With four children, we needed the income. My little sister would arrive as a surprise six years later. I can still remember Mom going around to the gas station and grocery on Saturdays after she was paid. I don't know how much she earned, but it surely wasn't much. She would take $20 and pay off what had been charged the previous week on our accounts.

The merchants in town ran nearly all their businesses on charge accounts. Of course this was before the days of ATM's and charge cards. As such, it was not unheard of for an unfortunate family who incurred too much debt to leave town in the dead of night. The many merchants would then be stuck with the debts. This remembers the many businesses that every small town supported back before the big box stores and the Internet. Our village was comprised of 1200 souls, more or less. The outlying farms added quite a few more. The 1960s were the heyday of the small farmer in the Midwest. Nearly every square mile supported six to eight families. Those families came to towns like Lenox for all their shopping, groceries, gas, clothing, and produce. At one time, Lenox had several gas stations, three groceries, men's clothing and women's clothing stores, four bars, an auction barn, and a healthy bank.

Well, that was then–times change. Today the vast majority of people have moved off the farms and into the larger towns and cities. Most farms are several hundred to several thousand acres, each, and the small farmer is a relic of bygone days. So too are the many merchants that were supported by the local

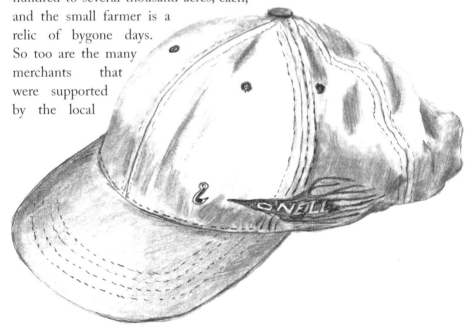

economies. Today it is a comfortable ride to the Walmart, or even easier, a mere log-on to have items delivered to your door. So, it goes.

I do recall one custom that has disappeared from the landscape of America: the counter check. If one went anywhere up to 50 miles from home, they rarely carried a checkbook. My father might drop into a tavern say in Corning, eleven miles from our farm. If he ran out of cash and wanted to stay longer, he'd merely point to the back of the bar and ask the bartender to write a check on the Lenox Bank. Stores generally kept a handful of check blanks from ten to twenty banks in their immediate vicinity for everyday use by patrons from other communities.

I can still remember the loud discussions that would ensue when Mom would balance the checkbook then express her opinion on the stack of $5, $10, and $20 checks that would show up from around the area. The man behind the bar would write out the amount, and Dad would sign the check. Often, his signature was barely legible, attesting to his lack of sobriety when signing. Yeah, nostalgia has its limits.

Nearly every business in small town America kept a stock of "counter checks" on hand; most especially bars. This is an image from the Gladbrook, Iowa bank circa 1929.

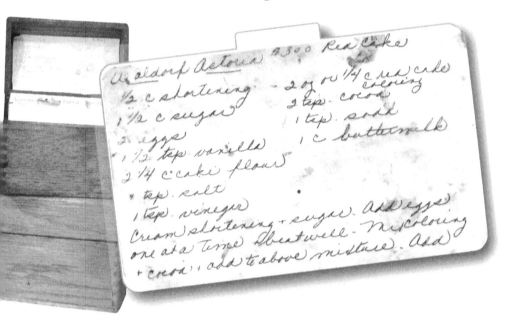

John Deere Cowboy and the Last Cattle Drive

"You better get to bed and get some sleep. We're driving a herd of cattle up to your granddads tomorrow. Your brother has to work in town, so you're going to drive the tractor." This terse instruction came from my father. It was the summer of 1962, and I was all of nine years old. The pasture on our 80-acre farm in Iowa could not support the number of cattle we had grazing on it, so we needed to relocate a dozen head ten miles north where Grandpa Gray had a large pasture and fewer cattle. Not wanting to pay to have them trucked, dad decided we (he and me) would just drive them ourselves.

Through the 1950s and early 1960s, the Cowboy was king in movies and on that recent invention, television. Like many rural families, we did not get our first TV until 1959. My dad wouldn't have one around, but us kids saved our money and convinced him to let us buy a used set. Trust me, I was glued to every episode of Roy Rogers, the Lone Ranger, Gunsmoke, and any and all western series or movies shown on that box. In fact, in 1959, you could still listen to Gunsmoke on the radio on Monday night and then watch a new episode on TV on Saturday.

Have Gun Will Travel, Rawhide, these and a host of others became my Cowboy Bible. You would seldom find me without boots, hat, and guns (cap guns, .45s of course) unless I was doing chores. When I chored, I had to put on my four-buckle overboots as stepping around the animal lots could be a messy event on a good day. My normal wear to chore in was an old pair of blue jeans with a hunting knife slung from my belt. I'd purchased the official Boy Scout hunting knife with the Green Stamps I'd managed to save, and the knife proved a useful tool. I used it to cut sticks, skin rabbits and squirrels, gut fish, and any task requiring a blade. Heck, I even slew the odd imaginary enemy with it. No matter where I went, there was also a pocketknife in my pocket. A habit I have to this day. As a matter of fact, I bought myself a new three-blade knife that year, and I still have it today. Of course, today, I have to make allowances for airplane travel.

The next morning I was up early and off to do my chores. Chores meant feeding the chickens, gathering eggs, checking waterers and hog feeders and refill if needed. Normally after chores on most summer days, I would have been free to loll around the farm, perhaps go fishing, or head off to town to swim, but today we were cowboying cattle on a real cattle drive. I'd donned working clothes, which consisted of work boots, jeans (with the aforementioned knives), t-shirt, and ball cap. In farm country, the ball cap was the preferred chapeau for most males young and old. There was seldom much variety.

You can bet if you met a local farmer, his cap would have one of a small handful of logos: Pioneer, John Deere, Garst, or IH. Thus, announcing their particular affiliation with an implement or seed company. If said caps were removed, which was only in bed and in church as far as I could tell, one was treated to a high white dome, where the sun did not penetrate. Young boys often wore the same type of caps as their dads, but as often as not, they might have on a cap with their school or Little League team logo. I sported a team hat that year when (if I remember correctly) I played for the Yankees.

Mom set out our breakfast, then headed off to town to her job at the feed store. Dad and I ate quickly and tossed our dishes in the sink. Ten miles is not very far, but it is a long way to walk a meandering herd of confused cattle. It was time to get started on our journey. I'd begun driving the tractor a year before, at the age of eight, and already I felt like an experienced hand. I could hook up wagons and drive them out to the fields and haul the grain back to the house. I was old enough now to drive the tractor while the men put up hay bales. On the farm, as soon as you were judged old enough for a task, you were "promoted" to that work and expected to get the job done correctly. Today I had been promoted to driving the tractor on the open road.

Of course, I'd been around farm animals all my life, so the cattle were like pets to me–stubborn pets, however. A bovine is generally not a mean thing, but they are headstrong. When they get it in their head to go somewhere, they usually just go in the direction they happen to be pointed at that moment. That, of course, was going to be the challenge today. To keep a small herd of large animals going where we wanted them to go, and not where they did.

Dad had penned our charges up in the lot the night before. All we needed to do to get started was open the gate and head them towards the road. It was the road that represented our looming challenge of the day. Where we lived was extremely rural, so traffic was not a problem. Drivers here were quite used to encountering livestock or large farm implements on the road and knew the routine of staying out of the way. In our case, we had ten miles of gravel road that were crossed by other roads at every mile, farmsteads with wide driveways all along the route. The last quarter mile to Grandpa's was on a highway and could prove to be treacherous as any cars we met would be traveling at a high rate of speed. Also, the steep ditch dropped away from the highway and was far too deep to get the cattle off the road.

Dad pulled his battered International truck out of our driveway, blocking the road going south. He ambled back down the drive and spoke. "Now you're sure you know what you're doing?"

"Yes, sir."

"You've got to drive real slow and keep your eye on the cattle and watch out for traffic at the same time. OK?"

"I can do it."

Today my horse was a Deere-green ten-year-old John Deere–B, parked next to the feedlot blocking the lane along the fence, so the herd had only one direction to go, out toward the road. The John Deer-B was, by today's standards, a small tractor. But back then, it was a full-sized field tractor. The B was a two-cylinder with four speeds and a hand clutch. We called it a Johnny Popper from the sound the motor made when it was running at full speed, and you throttled it back. *Ur, gurgle, Pop!, pop, pop, pop.* Dad walked back to stand by his truck, and I swung open the gate to begin moving our herd to greener pastures.

I walked to the far end of the lot and started gently prodding and pushing my bewildered charges out through the gate. I'd wave my hat and slap them on the rump barking, "Hi, you, get going, hey!" Once I got the first couple through the gate, the rest followed like, well… cattle. I worked the herd down the drive and onto the road. Dad then took over and moved them a few yards farther up the road past our open front yard. Jogging back, he jumped into his truck and waited while I climbed aboard my green pony. Pushing the starter button, the old B popped into wakefulness, and I eased the hand clutch forward. At the mouth of the drive, Dad pulled away and slowly drove his truck ahead of the cattle. I eased in behind the herd, shouting to keep them on the move. We were off and fortuitously heading in the right direction.

The first quarter-mile told the tale, as that was where the first crossroads intersected. As dad approached an intersection, he'd park the truck blocking one side, then hustle across the road to block the other. I came along behind, shouting and pushing. Once safely past, he'd ease the truck around the cattle again, taking the lead. Slowly, painstakingly we made our way, mile after mile. Periodically I had to stop the tractor and leap off the high seat to head one of the hardheaded calves back to their proper path. Farmhouses were the worst as they had driveways and no fencing in their yards with lots of open space. It was challenging to keep cattle from straying. At one farmhouse, three hard cases made their break for freedom, trotting back behind the buildings. It took both Dad and me to drive the Quick Break Three, the cattle that escaped, from around the outbuildings and back onto the road. One escapee would hide behind a shed, and when we'd move it out, it would break back, then all three would go in different directions. I can still see the face of the bemused farm wife watching us through her kitchen window, chasing strange cattle around in her backyard.

It took us all morning and into the early afternoon to walk those beasts the ten miles to Grandpa's farm, but by mile five, they were trail savvy. At mile nine, we turned the corner and headed straight west towards the highway. When we arrived at the crossroad, Dad sped the quarter-mile to Grandpa's drive and blocked off the road from any oncoming traffic. I puttered along on the tractor with my charges, knowing that I was only minutes away from one of Grandma Gray's famous workingman lunches. I knew she'd be ready to feed her "cowboys" and feed us well.

That was the one, and only, cattle drive I remember us doing on the farm. To this day, I'm not positive why Dad undertook to do it in such a fashion. I just remember that I was always proud that at the age of nine, I was trusted with such important work. Of course, when we finished our lunch, my task was not yet complete. Dad waved goodbye and said he'd see me at home. My job was to drive the tractor back to our farm by myself. And of course, I did. That was the first of many times I was entrusted to haul wagons and equipment between the farms.

You know, I still own a John Deere today. It's only a small garden tractor, but when I'm driving it, I sometimes get that same feeling I did when I was nine. Only today, there are no more cattle for me to move.

Rooin' Tootin' Cowboy – Christmas 1960.

15

Devils Food Cake
2 cups sifted flour
1 tsp. soda
¼ tsp. salt
½ cup sugar
½ cup shortening

¾ cup Karo
2 eggs unbeaten
½ cup cocoa
1 cup milk
1 tsp. vanilla

Sift flour once, measure and add cocoa, soda, and salt. Sift together. Cream shortening and sugar; then add syrup gradually. Add eggs one at a time and beat well after each. Then add flour alternately with milk. Add vanilla and bake in 2 greased cake pans.

Lessons from Old Yeller

Arliss Coates: *Why did you shoot Rosemary?* (the cow)

Travis Coates: *She was sick.*

Arliss Coates: *Well, you were sick. How come we didn't shoot you?*

Travis Coates: *That was different.*

I was four years old in 1957, the year the movie Old Yeller played on the big screens. In the typical fashion of the times, it took a couple of years for the film to make it to our little theater. Some critics have deemed Old Yeller the finest boy/dog movie ever made. Probably so.

For those few who may not be familiar with the tale, it is the story of a family on the Texas frontier, post-Civil War. Father is off on a cattle drive, so Mom and her two sons are left to tend the farm. From seemingly no-where, a large yellow dog appears and ingratiates himself into the family. He is christened "Old Yeller" and quickly becomes an indispensable member of the household.

In one pivotal scene, Old Yeller defends the older brother from a rabid wolf getting bitten in the battle. Confident that their now beloved pet will contract the deadly disease Old Yeller is quarantined in the corncrib, chained

16

to the wall. When Old Yeller exhibits symptoms, there is no recourse but to have him destroyed.

Travis: *No, Mama!*

Mama: *There's no hope for him now. He's sufferin'. You know we gotta do it.*

Travis: *I know Mama… But he was my dog… I'll do it.*

By the time the movie finally made its way to our tiny theater, I was six or seven years old. My sister Margaret Ann took me to town and sat through the movie with me. To this day, I can remember that we sat halfway down the theater on the left-hand side. I sat next to the wall, rapt with the story. In no small part because the little brother reminded me very much of myself. The life of a small boy running free on the prairie having adventures with his dog, I thought, was pure magic.

Then came the dramatic high point. There was no hope for the dog. Even at my tender age, I understood. I did. But… to be forced by life to give up the very thing you loved because it was best for the poor suffering dog? Well, that was just too much for one small boy.

Travis stepped up like the fine young man he was, and the deed got done. In typical Disney fashion, the movie ended on a high note. Cue the happy music and see the boy running with his new puppy, the progeny of Old Yeller himself. I sat stunned through the credits, then began to cry. Then sob. I was inconsolable. The lights came up, and we were the only ones left in the theater. Finally, Margaret Ann had to pick me up and carry me, still sobbing to the car and home.

I don't remember if I went home and gave our two old dogs a good pet, but if not, I should have. Most farms had at least one dog that served as ratter and house alarm against stray animals and strangers. Back then, we had two. Farm dogs rarely got treated like our modern house dogs are today. I don't remember Dad ever buying a sack of dog food. Our dogs only ate what they could find around the farm and the occasional scrap from the table. Of course, as all little boys do, I loved my dogs. They were constant companions anytime someone was outside of the house. They served as herd dogs, hunting dogs, faithful companions, and of course the aforementioned, ratter and alarm system.

The first dogs I remember on our farm were Skipper and Tubby. Skipper grew old and died in his time. Tubby ran off with a pack of coyotes and "went wild." For a while we would see Tubby swing through the neighborhood running across the pasture until one day we found him dead in the ditch along our road. It seems he developed a fondness for our neighbor's chickens and paid the price.

Not a boy to be without a dog, Cricket came into my life. Cricket was... well... Cricket was about everything one can throw into a dog. Medium-sized with a reddish blonde, medium-length coat of hair. Certainly, part Collie also parts of a few other breeds. Where ever I went, Cricket went. He was a good squirrel dog too. When we were out hunting and would spy a squirrel up in a tree, Cricket would worry that squirrel around until it moved to my side of the branch where I could get a good shot. I shot a lot of squirrels that way. I would just stand quietly, gazing up into the tree while Cricket ran to the other side barking until our quarry moved to get away from his tormentor.

In today's world of 24/7 electronic stimulation—and at the risk of sounding like the fogey I am—the joy of running across the landscape, unfettered and unsupervised, is a feeling that cannot be equaled. Especially not if your best friend Cricket is running by your side. We spent many, many hours conquering the world as both cowboy and Indian. In the summer, we fished and camped, and in the fall and winter, we hunted. It was nothing for me to fetch up my rifle and a pocket of shells, then Cricket and I would hike the mile across from road to road, through the fields and back, hunting all the way.

In 1963 Disney released a sequel to Old Yeller titled Savage Sam. It was a pretty good movie for a sequel, having all the necessary elements to make a small boy happy, a dog (of course), wild boys, wild Indians, danger, and adventure. I do remember thinking that Mr. Searcy's daughter got one heck of a lot better looking in four years than I thought was possible. I was flush with the adventure of Savage Sam. I couldn't decide if I wanted to be the boys, the man who takes the mile-long shot, or one of the wild Indians. It was, in short, the type of movie that fired my imagination and playtime for a long time to come.

I turned twelve years old on that farm with Cricket as my outdoor companion. Living miles out in the country, I had no one else to join me in my romps. Playing around the yard one day, I watched as our neighbor came barreling down our gravel road. This guy went everywhere at high speed. My folks had commented on it often. I only had a passing interest until I heard the Yelp! Cricket had charged into the road and was struck by the pickup as it barreled past our farm. I doubt if the driver even knew he'd hit the dog.

I gathered Cricket up in my arms and carried him to the house. Cricket was alive, but his eyes clouded with pain. His legs were not moving. He was very broken. It is impossible to know the extent of his injuries, but it was hard to imagine that the collision had not killed him outright. I asked my dad, "can we take him to the Vet?"

His response began with a sad look and a hand on my shoulder. "That dog is so broken I doubt he can be fixed. He is in pain. Further, you know we have no money to treat the animals that don't bring in money like cattle or hogs. Cricket will have to be destroyed. Go get me my rifle."

A sob caught in my throat. I knew what must be done. I also knew it would be wrong to leave this task to my father. This thing was my job to do. When I returned, I was carrying my rifle. I looked at Dad. Dad looked at my gun and then at me.

"Are you sure?"

I took a deep breath looking off into the distance. "I'll do it. I have to."

Dad went back into the house, trusting that I would do what was needed. I sat next to Cricket and lay his head on my lap. I stroked him and talked to him for a few minutes. He still had not moved, and the dull light of pain was in his eyes. I pulled the bolt and slipped the single round into the chamber of my rifle. I stood behind Cricket; his eyes did not follow me. I stared at nothing for a minute then raised the gun to my shoulder.

I put Cricket into the ground south of the house along the edge of the field of bluegrass, where he liked to run, chasing rabbits and birds. What was done was what needed to be done. I sat behind one of our outbuildings sobbing and sobbing until there was nothing left to come out. Then I put my rifle away and the sad experience behind me. I fully understood that it would have been far crueler to Cricket to try to hang onto him. It would have been selfish on my part–a lesson from Old Yeller.

In 1989 Karen and I were living in Kansas. We had two boys by then, Brad was a toddler, and GK was five. Today, it's hard to imagine at the pace technology changes, that the VCR was a pretty new invention. Instead of waiting for old reruns on late-night TV, one could rent many of their all-time favorite movies to watch right in their home. Magic.

Like many fathers, I wanted to share a bit of my childhood with my boys. I rented Old Yeller so GK and I could watch it together. He had already been walking with me on hunts since he was three. For his first five years, there

19

were dogs in his life. I knew he would love the story of the boy and his dog.

The two of us sat in our rec room watching this excellent story. GK crawled on my lap and watched wide-eyed. When the pivotal scene unfolded, there was not a single reaction from my small companion. Puzzled, as the credits rolled, I asked, "Did you like the movie?"

"Oh yeah," was his response.

I pressed on, "didn't you think it was sad that he had to shoot his own dog?"

A thoughtful look came over his five-year-old face, but his response blew me away. "It was sad and all, but he was sick. I would have shot him if he were my dog."

And there you have the lessons from Old Yeller.

Our dog, Skippy playing with Grandpa Gray after a winter snow at the Gray farm. (1959)
Over the years we had a procession of farm dogs, Skippy was a great one.

Poppy Seed Cake

1 package white or yellow cake mix
1 package (3 3/4 oz.) lemon or cocoanut
    cream instant pudding

4 eggs
1/2 cup oil
1 cup water
4 tbsp poppy seeds
    Mix ingredients. Bake for 45 min
    at 350° in a well greased pan

Have You Ever Seen the Rain?
(coming down on a sunny day)

From 1968 to 1972, Creedence Clearwater Revival was one of the biggest groups to hit Top 40 radio in America. "Have You Ever Seen the Rain? (coming down on a sunny day)" was their hit song that blanketed the airwaves in 1971, the year I graduated from Lenox High. Even to this day, so many years later, when I hear that particular song, I am instantly transported to a time that had significant meaning in my life. And that causes me to remember an incident from another era.

I grew up like a weed, running loose on a farm in rural Iowa. When the time came, I attended school in a one-room schoolhouse, one and one-half miles from home. As a youngster of five and six, I was perfectly content to consider this my entire universe. However, in 1959 the gods of progress deemed that all of the rural schools should shut down, and all of us "country" kids would attend town school. So dutifully, my older brother and I got up each morning and caught the big yellow school bus for the tedious ride to school.

Truth be told, after being forced into town (which is how I felt about it),

I chafed at school for many years. It was all a bit much for me. I wanted to continue to roam the fields and hollows, play in the creeks, and discover the universe on my own, without all of the rules imposed upon me by cranky teachers and some anonymous state board. But as things often are in this world, what we cannot change we endure. I made it through nearly all of my inaugural year in the big brick school. Even so, virtually every day brought a fistfight or a punishment from the teacher, usually for not having my work completed. I frequently sported a bloody nose and spent much of my year in the coat closet on punishment.

It was late in May, well into spring, the day we begged the bus driver to let us off of the bus early, many stops short of our home. In this day of constant surveillance and vigilance for our children, it is difficult to imagine how laissez-faire the world of a small town was back then. We clamored for the driver to let us off early. I'm sure he understood that our parents would merely shrug and say something like, "if they want to walk, then let them."

While we lived only three and one-half miles south of town, the bus ride, because of its route, was over an hour long. An interminable amount of time for a young boy who wants to get out and explore the new world after a long pent-up winter. Jack, our driver, pulled off of the highway two miles south of town and let my brother, a couple of neighbor kids, and me off of the bus. I am sure he was happy to see me off the bus early on any day as I was mouthy, loud and restless, and believe me, we were euphoric to be running free.

It was a stunningly, beautiful day in May. The kind of day I believe you can only experience on the vast prairies of the Midwest. The sun was out, and it felt like warm butter after the long cold winter through which we had recently passed. There was not a cloud in the sky when we pointed ourselves down the road for our mile and one-half walk to our home and our waiting chores.

We strolled along in a loose group picking up gravel to throw at old bottles and cans in the ditches, peering into the new grass for some sign of animal life. In half a mile, we stopped on a bridge to watch the high spring waters that raged down the creek, which was nearly out of its banks from the snowmelt. It was fun to see what was floating down the stream. We looked for errant fish or anything unusual that had been wash up onto the bank by the floods. Honestly, we liked to see the angry power of the usually placid stream, the awe of Mother Nature, if you will.

That's when it happened. It was a clear blue-sky day. As we turned to continue our homeward journey, one small cloud materialized just over our heads. It began to rain softly. Within twenty yards, we had walked into the rain, out of the rain, and back into the sunshine. I have now "seen the rain coming down on a sunny day."

1960 was a pivotal year for me in so many ways. And in some respects, it prepared me for the many other crucial years yet to come in my life. I am far from that dirty-faced little boy I was then, but whenever that song plays, I am transported back to a sunny, rainy day in May. 🏠

My family in 1954. Mary Pat (sister), Mom (Ruby), Dad (Bob), me at 6 1/2 months, Mike (brother), and Margaret Ann (sister). Margaret Ann would die from cancer in 1969. My younger sister, Stacy was still eight years away from joining our family.

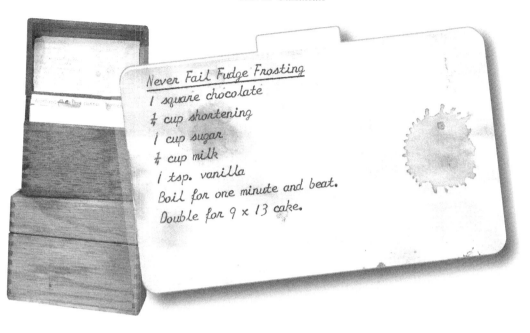

Never Fail Fudge Frosting
1 square chocolate
¼ cup shortening
1 cup sugar
¼ cup milk
1 tsp. vanilla
Boil for one minute and beat.
Double for 9 x 13 cake.

Phone Home

*This story, written before Smartphones, illustrates
how fast the world of technology moves. Enjoy.*

In my home, I count thirteen working phones. This number includes our two cell phones plus a fax but does not include the old waiting-to-be-used again phones in storage. Nor am I speaking of my kid's cells as I no longer pay their bills. Our entourage of phones for home and business includes the very latest in "beam me up Scotty" technology, several extension lines on portable phones, and a couple of faux and real antiques.

In our guest bedroom we have one of the old AT&T rotary-dial phones. It's black and made from some plastic-like material, Bakelite, I think, and it weighs a couple of pounds. I mention the weight, as it is the same type of phone my mother used to conk my father between the eyes. Oh, it still works if you can remember how to dial. You want to see a confused child? Few of them have ever used the old rotary-dial, and they don't know what to make of it.

Thinking about this reminds me of all the accessories made for use with phones and, of course, how they changed with phone styles. Gas companies sent out calendars listing local exchanges, there were special pens for dialing to save your tired fingers, advertising covers for your local phone books, pads for keeping important numbers at your fingertips. The list is long and now much forgotten. Somewhere in my basement is an old mirror from one of the filling stations in Lenox. The exchange was 25. Imagine in this day and age of ten-digit dialing and ever-shifting area codes just picking up your phone and dialing 25?

All this comes to mind because of our friend Greg. When Greg decided to move from San Francisco to Hawaii, he discovered the need for a garage sale. He was in possession of an old oak, crank-style telephone, precisely the type of phone we had in our home back in the 1950s. He made a gift to us of the old phone. A very generous gesture as they command premium prices today. If you are old enough, you may remember them, or you may have seen them in the movies, or for sale in an antique shop. They weigh about ten pounds and are eighteen inches tall. A large black speaker thrusts from the front. An earpiece hangs on a hook on the side of the phone. Classic.

Back then, it was a rare home that had more than one phone, and not so rare to find a home without any phone at all. Out in rural Iowa, our town had a Central Exchange. This department was a part of the Municipal building that housed an incredible tangle of wires and the mainboard. A full-time operator manned the board wearing a headset plugging and unplugging connections almost continually. If you wanted to talk to someone you picked up the receiver in your home and clicked it a couple of times–the operator, in Lenox, would ask who you wanted to speak to, then connect you to your party. It was not unusual to have the operator say something like, "I can connect you to Doc, but I just saw him going down the street, and I know he's not at home" or some other such thing.

Most rural homes were on party lines, eight or more families on the same switch. When the operator rang your phone, they used a unique code. Our family's "ring" was one long and two short. Quite simply, if I were at the neighbors and wanted to talk to my house, I'd pick up the receiver and roll the crank around three or four times, pause, crank it once, pause, crank it once more. One long, two short. If anyone were at home and heard our ring, they'd pick up the receiver. When the operator was connecting a call from outside the neighborhood one long, two short was our signal to answer.

Of course, when your phone rang, so did everyone else's on the party line. The idea was that with your particular ring, you would be the only person to answer. Truly. I remember very clearly that if you were talking and signed off, then hesitated before you hung up, you could hear all the other receivers clicking off throughout the neighborhood. There were times when you might have to ask a neighbor to hang up, so you could make an urgent call. And, although rare, I have heard the people who were listening in get so incensed at what was being said, they'd break into the middle of another's phone call. I've even heard my mother say something like, "Oh, for heaven's sake Mabel, would you please get off the line? This is a private conversation!" I must admit my childish curiosity got the best of me, and I was known to listen in from time to time myself.

In 1971, I'd managed to secure myself a place at Graceland College. Karen graduated from Lenox High the following year and was off to Drake University in Des Moines. I had applied there in the spring, and we became study buddies at Drake.

In the fall of '72, we were home from college, and my mother invited us out to the farm for dinner. When we arrived, she cautioned us not to mention the slight mark on Dad's forehead, as he was a bit embarrassed. When he appeared for dinner, he had a goose egg complete with a two-inch gash smack between his eyes. It lit up like Times Square on New Year's Eve. As promised, the four of us spent the entire evening without mention of the nearly fatal wound shining directly across the table. Seems Mom "got her Irish up," and when Dad came across the room too fast, she picked up the phone and cracked him. If the darn thing wasn't wired into the wall and hadn't hit the end of the cord, she might have killed him. Until they both died, we never mentioned it in front of them, but we got a few private chuckles out of that dinner.

Oh yeah… the good old days. The old black phone still functions in our home, and every time I see it, I think of my father and his goose egg. The antique wooden phone has a treasured place with our other antiques. It is no longer in operation, but I swear, sometimes, when I walk by, I can hear "riiiing, ring, ring." "Mabel, would you get off the line!?"

The antique crank phone that graces our home, like the one that hung in our farm house.

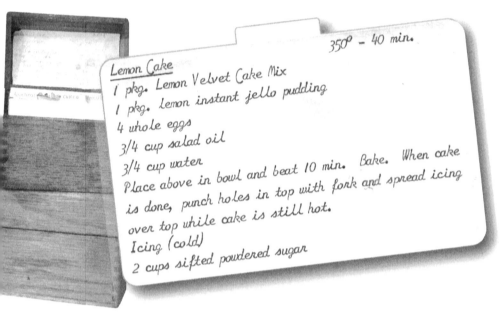

350° - 40 min.

Lemon Cake
1 pkg. Lemon Velvet Cake Mix
1 pkg. Lemon instant jello pudding
4 whole eggs
3/4 cup salad oil
3/4 cup water
Place above in bowl and beat 10 min. Bake. When cake
is done, punch holes in top with fork and spread icing
over top while cake is still hot.
Icing (cold)
2 cups sifted powdered sugar

Grade A Produce

I was three-years-old in 1956, the year my mother took a job at Terry's Produce. Or so I am told, as I was too young to remember. My sister tells me that Mom worked at Terry's before I was born and that after I had arrived, she did not go back to work for three years. I suppose due to economics, Mom needed to return to the workforce, so my sister took over the task of rearing me, at least until I was old enough for school. As I grew older, hanging around the Produce building became a regular part of my life. The tiny entry room where my mother sat behind the counter, answering phones and customer inquiries, also contained shelves of medicines for various ailments in chickens, hogs, sheep, and cattle. I remember one day when Mom tilted my head and pronounced, "You have Pink Eye." She reached on the shelf and opened a bottle of Pink Eye medicine labeled for cattle, and then she proceeded to squeeze a powdered substance into my eyes. After a few treatments, my malady disappeared.

Periodically, on any day except Sunday, rough-dressed farmers would shoulder their way through the door and place orders for feed, seed, medicine, or they would deliver eggs and cream to be sold. Most paused to engage in a little gossip about crops, prices, the weather. In the depth of winter, they often lingered around the red-hot stove, reluctant to venture back into the Iowa deep freeze. Farming done for the winter, they did not need to hurry home. I don't now recall each of their names, but of course, they were the fathers and grandfathers of my schoolmates, so I knew them. I do remember they each possessed distinct personalities. If they were naturally cheerful, they would charge through the door with a loud greeting and a smile. If taciturn, they would come in quietly, using as few words as needed to get back outside and on with their life. Some were just plain grouchy, as if they were always sitting on a burr; nothing in life seemed to please them. It was an excellent place for a small boy to collect all of the personalities of our tiny community.

In the summers, especially, I would chase through the various rooms, the egg candling room, the refrigerator room, and the cavernous back room piled high with palettes of bagged feed for numerous types of farm animals. The Produce sold Garst and Pioneer seed and Gooch's Best feeds. Gooch's Best was a mill in Nebraska, and along with their extensive line of animal feeds, they sold grocery items such as flour and pancake mix. I remember my mother using Gooch's products for cooking, I am sure from loyalty to the brand, but also to get the coupons on the bags. As an enticement, Gooch's Best printed on bags coupons of various values, 25, 50, and 100 points. These coupons could be cut off and redeemed by kids eighteen and under at the Gooch's Best Auction in Salina, Kansas, each summer. The tokens acted as money, and kids bid according to how many "points" they collected. I recall that it took a whole lot of points to buy a steer, many thousands. In the early 1960s, my brother bought a beautiful steer at the auction. He fed it up to a prizewinner. A few years later, I purchased a Duroc sow and began raising my own hogs.

Bill Terry, who opened the store in 1945, Mom, and several local youths staffed the business. At such an early age, I paid little attention to who those young men were, but one was Mervin Shawler, and in 1959 Terry's Produce became Shawler's Produce when Bill retired, and Mervin took over the business. By then, I was getting old enough, and my mother thought if I were going to be hanging around, I should be do some work, I was eight. I was

28

sent on errands to grab needed items from the back, but my primary job was candling eggs. The eggs came in from the various farms in the immediate area that still raised chickens. Each egg placed onto a small projector that shot light through the eggshell. That way, one could see if the egg was fertilized, or if it contained a spot of blood, those eggs discarded. The good eggs then graded by size, medium, large, extra-large. We had a hand stamp and stamped the boxes of eggs Grade A, Grade B, or Grade C. It was a bit tedious, but I enjoyed it anyway, and I felt I was a real help.

Mervin Shawler had a younger brother, Galen, who was in high school. I remember Mervin employed his brother and Donny Young to load and deliver the heavy bags of feed. Galen often drove the panel truck, making rounds to farms where he would deliver a small quantity of feed, and, more importantly, pick up eggs and cream for those who did not want to drive into town. I often accompanied him on his route. I was a young boy learning the invaluable secrets of older boys.

I don't think it will come as a surprise to anyone who knew me growing up, but I was an ornery little cuss. Quick and mouthy, I loved to taunt Donny and Galen. I was much younger but quick as a cat. Unless they were less than arms reach away, they could never catch me. Sometimes they would even chase me into the stacks of feed bags stacked in the back, where I would scramble into the rafters and perch until they got tired of waiting for me, and they had to go back to work. Inevitably when one of them got fed up and Mervin or my mother were not around, they would get me cornered and grab me. One would pull down my pants and the other stamp Grade D on my butt with indelible ink. My punishment regularly ended with them throwing me into the cooler. The cooler had a huge wooden insulated door that locked from the outside. I would be tossed inside and left for an extended period. Usually, I was wearing jeans and a t-shirt. Brrr, I can still feel the cold. Of course, it was all in good fun. I figured someone would find me, eventually. Although, there were a couple of times…

A few more years passed, and the boys became men. Tragically Donny was a fragile diabetic who eventually became blind and later passed because of his disease. By the time I was in high school, Mervin had employed me, part-time, to heft the bags of feed and help load and unload the straight truck as we made our way around to deliver to various farms. It was a great way to stay in shape for football and wrestling and earn extra pocket money. Time went by; Mom got sick and had to quit working. I would still help Mervin when he called, usually when he had a delivery of a couple of tons of feed. Soon enough, I too was off to college, and my days at the Produce finished. Sadly in 1988, Mervin died while working at the business where he had spent so much of his life. After Mervin's death, the Produce closed, and the inventory liquidated. A 43-year institution in Lenox faded into history.

In 1990 the old building was sold to Larkin and Johnson to become a funeral home. Eventually, becoming Larkin and Shelly and today Ritchie. In 1997 my father, Bob, passed after being bedridden for several years. The irony was certainly not lost on me when the funeral home that did his service was in the old Produce building. It seemed to me to be a most fitting exit from this world. After all, it was all in the family.

The original building of Terry's Produce. It became Shawler's Produce and today it houses Ritchie Funeral Home. To the right is the historic Lenox Hotel built in 1874 and destroyed by a fire in 1912. The hotel was rebuilt in 1916 serving traveling salesmen and a few locals until it closed in 1979.

The Bull Riders

When I was a small boy in Iowa, way back in the 1960s, summer was a wondrous time. My father farmed, and my mother worked in town. So the entire world was mine to explore, just as soon as my chores were finished each morning. I filled my days with fishing, swimming, and pretty much running loose across the land. It is almost impossible to imagine a child today allowed the kind of personal freedom many of us had back then. Like school children at any age and time, Summers held great promise of fun and excitement. For me, the two most exciting happenings in the long, languid summers in Iowa were the arrival of the Carnival and the Rodeo.

Rodeo, in Lenox, back before the sport moved into venues like Madison Square Garden, attracted the biggest and best riders in the country. As a boy, I was able, each year, to see the World's Champions in bronc riding, bull riding, roping, all the events. These itinerant cowboys traveled around the country on four wheels, looking for a few hundred dollars prize money to get them from one rodeo to the next. In August, they came to my town.

Born and reared on the westerns of the day, like many, many children of the time, I fancied myself a pint-sized cowboy. All year 'round really, but the anticipation of the rodeo only heightened my galloping pursuits. Out on the farm, I wore my chaps and hat, carried silver six-shooters, and practiced

31

my bronc riding and roping daily. I rode out of a chute fashioned from old farm equipment, galloping and bucking as only a little boy on his own two legs can. I roped anything that would hold still long enough, which included posts, dogs, chickens, and all objects animate and inanimate. When I could spend days in town, I ran with a group of boys who would chase each other all around the place playing Cowboys and Indians. This, of course, was way before PC speech.

We also practiced our riding skills. One of my friends had his father rig us our very own bucking bronc. He strung a strong rope between two small trees. The cable passed through a fifty-gallon drum opened at both ends. A blanket tied on the barrel, and when you climbed on board, one boy would pull on the rope, sawing it between the forks of the tree to simulate a bucking horse. It was quite a ride. In reality, there was a lot more falling than there was riding.

One year, I think I must have been around eleven years old. I spent two weeks at my cousin Donny's farm. Donny lived several miles north of a neighboring town, and each summer we would spend time together at his farm or with my grandparents at their farm. Life was pretty much the same there. After the chores, we had the day to play, unsupervised.

One Wednesday (yes, I remember clearly) it was a bright, hot, muggy Iowa summer day. We were choring out in the cattle yard. Farms at that time had fenced-in lots to hold cattle and hogs for feeding, vaccinating, and herding into trucks for shipping. Most of the time, the livestock would be turned loose into an open pasture to graze. In the morning and evening, they would file up to the lot for their processed feed scooped into bunks, long shallow tables that set about three feet off the ground.

These lots were always solid dirt as any semblance of green was long since eaten or trampled underfoot. In dry weather, the ground was hard-packed and covered in a couple of inches of loose dirt in shallow areas where the cattle would sometimes lay. If there were trees (and there were), the knots of shallow roots would poke out through the packed landscape. Four strands of barbed wire fenced the lots, sharp, rusty, nasty stuff that would cut skin and rip clothes if you weren't careful. Today the cattle lot held two baby bulls born late in the year and not yet made neutral by the local vet.

As these baby bulls were still young, they were hand-fed using a five-gallon bucket that had a large nipple on the side and filled with milk. One of our chores was to feed the babies a bucket of milk each, twice a day. Suddenly

I taken with the idea that we should take up bull riding and practice our considerable rodeo skills. It would be fun. Now while the baby bulls were suckling on the nipple, they were calm and easy to maneuver. You could even climb onto their backs and sit on them. No problem.

"Hey, I'll climb on board, and when I give you the signal, you pull the bucket away."

"Okaaay…"

"Ready?"

"Ride 'em, cowboy!"

Time froze for a long second until my "bull" realized he was no longer getting breakfast. "Bwaaa!" he bellowed and began running and kicking. I'd love to tell you about the great ride, but I lasted about ten good feet before I went up, then down onto the hard-packed dirt.

"Oof," I said, climbing slowly to my feet. "That was fun; now it's your turn."

Donny eyed me just like the baby bull had done, just after Donny jerked his bucket away.

"Aw 'common, you chicken 'er sumpin'?"

"Yeah, yeah, OK."

I grabbed the bucket and stuck it out to the second little bull. He immediately latched on to the nipple and began a mighty pull on the contents. Donny gingerly climbed on board and grabbed a handful of hair. I whipped the bucket away and *whoo wee*! That baby bull got mad. He pitched a buck, and poor Donny went about six feet straight up. Then he came the full six feet straight back down. Of course, he would land right on one of the knobby tree roots and his arm.

After copious tears with much wailing and a ten-mile trip to the doctor, it turned out to be only a partially dislocated shoulder. Donny got a sling, lots of sympathy, and out of doing chores for a week. I got holy hell. Then I was elected to do all the chores Donny would be missing. But it sure was worth it, 'cause now I'm a real bull rider.

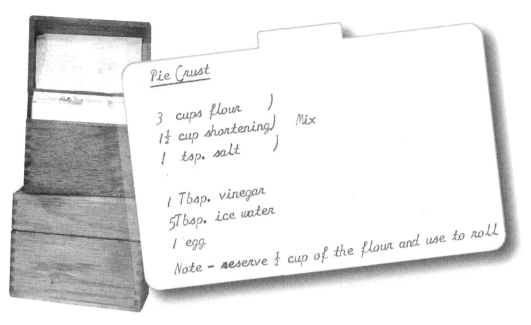

Pie Crust

3 cups flour   )
1½ cup shortening)   Mix
1 tsp. salt   )

1 Tbsp. vinegar
5 Tbsp. ice water
1 egg
Note - reserve ½ cup of the flour and use to roll

Underground Railroad

I have always loved history, especially the history of the Early American West. Perhaps it's because I was born on the edge of the West, or perhaps that my great-grandfather was an early settler in Iowa after the Civil War. I am positive the spate of westerns on TV and the movies that were popular in the 1950s and 60s fueled my fertile imagination. Way back before the Civil War, the Mason/Dixon line divided the nation. This imaginary and seemingly serendipitous line meant that states north of the line were free, those south were slave states. Missouri, twenty-five miles south of Lenox, Iowa, though technically free, was, in actuality, a slave state. It was also an outlaw state spawning, among others, the greatest outlaws of the west, the James brothers, Jesse and Frank. It was rumored that when they made their infamous bank raid into Iowa, they rode up our road. Lenox was so rural that over the years, many natives of the area developed what amounts to a soft southern accent in their speech. We have a slight but noticeable drawl.

One morning on a bright summer day, I was riding down a dusty gravel road with my father. We were bumping along in his old Dodge pickup when he turned to me and inquired if I knew about the Underground Railroad. I must have been about ten years old at the time, and I had been introduced to the concept in school, so I allowed that I did know about it.

Want to see it?" queried Dad. "I can show you."

"Uh, sure. I guess."

In truth, I wasn't sure what to expect. Dad headed straight up the road until it intersected with the paved road that ran into our town. Lenox has two paved roads that dissect the town; the main highway runs north and south. South is Missouri, and seven miles north of town, the road tees into State Highway 34. State 34 runs east and west and roughly follows the old Mormon Trail coming out of Illinois, crossing the Mississippi River running across the lower third of Iowa and crossing the Missouri River into Nebraska. A few miles south of Omaha/Council Bluffs is where Lewis and Clark had their famous pow wow. Back in 1868, my great-grandfather homesteaded a couple of miles to the west and just south of the intersection of Highway 34.

The paved road Dad turned onto ran east and west. The gravel crunched as Dad stopped the truck at the paved highway and turned east away from town. He drove less than one half-mile and turned into a driveway. An old grove of trees stood testament to the fact that there had once been a farmstead here. The trees and the humped grassy swell of an abandoned root cellar were the only visible evidence that a family once called this home. I was eager and excited as I jumped out of the truck. I was ready to see a railroad. In my mind, I could readily imagine the whipped and cowering slaves making their way from the "South" to the "North" to freedom, a freedom that began here in Iowa. I felt a kind of pride thinking about that. Dad walked over to the large door that was flush with the ground and lifted. He flopped it back on the grass, and we gingerly made our way down the half-dozen decrepit wooden steps to the dirt floor below.

The morning light filled the old cave, and I peered into the soft shadows in the back at a black wall of earth. Puzzled I turned to Dad. "Where are the railroad tracks?" I'd expected to see a railroad running underground from "down south" up to Canada. My dad roared with laughter, and then patiently explained how the real Underground Railroad worked. Boy, I felt like a knucklehead. But I still thought it was cool about the Underground Railroad and that it had run through my town. That was pretty neat. It wasn't until years later and grown that I realized maybe I should have probed a bit more. You see, the closest town to Lenox was Bedford, twenty miles south of Lenox. Bedford was founded in 1856, five years before the Civil War began. Bedford was located a mere five miles from the Missouri border. My great-grandfather came to our area in 1868, three years after the Civil War ended. The actual town of Lenox? It was founded in 1872, seven years after the hostilities over slavery had ended. So, you may ask how could this have been a stop on the Underground? Darned if I know.

Ranger Cookies   at 350°

1 cup brown sugar   2 egg
1 cup sugar   1 cup shortening
1 tsp vanilla   2 cups oatmeal
2 cups flour   2 cups Rice Krispies
1 tsp soda
   Add m&m's, raisins, choc. chips etc.
      bake for 3-5 min. - cool before
removing from pan

Making Donuts

A friend sent us a new set of knives. They're beautiful knives, sharp as razors, and ready to do any job in the kitchen where a knife is needed. In the process of cleaning out a drawer in which to store them, I found it. It's only a little piece of tin, but when I picked it up, the memories flooded over me. It's round, shaped like a flat cup and 2.75" across with a smaller identical cup attached inside that is 1" across. It has a black plastic handle on the top, and the inside cup is removable. It's a donut cutter.

When I was a small boy on our first farm in Lenox, my mother and grandmother would bake every day. They made bread, cakes, pies, and sometimes donuts. Donuts were Mom's special treat because she always made the first batch in the fall after we'd butchered a hog.

Late October–usually after the weather cooled–and we'd had a good freeze was the time to butcher. A particularly fat hog would be chosen for slaughter by my dad. Freddy Strunz would drive out to help with the butchering, which was done down in the old shed, just a lean-to with doors, attached to our barn. Later the meat from the hog would be taken to Freddy's locker in town. Back then, folks had meat lockers like we have safe deposit boxes today. Not everyone had a freezer, and even so, if you butchered a steer and a hog, it would take more than one large freezer to hold it all. Renting freezer space made a lot of sense.

Once back at Strunz's Locker, the porker got cut into pork roasts, hams, pork chops, ground pork sausage, and the ubiquitous side meat. For the uninitiated, side meat is merely cured but unbrined bacon. The fat and meat cut into finger-thick slices three inches wide and three to six inches long. Mom would, of course, fry it with breakfast or cook it in with green beans or other vegetables. My mouth is watering with the memory—the rest of the hog rendered for the lard. Fat boiled down and allowed to cool, to you city folks. Each year the hog gave us several five-gallon tins brimming with a substance that looks like Crisco but is just pure pig fat.

Mom, and every other mother I knew cooked the bulk of her meals using lard. She fried chicken, steaks, eggs, potatoes, and in some ultimate irony, even the meat from the same little pig in lard. Back then, the moms I knew cooked in two ways: fried or baked, period. Boiling was for vegetables and mashed potatoes. The thing is, everything tasted *sooo* good. I know it clogs the arteries and all that, but wow, it was good.

This part is where the doughnut cutter comes in. It was always like a ceremony. The first can of lard was opened and used to make a batch of donuts. Mom would roll out the dough flat on the tabletop, and I would cut out the dough. The little piece in the middle of the cutter made the holes. She would drop them into a deep pan of boiling lard, turning them with a long fork. It only took a minute, until they were pulled out sizzling and golden brown. Still oozing oil, the beautiful little hoops and balls were rolled in white sugar and placed on a rack to cool. Believe me, the first bunch never got cool before they were gone.

Well, of course, those days are long behind me. No one eats lard anymore, and after Mom started her job in town, baking became much less frequent. We began to eat what we called store-bought bread. Eventually, Strunz's went out of business, and time crept on in its inexorable way. I am, however, left with this precious little memory in the guise of an old donut cutter. Oh... you may ask, "why was the hole cutter removable?" Without the inside, it was used to make biscuits— homemade biscuits, with egg noodles, and home-canned chicken. But that's a whole 'nother story.

Grandma's Sugar Cookies
1 cup powdered sugar
1 cup shortening (mostly butter)
1 egg, beaten
2 tsp. vanilla

375°
2 cups unsifted flour
½ tsp. salt
¼ tsp. soda
½ tsp. cream of tartar

Sift dry ingredients and cut in shortening, as you do for pie crust. Add beaten egg and vanilla. Form into little balls. Roll balls in granulated sugar. Place on unoiled cooky sheet and flatten with tumbler bottom dipped in sugar. Bake about 10 to 12 minutes.

Scared Straight

It was a dark and stormy night. (No, really, it was). It was mid-summer in 1965. I can be sure of this as that was the year we moved from the farm where I was born to a new farm. I was twelve. Our new house felt fresh to me as it had indoor plumbing, a bathtub, and small gas heaters along with the big gas furnace in the living room. Our previous home had only one heat source and no bathrooms, only a creaky outhouse. Expanded over the years from an old one-room cabin to a ramshackle multiroom affair, I think it was only held together by years of accumulated dirt. Of course, our new house wasn't very new, as it would soon be a 100-year-old farm. As a matter of fact, the building, dated by the summer kitchen, was built many years before central air. Summer kitchens were used just as they were named. However, ours was long out of use. It yet housed the wood cookstove but had, for years, been a store place for discarded objects–a history lesson of broken cabinets, kerosene lamps, and myriad objects of a bygone era.

In 1965, our family was shrinking. My two older sisters were married with families of their own. My brother was recently graduated and off to the Army. His departure left Mom, Dad, baby sister, and me in our new abode. Within a year, Dad would add a small mudroom to the concrete slab in front of the main door that opened into our kitchen. This night I stepped out of the house into the darkness onto the bare concrete. I was home alone. I do not recall where Mom, Dad, and sister were. Having spent my first twelve years on an isolated farm, being alone was normal. But tonight felt different. I stepped out into the quickly rising turbulence of a prairie summer storm.

I must mention that a few months prior, I had asked, then begged, my father, to let me see a horror movie at the local cinema. He relented. I think because it gave him an excuse to sit at the tavern for a few hours while I was occupied being frightened out of my wits. The movie was Straight-Jacket! A Joan Crawford vehicle made in her waning years. The film described by one critic as a "...disgusting piece of claptrap." Of course, the point for me was that the story took place on a farm. I lived on a farm: chicken house (we had those), axes (we had those too!) People kept getting chopped up. Murderous people came out of seemingly empty closets and abandoned buildings hacking innocents while Hitchcockian music pulsed in the background. To be honest, it scared the living hell out of me, and does even to this day. The movie had me looking in closets, under beds, and jumping at shadows.

Of course, this describes my state of mind when I slipped outside to inspect the coming storm. It was around eight at night, darkness arriving a bit early because of the increasing clouds. The wind was blowing strong, running through the ancient pines, making a pitiful sigh as branches shook and swayed. The dark was near-total, but flashes of lightning illuminated even more ominous clouds roiling overhead. Rumbles of thunder building in crescendo and shaking the ground added to the operatic quality of the night.

I turned from the yard and sprang for the shelter of the house. The rain felt imminent, and the storm, along with memories of the movie spooked me. You know that feeling one gets? The feeling often called "the willies?" That's just how I was feeling. My hand reached for the door latch. At the very moment I placed my hand on the handle from out of the stormy dark something goosed my butt. I screamed. Yes, I hate to confess, but I screamed. Also, I think I made the highest jump I will ever make.

My feet hit the ground the same time my heart and stomach hit the back of my throat. I spun around and saw nothing. Then I looked down at the ground. Sitting expectantly, staring at me was the neighbor's large Collie, happily wagging his tail. He had wandered the half-mile to our house seeking affection, something he often did. It was his long patrician nose that had caressed my startled backside. After my panic had subsided, I petted my friend and practically leaped into the waiting arms of our new home. Scared Straight. 🏠

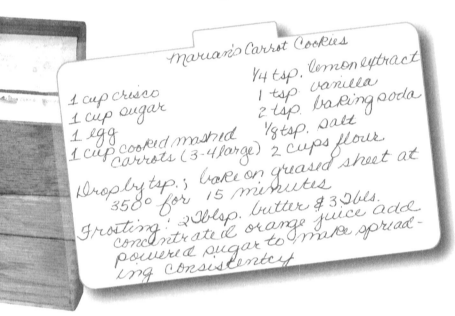

Marian's Carrot Cookies

1 cup crisco
1 cup sugar
1 egg
1 cup cooked mashed
   carrots (3-4 large)
¼ tsp. lemon extract
1 tsp. vanilla
2 tsp. baking soda
⅛ tsp. salt
2 cups flour

Drop by tsp.; bake on greased sheet at 350° for 15 minutes

Frosting: 2 Tblsp. butter & 3 Tbls. concentrated orange juice add powered sugar to make spreading consistency

Dogs, Hogs, & Moonshine

The males in my family have a long, proud, and storied history of misbehavior, most particularly with alcohol. My father led the charge, but my brother and I didn't do too badly, especially when you consider our early education at the feet of a master. Dad was reared up rough, and that's for sure. His father was an abstentious man, but he died when Dad was merely twelve. The years that followed coincided with the Great Depression and found my dad on the streets stealing food to eat. In a single encounter with a gang of bullies, Dad discovered his lightning left and found his true calling for many years to come. He was a boxer and a drinker. He fought in and out of the ring. The slightest hint of an insult brought to the surface deep feelings of shame at his early poverty and would find Dad in someone's face asking him to step outside. His amazing abilities in the ring brought him notice and an ever-increasing cadre of fellows who would buy him a drink. I never saw him turn one down. He was, as the Bard would say, a hail-fellow, well-met.

Of course, all of this took place a whole lifetime before I was even born. But it did set the stage for the father I knew. I understand from the conversations of both my parents and others that early on, they were typical young lovers. Soon enough, more children than money came into their lives, and my mother got tired of hanging out in taverns while Dad drank with his cronies and sometimes fought. Soon the lovers fought. By the time I came into the world, the only fighting was with my mother. It was kind of like living next to the ocean; there was always a regular rumble of crashing surf with the constant threat of a big storm.

Who knows how we, each of us, scratch the grooves into our lives. I've been married long enough myself to understand that love, hate, passion, and other people's relationships, even my own parents, are not to be easily understood. Like two cockleburs stuck together with their backs on fire, my parents clung as one, as they destroyed each other. You could never doubt their love, but that love took on some decidedly odd appearances on a daily basis.

I was three years old when my mother took a job in town. As a consequence, I spent the next fifteen years being with and very close to my father. Where ever he went, I went. By the time I was five, I knew every bar, saloon, tavern, and dive within a fifty-mile radius of my hometown. To mine the history of my parents, especially my father, I found an ideal classroom. For years I met men who could and did tell me stories of my father and mother that I could have heard no other place. I also met the formerly-great, should-have-been-great, and would-have-been-greats that spread across this land in every little nook, happy to tell their story to anyone who would listen. I listened.

I wasn't very old by the time I learned to tell how much my Dad had had to drink merely by the angle of his ball cap. But once he walked into the kitchen, he might as well have had twenty beers as two. The battle was on. Mother had reached the point where she could no longer tolerate drinking, either one or twenty. This total lack of détente merely stiffened my father's resolve not to be told what to do, forcing him to do his drinking in town away from the farm. However, he would sometimes keep a bottle in the house and was also known to stash them around the farm buildings. A very poorly kept secret indeed.

This prequel, of course, brings me to my story. Early in the summer of 1968, I turned fifteen and acquired a new pup. This dog was no mongrel; this was a full-blood Black Labrador Retriever. The first real hunting dog I'd ever owned. I don't remember where I got Lab, but I paid a lordly $45 for him. A fortune for a farm boy who labored at $1.50 an hour. By late summer, he was about half-grown with a teenaged personality to match. He lived outside and would roam the farm poking here and there. I had to break him from chasing mom's chickens and sucking eggs, or he would have to lose his happy home. He was also a quick learner.

One pleasant summer afternoon Al O'Dowd rolled into the drive for a little visit. Al was one of my Dad's oldest friends, and as a result, one of his oldest drinking buddies. We said our howdies and Dad gave Al the "wink." "Got something to show you down here in the shed," he says. Off they headed to the old garage. In about two minutes I heard "God damn it!" followed by my name. Now I got to tell you until that moment I had no idea the Old Man had a bottle stashed in there. The garage had a dirt floor. He'd slid it down an old hole probably made by the rats, so it looked like discarded junk. Pretty clever, but not clever enough.

"Have you seen my bottle?" was the query.

"You mean the one my dogs a chewin' on out there in the yard?" I responded as laconically as I could muster. Then I doubled over in laughter.

Al O'Dowd went over and nudged the dog with his toe. "Why, this dog's drunk!"

It seems the pup was curious about the neck of the bottle sticking up out of the corner of the garage floor so, unnoticed, he drug it out to the yard where he chewed off the top and proceeded to lap up some of the contents. He was one drunken pup. Fortunately, there were no lasting ill-effects to my future hunting buddy.

The following year was a banner year on the farm. Farmers were bringing in more corn than could be stored in the town's elevators or their farm bins. The result being that excess corn had to be piled outside until it could be safely stored away from the elements. We too had a few hundred bushels piled on plastic tarps. Of course, it rained before all the corn could be moved and some slid off the tarps onto the grassy ground. And of course, it couldn't be recovered so there it lay and began to rot. After a couple of weeks, we cleaned up as much as we could, then we let the hogs out to clean up the rest. The soggy corn didn't merely rot, it, in fact, fermented into a lovely sour mash. The pigs ate it with glee and immediately became drunk. Then they got rowdy. Just like any good drunk they'd snort and squeal, chasing each other around then sink to the ground in a drunken stupor. We'd never even imagined such a scenario. Drunken dogs and drunken hogs, sounds like a country and western song, doesn't it?

At sixteen with my license, I must confess that I, too, was drinking with the boys by this time. It wasn't too hard to get, mind you. My biggest fear was being picked up by the cops and losing my athletic eligibility. The neighboring state of Kansas was a hard and fast two-hour drive, and the legal limit to buy 3.2 beer was eighteen years of age. Someone from school would always shoot down to Wathena on the weekend, pick up a few cases of Coors, then resell it for double their cost to those of us too young to buy. There were plenty of older brothers home from college or the army who would pop for beer or liquor as well.

North of our town, about 15-20 miles, was Williamson. Not much more than a crossroads–there were lots of little places like that in Iowa back then. They were places that had a name and nearly no people. There was perhaps a grain elevator or a station, or in the case of Williamson, a supper club. At that time, it was a happening joint, in particular, on the weekends. You could find dinner, drinking, and dancing 'till the wee hours, which meant that they kept a well-stocked back room. Seems like those Iowa farmers could really drink when they cut loose. Well now I knew some guys, close friends actually, that got wind of this fact. One night they shimmied through a small window and made off with twenty cases of whiskey. They stashed their store all around the countryside in haystacks and culverts and would sell it for $10 a bottle, 100% profit if you're counting. These B&E boys were never caught. Heck, they were never even suspected. And yes, dear reader, it was grand theft by any name. Another close friend and I were invited to participate, but we both firmly said no.

I had three very close friends, and we were together almost constantly, even on dates with our girls. Drinking did occur. Back before their Great Whiskey Raid, and during a severe drought of beer, we needed a solution to our no-alcohol problem. It came from a most unlikely source. One of the members of the wrestling team was a Seventh Day Adventist; his entire family was very religious. His father liked to make a little wine for religious purposes, you understand. He learned from his Dad. He would produce several gallons of red wine aged just long enough to kick you over the barn, then sell it for $10 a jug. Well, it turns out he'd made a batch that was, just to be honest, really nasty. He offered us two gallons for the price of one. We struck a deal. But somehow, it just needed a little something. One of the guys motored down to northern Missouri and picked up some moonshine. Yep, that's right, honest-to-God moonshine. That stuff would make great turpentine. You could find home-stilled liquor if you knew where to look, and we did. There were some pretty rough old boys down there south of the border. I knew because I used to go on raccoon hunts with a few of them. We added a pint of moonshine in each gallon of wine. We now had some Old Head Buster, *fer sure*.

You could drink this concoction, but it took some courage. We had it, no brains, just courage. We'd already worked our way through one whole gallon and part of the second. One hot summer day, we decided to spike a watermelon. We cut the hole, and all that night, the liquid fire soaked into the juicy melon. The next day was a Saturday, and there was a carnival in a neighboring town. We spent the morning and afternoon drinking beer we'd managed to score, and eating every bit of that melon. I believe we even ate part of the rind. We were a little stupefied by then. Later (as may be imagined), one of the guys got sick. The resulting effusion was bright red and witnessed by none other than his parents. They became convinced their precious son had a bleeding ulcer, so they rushed him off to a doctor. He certainly was not about to cop to drinking or excessive ingesting of spiked watermelon. I never did find out what they said when they discovered he was merely intoxicated.

I never had no summertime blues.

Stoneware jugs like this one were often used to store homemade liquor and inspired the song "Little Brown Jug." In my first design job I put together books on antiques and collectibles for Wallace-Homestead in Des Moines, IA. One of the books I designed was on Redwing pottery. I have been collecting stoneware since I did that book.

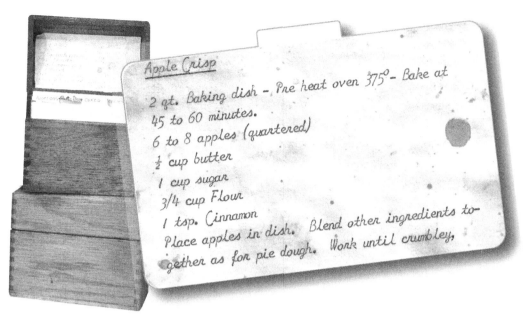

Apple Crisp

2 qt. Baking dish - Pre heat oven 375° - Bake at
45 to 60 minutes.
6 to 8 apples (quartered)
½ cup butter
1 cup sugar
3/4 cup Flour
1 tsp. Cinnamon
Place apples in dish. Blend other ingredients together as for pie dough. Work until crumbley,

A Whiter Shade of Pale

It was a well-hit line drive. The ball traveled between the first and second bases and between the center and right fielders—a sure hit. I shot down the first baseline, not stopping as the coach gave me the windmill. I rounded first and closed in on second with time to spare. The ball was coming in, but I knew I would beat it. I went into a classic slide several feet from the bag. My right foot pushing dirt. Until. Until that is, my cleats got caught on a tuft of grass no bigger than a fist. My right foot held like super glue to the ground. My body twisted to the right, snapping both bones in my lower leg, pushing the bone through my shin. I screamed in pain as my leg flopped around like it had a mind of its own. Several adults gathered to assess the situation. One of the fathers suggested it was a dislocation, thinking to pull and twist. Thank goodness more level heads prevailed.

That broken leg was the beginning of the summer before my freshman year in high school and the end of my baseball career. As ephemeral as it had been. While not the best player, I liked the game and still hold the distinction (?!) of being the only Little League player traded by my coach. He could not stand my enthusiasm (read, big mouth) and negotiated a trade, to the first-place team of that year. So, I was a Little League champion. Dubious as it was.

After surgery and a week in the hospital, I spent most of that summer on crutches. My cast was off in 8 weeks. However, I was admonished by my doctor, "no football for you this year." I was really looking forward to playing in high school. Of course, at the age of 15, I was a mighty five-foot-four and weighed (at least) 112 pounds. I was sure I would have been fearsome on the field. I was all prepared for high school. Well, sports at least. I had my Letter Jacket and school spirit to spare. Alas, my Friday night role this year would be in the cheering section.

Still, I made it to all the games, both home and away. As it turns out, one of my favorite memories from that year was the time between when school was out on Friday and the home football games. After school, I hung around town for a few hours, footloose and free. At six, I would take a seat at the counter in the Lenox Café. Mom gave me $2 to buy dinner, always the same meal, a hamburger with fries, and a Coke. I was a purist back then and only wanted my burger on a plain bun with ketchup. Watching the cook fry that meaty orb, the sizzle, and the aroma—so enticing. But then, the buttered bun went on the grill and toasted to a nice crispy golden brown. Perfection. Shortly, my burger and French fries appeared before me, arrayed on a thick white china platter. A bite of burger. A fry dipped in spicy Heinz. A sip of sweet, bubbly Coke. How could it get any better?

In 1968 two songs were still chart-toppers on the radio. They were Procol Harem's A Whiter Shade of Pale and Keith's 98.6. Those two songs stay in my memory vault. Even today, a half a century later, when I hear those songs, I am instantly cast back to that pre-game time of my freshman year. The taste of those hamburgers, the bands, the crowds, the cheering, the smell of dewy grass on cool fall evenings of September and October, are yet with me.

Grandpa Gray loved to play baseball with the grandkids. Here we are circa 1960, that's brother Mike catching, cousin Donnie batting, cousin Jim in the field, Grandpa pitching. God knows what I was doing?

A Broken Knife

The ubiquitous entertainment known as The Western dominated the decades of the 1950's and 1960's. Some of the great classic Westerns were made during this fertile period right after World War II up to the Cold War era. But it was the fledgling medium of television that really showcased the Western genre. Back then, there were three channels on TV. And, believe it or not, they signed on in the morning and off late at night—no 500-plus channels of around-the-clock entertainment. Daytime was reserved for news and soap operas, and evenings for news and prime-time entertainment shows.

In the year 1959, there were 26 western shows on prime-time TV. A partial list includes such classics as Gunsmoke, The Lone Ranger, The Rifleman, Wanted: Dead or Alive, Have Gun-Will Travel, Bonanza, The Virginian, Wagon Train, The Big Valley, Maverick, The High Chaparral, The Gene Autry Show, Sugarfoot, and Cheyenne. Also, the show that introduced Clint Eastwood to the world, Rawhide.

Growing up as a young boy on the Iowa prairies, I was much influenced by all of this western mayhem that came my way via the big glowing box in our living room. In my spare time, I was a rootin' tootin' cowboy, a mean gunslinger, an Indian fighter, and, often as not, the whole Indian tribe. Yes sir, I galloped, shot, fought, stabbed, and stampeded across a wide swath of

Iowa sod.

My glee in my chosen profession (at least that is how I saw it) of being a full-time Westerner was stoked by discovering a couple of facts about my family history. First, it was rumored that the farm where we lived was located on an Indian burial site. I could not prove that, but it was a regular and frequent occurrence for us to pick up stone implements in the field just east of the house, which lends some credence to the story. Second, my great-grandparents were original settlers of southern Iowa, homesteading on 80 acres, miles away from any town or settlement.

Great-Grandpa Gray came to Iowa, and the newly decommissioned Iowa Indian Territories, with his family three years after the Civil War where he homesteaded just south of the Old Mormon Trail (now Highway 34) on 80 acres, at $2 an acre. Grandpa Fin (Alvin) Gray was born on the family homestead in 1883. As a boy, I still recall some of the older men talking about how their fathers were impressed with the bravery of these original settlers living so far away from any town. In truth, these hardy families had little to fear from marauding Indians. The Ioway, Sac, and Fox had by then relocated to reservations in Iowa or Indian Territory in Oklahoma, the mighty Santee (Sioux) had fled to the west in 1862, and the Kansas and Pawnee had long since moved west across the Missouri River.

No, the real dangers were much more prosaic and came from things like disease, violent weather, accidents, and the like. Ten, twelve, twenty miles doesn't seem like much today, but back then for those early farmers, it was a day's travel to and from civilization. There were no convenience stores on the corner for groceries, and travel was by foot, horse, or wagon. A doctor, replenishing supplies, or even the law for that matter was "a good ways away." Creston was merely a railhead in 1868, Lenox would not be a town until 1872, Corning in 1883. The closest real town was Bedford, originally called Grove, a small community with a post office that began in 1855. Families had to be self-sufficient or move to a town.

During my childhood, I was very privileged to be able to spend much time with my grandparents. I loved spending days, even weeks at a time on their farm north of Lenox. Grandpa Gray was a great man, a good farmer, and known around the state of Iowa as a famous rough-and-tumble wrestler from back in the early 1900s. His best friend and wrestling partner was Mr. Ed Briles of Corning, father of the future State Senator Briles.

My dad farmed Grandpa's land by then, so as I grew enough to do farm work, I spent time there for different reasons than play. For as long as I could remember, and certainly longer than even that, when we would come inside for lunch or dinner, the yard just outside the back steps was a space for clean-up. There was always a big wash pan and soap next to the hand-pump. Stuck in the ground was an old knife with a black handle and rusty blade. Back in some lost decade, the point had been broken off, leaving a jagged end. For all the years I had been coming to the farm, I never gave it much thought, it was just there, used as a tool. We used that old knife to scrape the mud from our boots before we were allowed to step into Grandma's spotless kitchen. Once we finished that task, it was shoved back into the ground, where for all I knew, it had grown there like King Arthur's Sword in the Stone. It was just always there.

In 1970 Grandma and Grandpa celebrated their 50th wedding anniversary and the installation of an indoor bathroom on the old farmstead. Grandpa was 87 that year and starting to show signs of aging. When he was 85, while shingling the roof in a windstorm, Grandpa fell off the roof onto his head. That fall initiated his health problems. One week after celebrating his 50th, he had a stroke and passed.

After Grandpa's death, Mom and Dad purchased the farm. Grandma was set to move into town. During the move, I just happened to pick up the old knife and asked Grandma about it. "Oh, that old thing, your great-grandfather Gray carried that when the family homesteaded here in the 1800s."

"Really? Can I have it?"

"Of course, take it, but I have no idea why you would want that old thing."

Well, she was right; it was not much. But, what it was to me was a direct connection to my families' pioneer past. I took it home and kept it in my room. Several years passed, and I was now in college. The old knife was one of the few things that went with me to my new life. I was stocking shelves at night at a grocery chain and happened to have a conversation with our produce manager about old guns and knife making.

This era was a period in America when there was a renaissance in the art of shooting muzzle-loading guns. The guns and all their accruements, powder horns, knives, etc., were popular in the shooting community. It turns out that Don, our produce guy, made hunting knives. I mentioned the old knife, and he asked me if he could clean it up for me? Sure.

When Great-Grandpa's old knife was placed back into my hands, I could not believe it was the same one. The black handle turned out to be a big surprise. It consisted of alternating leather and brass rings. Polished up, it is a thing of beauty. Since the blade had broken off square, Don honed it down to a nice pointed blade that shines in the light. It is sharp and has acquired a new functionality. Many generations used this old knife even after being broken and serving as a boot scraper for decades.

In my home, I have a neat little room that holds my collection of antique arms and various accruements acquired over the years. Hanging on the wall is a frame containing family memorabilia. Inside the frame are old coins of decorative value, and several family photographs. One of the photos is of my great-grand parents in middle age; Great-Grandma wears a severe black dress and frilly white collar; Great-Grandpa, sports a full beard and a receding hairline. In another photo, are my grandparents holding my mother at around six months of age? My grandpa looks like his father, hairline and all. A third photo shows my grandparents in the identical pose, but in this shot, they are holding me, at six months of age. My connection to my families' past is palpable.

Over the years, Great-Grandpa's old knife has maintained a place of honor in my collection. I hung it together with an antique .44 pistol, replete with brass cartridges–the items wired onto an old barn board. I cut the board from one of our aged corncribs that I helped dismantle in 1977. Just glancing at the primitive sculpture provides me a physical and emotional link between my childhood, my Grandpa Fin, all the way back to Great-Grandpa Gray, and the old homestead out on the virgin prairie of southern Iowa.

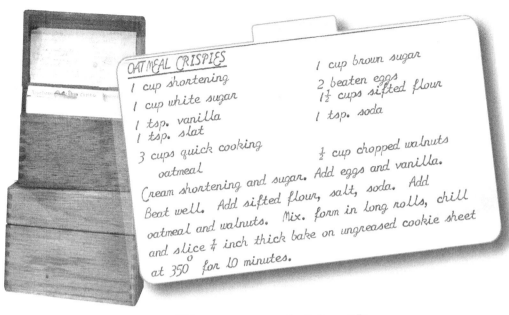

OATMEAL CRISPIES
1 cup shortening
1 cup white sugar
1 tsp. vanilla
1 tsp. slat
3 cups quick cooking oatmeal

1 cup brown sugar
2 beaten eggs
1½ cups sifted flour
1 tsp. soda

½ cup chopped walnuts

Cream shortening and sugar. Add eggs and vanilla. Beat well. Add sifted flour, salt, soda. Add oatmeal and walnuts. Mix. form in long rolls, chill and slice ¼ inch thick bake on ungreased cookie sheet at 350° for 10 minutes.

Grape Hi-C

Gentle Reader:
To keep this story a manageable length, I chose to truncate several wrestling matches,
which took place in the season of 1970-71 and write them into a single day.
To the best of my recollection, and (with help from my scrapbook), the matches unfolded as
I have written. For those of you who read this and were there with me, I hope you enjoy
my story. Because in so many ways, it is your story too.

I think of it. Not all the time, but often enough. I am many miles and decades removed from the boy/man I was in 1971. Regardless, periodically it comes to life in my mind. Perhaps it's a bit like the Bruce Springsteen song *Glory Days* in which Bruce sings of the nostalgia of glorious days gone by for the athlete and the beauty queen. Perhaps. But that would only be a small part of my thoughts. No, mostly it just remembers the person I was, and in so many ways how it propelled me into my future life. Come with me on a journey into my past. It's a mere 24 hours with a few asides thrown in. I will attempt to describe how it was for me so many years ago.

It was mid-January 1971, and it was one of the coldest and snowiest years on record in the state of Iowa. And that is saying something. The entire upper Midwest was blanketed in deep snow and crushing cold. My world, however, extends only to something like a 50-mile radius outward from our farm located in a very rural part of a rural state. So much snow has fallen this winter that driving the gravel roads is akin to being in a maze. The plows have pushed the snow into ten to twelve feet high banks in most places, except where the wind blows the ground bare. Temperatures hover down around zero, and many nights drop to ten to twenty degrees below zero. Tonight would be one of those nights.

Friday night, and I was home early. Tomorrow was a wrestling day. It's a big one–the Creston Invitational. Creston is only 24 miles away, but it is roughly twelve times larger than my hometown of Lenox. At the larger invitationals, small schools compete with large schools on an even basis. I was in my senior year, so there are only a few matches left before my high school career is finite.

1971 is the year of the 119-pound weight class in southwest Iowa. There are five, maybe seven, top wrestlers, each who are capable of beating one another in any given match. Most likely, the State Champion will come from our area this year. Most of those guys will be at the tournament tomorrow. Whoa yeah.

And, oh yeah, I'm one of the five.

This morning began for me as most do at this time of year. I was out of bed and doing chores before first light. Then I drove into town to the grade school where I swept floors and straightened classrooms for an hour. I hopped into my car and drove across town to the high school in time for First bell. School dismissed early for a pep rally to cheer us on and wish us luck in the tournament. All 200 hundred students, plus faculty crowded into the gym, excited to be let out of class early. The pretty cheerleaders were all cheering for us guys. The pep band played between cheers–it made us feel pretty darn special.

For practice, we had a light workout, merely rolling around on the mats and getting instructions from the coaches. Then we weighed in. Damn. I am 1½ pounds over my scratch weight and less than 12 hours to weigh-in. Ordinarily, I could sleep off that much weight, but not at this time of year. I started off in November just after football season at 139 lbs. In a week, I lost 10 pounds, and by the first dual meet, I was on weight. I'd taken off 20 pounds, but now I had to hold at that weight until March. For nearly four months I would rarely eat a full meal. On tournament weekends I could afford to eat on Saturday and Sunday. By Sunday night I was back on a regimen. Drinking? Forget it. I took in just enough water to survive. Occasionally I would allow myself to suck on a cup of ice cubes. One and a half pounds now was a lot harder than ten in November. But I knew how to get it done. I'd been here before.

So as my buddies prepared to go out and hit the town and howl, I was off to home and a bit of regimen. The coach cautioned us not to eat or drink, especially if we were overweight. I was. I wouldn't. Why, you may ask, did I do this to myself? The answer is at once both straightforward and complicated. The simple answer is I wanted to compete. Why is much more complicated. I loved to wrestle. Since I discovered the sport in 8th grade, I'd been in love with it. I was good, not great mind you, but good. Better than most, but I knew I would never be at the major college level. The thing is, it's one-on-one combat. No excuses. Make weight, and you wrestle. Win. Or lose. Your choice. Regardless, I wanted to compete.

There is one stark reality in wrestling: there is only room for one wrestler at any one weight. Pretty simple, and very final. We had a solid team this year. I might have preferred to wrestle at 126 lbs. I might have preferred it, but Tom was there. He and I were like peas in a pod. Eight of us on the team also played football together. Tom was left guard, and I was right. He was a bit taller, and we weighed nearly the same. When we wrestled together, he almost always beat me. We would roll and tumble, and at the end of six minutes, it would be 4-2 or 6-4 or sometimes 8-6. It made no sense for us to be at the same weight, so I went down the extra 7 lbs. If this seems brutal, consider that Herm had to drop to 112, or for him, more than twenty pounds. Or beat me. I wanted to compete. No one challenged me at 119, not seriously at any rate.

We had lived in this old farmhouse for five years, and it wasn't much of a house. No central heat meant that the upstairs bedrooms were not heated. If it was 20 below outside, it was 0 inside my room. I once placed a thermometer there to prove it to my girlfriend. However, I had a secret weapon, a heat blanket. This house did have one other thing I truly liked, an indoor bathroom. The bathroom contained my real secret weapon. It had a small gas heater that would heat the little room like a sauna. I would need every BTU it could put out tonight.

Right at this particular moment, I was standing in front of our refrigerator, which was in our dining room. My parents were already in bed, and the house was nearly dark. The light in the dining room came from a 40-watt bulb that strained to send light through an orange-colored shade. It

"Inside the Magic Circle"

made your eyes hurt. The real light was from the open refrigerator door. I was hanging on the door staring at a full quart can of grape Hi-C. On Monday, every Monday during wrestling season, my mother would put in a new can of Hi-C, always grape. After I made weight, it would go down in one long drink. The liquid flowing into me and restoring the desert my poor cells had become in a week of little water.

I'd been standing there long enough for moisture beads to pop out on the surface of the can. The shiny wet beads only stimulated my imagination further. I could have reached in and drunk the can of juice right then. I could have eaten a full meal on the leftover roast and potatoes. Who would have criticized me? I would be just another wrestler who didn't make weight. Try again next week. I could have, but I didn't, and I knew I wouldn't.

From the back bedroom, I heard my mother. "Are you standing in front of the fridge with the door open?"

I closed the door quietly. "Not anymore, 'night Mom."

In my head, I'd been going over a checklist. My bag was laid out with toiletries, uniform, shoes. My car was plugged into the block heater, so I was certain it would start in the subzero early morning. My clothes laid out so that it was a direct line from my warm bed to fully dressed in a couple of minutes. I would snag my clothes, hustle down the stairs and dress quickly in front of the furnace. My alarm clock was set for 4:30 AM. Once, as a freshman, I'd slept through a tournament, waking too late to make the team bus. After that, I purchased an old-fashioned brass clock, which I wound faithfully. It had a bell alarm that could wake the dead.

Everything else done and ready, it was time to go to work. I'd lit the gas stove some time ago and had filled the tub full of scalding hot water. I had on a set of cotton sweats with plastic sweats over the top. I slipped into the bathroom quickly as not to release any more of the warm moist air than was necessary. I began by shadowboxing in front of the full-length mirror, moving my body, throwing punches into my own image. Moving, moving, moving. I did jumping jacks, toe touches, I danced, I jumped, I moved.

In a few minutes, the sweat was flowing. I don't know where it came from as I had little fat content in my body, only lean, hard muscle. Still, I was sweating, and that was what I needed. I didn't want to wear myself out. This romp was just a bit of light work. I stripped off both sets of sweats and sank into the tub, the water now merely hot. My sweat output increased. Water ran down my face, so I had to keep wiping it from my eyes. After about fifteen minutes of soaking and sweating, I toweled off then headed up to my toasty bed, where I hoped to sweat some more as I slept.

Right on schedule, the alarm jangled me out of a sound sleep. I felt for the string attached to my bedstead, and the single overhead bulb popped on, helping drive the sleep from my head. I switched off the irritating alarm and slid sleepily out of my warm cocoon. My bare feet hit the ice-cold linoleum floor, and I was fully awake. I switched off the blanket, grabbed my clothes to head downstairs. I shrugged when I saw the small mound of snow that had collected under my window during the night, blowing in through the gap in the window frame. The heat blanket kept it from accumulating on my bed. It could have been worse.

Dressed, Hi-C in my bag and bag ready, I was pulling on my Tiger-gold hooded sweatshirt that I wore under my letter jacket when Mom came sleepily into the kitchen.

"Good luck today, your Dad will be up in the afternoon."

"Thanks, Mom," I murmured as I kissed her cheek.

I pulled on my jacket; the wrestling medals from previous tournaments made a soft clinking sound against each other. Donning stocking cap and gloves, I slipped out into the frigid pale illumination of the yard light.

Thanks to the block heater, the car started on the first turn. The drive to town took less than ten minutes. The cold was so intense you could hear the snow crunch under the tires. I said a prayer that the car would start tonight when I came back. Well, I had other things on my mind.

Gathering at the gym, the team piled into school cars for the 24-mile drive to Creston. I huddled in the backseat with Tom and Marty. I had a pack of gum, and an empty coffee can. I would shove a new stick of gum in my mouth, chew quickly then spit into the can. I would repeat this process until we arrived at the tournament with a half-full can of spit. Every drop counted.

Early Saturday morning and the sun was struggling to make its presence known in the mid-winter cold. The parking lot of the Creston school was already bumper to bumper with cars and school buses from all around the area, even as far away as Des Moines. I loved this part of the tournaments. I would see boys today that I had known for years. I'd wrestled some of them to be sure, and knew them from wrestling, but I had also played football and ran track against many of them. In the way of small towns, we'd even occasionally had the same girlfriends.

Then there was my competition. Those I knew and those I didn't. Swoyer from Greenfield was a likely state champion, if not this year, then next. I'd wrestled his older brother and his cousin in the past three years, losing to each in turn. Wetzel from Bedford was good. I was better. He'd driven through town one day and made a pass at my girlfriend. I had a particular thought for him. The guy from Mount Ayr was very good. Like I said, 119 this year was a real challenge. Then there was Conard from Creston. Conard was a very particular case. He had an older brother, and they looked like twins. Both were excellent wrestlers. Barely five-foot-tall, they were built like Charles Atlas and had the attitudes to match. Creston was his town, his gym. Everyone in the area knew the Conard brothers were rough, running with a tough crowd, and also, they were bullies. I didn't like bullies.

Of course, my likes and dislikes meant nothing on the mat. I didn't know it yet, but this day was going to teach me some lessons. I would learn the kind of lessons that come through heartbreaking defeats and soaring victories. Experiences that put a glow in your father's eye that you will never see again. By the time today was done, I would be fully wrung out, and, in many ways, a better person.

First, I had to get through the weigh-ins. If you were at all modest, wrestling would not be for you. If there was the slightest doubt about making weight, you would never weigh-in with a stitch of clothes on. I am not modest. Besides, I wanted the other wrestlers hanging around to see me. I was ripped, broad shoulders, a six-pack for a stomach, and biceps that popped. OK, I was a strutting rooster. Yep. I was.

I earned every muscle that popped out of my short little body. I ran and worked out most of the year. Starting with football in the late summer and continuing through track season in the spring. In the summer, I threw hay bales; in the winter, we lifted weights. I also, among my other jobs, worked for my Mom's old boss. He had the feed store and would pay me to move feed when he had large orders come in or go out of the warehouse. Most hogs and cattle feed came in 50 lb. bags. Local farmers would order 200, 500 even 1,000 pounds of feed to be delivered to their farms and stacked. I would bring them down from the loft, put them on the flatbed truck then do the same in reverse when delivered at the farm. I usually moved two bags at a time. I didn't mind.

This strength didn't make me stand out on my team. We were mostly farm kids. We all worked hard. Once at a tournament a boy from a distant school wandered over to our group. He inquired as to our weight-training program. We all looked at each other, laughed, and answered in unison, "hay bales!"

An official called my name, I dropped my towel then stepped gingerly onto the large set of scales. The lever trembled, hovered between the top and bottom then clicked up to the top. Coach Bunch's face fell. My heart skipped a beat. I could not be more than a couple of ounces over. But in the real world of wrestling, over is over. I heard groans from my teammates and noticed a few smiles from the rest of the crowd. I stepped off the scales. Tongue on the roof of my mouth, I licked out my partial plate. I had not had my upper front teeth since I was in 4th grade and had worn a partial since junior high. A situation like this had never come up before.

I placed my teeth on the scales out of the way. Slowly, like a condemned man, I eased back onto the platform. The bar rose, hovered in midair. "Good!" exclaimed the official. A shout arose around me. I left the room with my coach and teammates smiling and the officials ruefully shaking their heads.

I walked straight back to my assigned locker, reached into my bag for a key, opened the grape Hi-C, and gulped down the entire quart while standing there stark naked. Whoa! That felt gooood. I dressed, and several of us went off to find an open restaurant for breakfast. We had time before the early rounds started. Today was a big tournament, and it would go four rounds. For some of us. If you lost in the first rounds, you were done for the day. You keep winning, and you keep wrestling.

Back in the gym, we slipped on our wrestling singlets and warm-up jackets, then gathered in the middle of an empty mat. At any major tournament, this is akin to putting out a sign: open for callers. Soon the boys from Greenfield wandered over, and we started a game of cards. We teased each other about girls and football. We'd beaten their team for the past two years. In this gentle way, we made friends. I knew the Swoyer boys, two brothers Tom and Don, and their cousin Dan, Brian Tracey, and several others. They had a fantastic wrestling program. I knew I was talking with future state champions and All-American college wrestlers. With luck, I'd see Don later today. For now, we just kidded each other.

Don looked across the mats at Conard from Creston. "What an ass," "Yeah," I replied, "a tough little ass."

Soon enough, it was time to get this thing rolling. We had a good team this year. One of the best Lenox had been able to field since wrestling began as a sport five short years ago. At 98, Sims was not our toughest boy, but Gail (Ettard, we called him) was at the next weight up, then we got to 112 and Herm. From 112 through 119, 126, 132, 145, we could hardly be beaten. Then there was Jim, Marty, and Dave at the heavier weights; they won more often than not. Especially Dave. He was our right tackle, right next to me on the football field. He was affectionately known as "the Hun." The year we all showed up to register for freshman classes, he came sporting a full beard. With his shirt off, he looked like a big black bear.

I wandered over to look at the pairing for the morning and see where I fell in my bracket. At 119, all matches were full, with no scratches. No one would get a bye early on. I pulled a kid from a town west of here. I looked over at their team. He looked like a frightened freshman. We called those types *fish*, after the term, *fresh fish*. I smiled. At another time, I might have felt some sympathy for the boy, but today I smelled raw meat.

I spent the next 30 minutes, warming up and getting a real mad on. I would shoot against a back wall. Growl, move, be in constant motion. I heard my name called and bounded to the scorer's box, and was handed a green ankle band. One wrestler wore green, the other red. The official merely had to indicate one color or the other to keep track of scoring, penalties, and who was on top or bottom.

I straightened, and at the referee's command, I crossed the circle to shake hands with my opponent. He had a deep, deep fear in his eyes. I went into my crouch, and as the whistle blew, I shot across the mat and launched myself into my opponent. I did not need my usual moves. This boy probably had to eat his way up to 119. My charge overpowered him, and he went down on the mat. Two points. I didn't want this to end too soon, being all keyed up. I wrapped my left leg around his left leg, snake-like, clamped his left wrist in my left hand, and pushed his right leg out with my free hand. He had nothing to hold him up but his free right hand.

With my chin, I worked it into his upper back just between the shoulder blades. Done properly, it is perfectly legal and causes excruciating pain. I pancaked him to the mat. Then I let up. I let him get to his feet and turn, one point for him. Then I took him down again. This time, I snake locked his leg, bunched him forward, and reached both hands underneath him. I clamped them around his head and pulled him toward the mat. Involuntarily he curled into a ball, and his shoulders touched the mat. He squirmed, but the outcome was inevitable. The ref slapped the mat. Pinned 1:29. The boy struggled to his feet, shook my hand and fainted.

It was not that I wanted to hurt the boy; no, that wasn't it. It was that I wanted all the other 119 pounders to witness my fury. I wanted them to worry. The ref raised my hand in victory, and I sprung off the mat to the smiles of my coaches and teammates. Then I watched Swoyer and Conard similarly destroy each of their opponents. Wow.

At a tournament, you spend long stretches containing your excitement and energy. I had to sit through all the other weights and then the break until the next round. Most tournaments run at least two mats, sometimes four for the early rounds. This arrangement helps move matches along at a good pace. Still, I was barely breathing hard, and I was ready to wrestle. I walked over to look at the boards. In each tournament, large cardboard sheets were carefully drawn out, showing each weight class and their brackets. In a sixteen-team match, there were eight names on one side, eight on the other in a progression until there was only one name at the top. The top is where you want to be. This is the ideal. The reality is that only one can get there. If you must stumble, or make a mistake, then do it in the third round when you are guaranteed to finish no lower than 4th, earning a medal and more points for the team.

The second round was underway, and I'd drawn Wetzel. Good. He was good, but I knew I could beat him. I had absolutely no doubts. Besides, the aura of righteousness was on my side. He'd insulted my honor. He was, however, a bit tougher than I'd given him credit.

The match began just as I wanted. Wetzel came in to tie me up, a wrestling term for both hands-on. In the stand up position, each opponent grabs neck and arms and tries to find a weakness to throw the other off their feet. I never got thrown off my feet. Not from this position. He was strong though, so it would be risky to try and muscle him off his feet. You can do it, but if you lose balance on the way down, you'll find you are the prey, not the hunter. Besides, my best move on my feet was a single-leg takedown. I was as good as anyone in several weight classes at this move. I'll try to describe it.

First, I would go into a half-crouch, legs flexed. Right leg and arm slightly in front of the left. Then I move, forward, sideways, in a kind of crazy shuffle dance–sort of a stutter step. This movement confused my opponent, and he wouldn't know if I was going to shoot into him or back off and circle. I stutter-stepped he moved back to defend. What I did, though, to get him off guard, was bump with a head slap. You can't hit an opponent or knock his head aside, but you can use the heel of your hand and bump his forehead if he's stupid enough to let you in that deep. Many opponents are just that stupid.

Here it is: stutter step forward, back away, circle, stutter-step, forward. My opponent's eyes moved, just a flicker, but he took his eyes off me–a mistake. My hand moved forward like a snake, strike, whap, and it hits his forehead, his eyes shot to the ceiling. At the same instant, I dropped down to his exposed leg. My left leg wrapped around his, and my hands reached for his free leg. I planted one hand behind his heel and the other on top of his instep. I leaned forward and pulled up. At this point, he had absolutely no center of gravity. I drove him to his back and took my points. A pin position; at least two points.

This precise move is what I did to Wetzel. He came in ready to tie up again. He moved in too close. In turn, I moved into him, popped his forehead, and shot for a leg, 2-0. We stayed locked together until the end of the 1st period. I could not turn him; he could not escape. He started period two in the bottom position; lunging at the whistle, he broke my grip and scored, 2-1. We circled, locked, this time, I was confident, and he was afraid to work too close, yet he still wanted to tie up.

I worked my right hand down and got a firm grip on his elbow and pushed him back. We were chest to chest. I moved my left hand under his armpit and suddenly jerked him toward me. I hip-flexed and threw him to the mat, my right hand locked on his elbow. He landed on his back and stayed there long enough. 6-1. I was in control, but not for long. He stood up. *Damn, he is strong,* I thought. He turned away, and it is 6-2. We finished the period. I was now in the bottom position.

Wrestlers look at this in two ways, one, you can escape or reverse your opponent to make points; or two, if you are good, it is a chance to turn your man and get a pin. Today was not a day for me to be pinned. At the whistle, my legs shot across the mat into midair. He was quick but not quick enough. As I reached full extension, I twisted my body and rolled away. Scrambling to my feet, the score was now 7-2. At this point, I felt good; I knew I was in control. I slowed down the match and began circling, tying up. He shot into my legs, and I'd crow-hop back away. I was only catching my breath. The match ended, I was on to the next round.

We had a nice break for lunch. A rare treat for me this time of year. I could find a restaurant and get a hamburger and fries, with a coke. Food. All I wanted. Today I could, tomorrow maybe, but not after tomorrow night. Not for a few days anyway.

Back in uniform, I was working hard to get my mind centered. I had drawn Don Swoyer for the 3rd round. Round three left only the best in each weight class, so it made sense. I would either go into the finals under the lights tonight or find myself wrestling for 3rd or 4th place later this afternoon. Several of our guys had been knocked out. Herm, Tom, Johnny, Elis, Dave, and I were all still in the hunt for medals and points. We would all place, but where?

For this round, they wrestled on two mats. This arrangement meant that win or lose you wouldn't get an opportunity to watch your next opponent wrestle unless you scored a quick pin. Most of the easy matches were in the first two rounds. I heard my name called. Herm had lost and would wrestle for 3rd. I bounded out onto the mat. Don was a big 119. It was evident he was still growing. His older brother, who I'd wrestled as a freshman, was now 6'4" and wrestled at 185. Don was strong and athletic, but so was I.

We started in the usual way, feeling for strengths and weaknesses; I was not finding any weaknesses. We circled, grabbed, threw each other like small dogs worrying an old sock. I would shoot and get a leg; he'd squirm free.

He'd shoot, and I'd drop the weight of my chest onto his back and pivot. He'd throw up an arm to block my spin, and we would scramble back onto our feet and begin again. The air was electric. The entire gym was starting to pay attention to our match. Could these little Titans keep up this pace for six full-minutes? It didn't seem likely.

The 1st period ended 0-0. I was on the bottom. Don's left hand felt like a vise-grip on my wrist. I sat back, reached around to perform a switch. I arched my back and leaned into him. The pressure brought both my feet off the floor. Just as I was achieving separation, he pulled me back in–I could not break his grip. We struggled off the mat. The ref repositioned us, whistled again. This time I shot straight up, clawed furiously at Don's hand, ran toward the mat's edge, and turning, I was free. It was 1-0. We circled each other warily. He shot at my legs. Boy, he was quick. Just in time, I threw both ankles back out of reach of his hands. I pancaked onto his back, pivoted while pushing his shoulder down. I was behind him and in control, 3-0. The euphoria didn't last long. I tried to turn him over for a pin, or at least back points. Don rolled away and got to his feet. Just as quickly, he shot into me, and now it was 3-3 at the end of the 2nd period.

When the whistle blew for the final two minutes of the match, I had a death grip on Don. I snake-wrapped his left leg, vise-gripped his left wrist, and every time he'd try to move, I'd knock his right leg out from under him. Scrambling toward the edge of the mat, he tried to break my hold. I'd pull him down or run him off the mat. The ref would bring us back to the middle and restart the match.

I stayed on his back like a cocklebur. Great, but whenever I tried to turn him, it was no go. I could not get enough leverage to get him on his back. This match was going fast and furious. The other match ended, and the officials were not starting the next set until this one finished. The entire gym had stopped to watch. I had never been in a match where there was absolutely no let-up. There had not been more than a quarter of an inch between us since the ref blew his first whistle.

Then it happened. I was moving to try and leverage Don onto his back, and I reached too far. Probably not more than a fraction of an inch, but that was the only opening he needed. We rolled, and he snaked around behind me. As I moved through him, my shoulders contacted the mat. 3-7. Damn, I was mad at myself. I also thought those were pretty quick mat points, but now was not the time to be a crybaby.

63

He smelled victory and started to push me, trying to turn me over for a pin. I sat back into him and used a Japanese whizzer, or what some called a head switch. I reached back and grabbed the back of his head. Then I tucked my chin in and rolled him over on top of me. This move has obvious risks as pulling your opponent on top of yourself can be dangerous. It also has great rewards if it works. It did.

As Don's body rolled over the top of me, I retained my grip in his neck. When we stopped moving, he was on his back, and I was on him. 7-7. He continued to roll through, and the final whistle sounded. We were tied. There were no riding points, so the match went to overtime. We went after each other like it was the end of the world. The crowd cheered, but on the mat with our headgear on, it was only a dull, constant roar. Once, the crowd went silent. Then I heard a voice from the stands, "Come on, you little Irish son of a bitch." That's when I knew my Dad was there. At the end of overtime, it was still 7-7. The officials and the ref put their heads together. They raised Don's hand.

Well, I didn't have a lot of time to worry about what might have been. Don was off to the finals, and I was to compete for 3rd place. So be it. Many, many people, lots I didn't even know, came by to tell me what a great match it was. Even the ref came over to console me, saying he honestly didn't want to have to choose. But that's the thing, isn't it? There can be only one winner, after all.

It turns out there were big doings on the other mat, too. The boy from Des Moines had beaten Conard, the hometown favorite. It was close, but Conard lost and would be my meat for the consolation match.

For some reason, I would never understand, even after what should have been a soul-crushing defeat I still had utter confidence. Even understanding just how good Conard was and could be I would put a whippin' on this boy. (He would beat Don Swoyer a couple of weeks later.) I was not tired, and I was not defeated. I felt powerful.

I had another chance to win.

Facing with Conard he charged across the circle to knock me off my feet and give notice that he was bringing the match to me. He should have stayed on his side of the circle. He came in low and fast. I met him chest to chest and stood him straight up. I could see the light go out of his eyes. Right then, I knew, without scoring a single point, that this match was mine.

I worried him to the mat, chinned him and stayed on top of him. He could not catch a breath. I twisted his arms, assaulted his legs, and just generally made him hurt. He was too strong to turn and too much of a savvy wrestler to give up much. By the middle of the second period, he was spent. His coach asked for a timeout. Nearly unheard of, unless you are bleeding, or something is broken. The ref glanced at my coach for affirmation, and the coach nodded his ascent.

I withdrew to my corner of the mat. My father came up and stood beside me. Dad had that glow in his eye. A light that said to me, you are my son, and you will never do a better thing. "You've got him, son, just keep it up." The coach rubbed my arms and legs to keep the blood circulating. I never took my eyes off Conard. If anything, after his rest Conard had become more of a dishrag. I continued to maul him mercilessly until the final whistle. He slapped my hand instead of shaking it. It made me feel better that he would continue to be a jerk.

It was a day filled with highs and lows, victories, a defeat, then standing up against it for a final win. It was life, plain and simple. Looking back it was merely a warm up for adulthood. This day was an opportunity to pick myself up and realize my limitations and, more important, my strengths. Then move forward. So many years ago, I could concentrate my focus and goals into one single can of grape Hi-C. Winning and losing were merely tangential to competing and moving my life forward. I did.

Just enough to "clink."

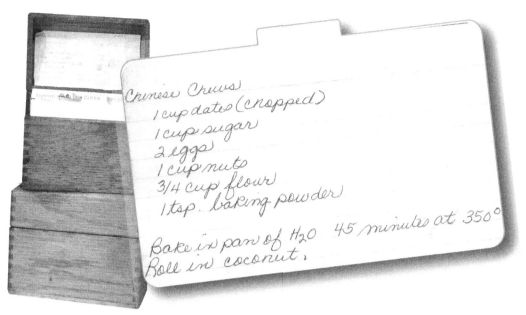

Chinese Chews
1 cup dates (chopped)
1 cup sugar
2 eggs
1 cup nuts
3/4 cup flour
1 tsp. baking powder

Bake in pan of H₂O   45 minutes at 350°
Roll in coconut.

The New White Couch

It was New Years' Eve 1969; I was sixteen years old. There was a fresh blanket of snow on top of the Christmas storm that came our way a week ago. The thermometer hovered close to really damned cold. Outside it was bright and crisp as the new moon filtered through the tree branches reflecting its light off of fresh snow–a typical Iowa winter scene. In a few hours, the clock would roll over to 1970, and the party was on. My girlfriend at the time, I'll call her *ma Chérie* or *Chérie* for short, had convinced her mom and dad to let her have a few friends over to their house to celebrate New Year's Eve. It would be a quiet affair, only a few close friends, and no drinking. Pu-leeeze! Promise. Promise. Promise.

Chérie's very strict parents relented, and the party was on. The one caveat, Mom and Dad would be home early, as they too were invited to a party but would return by one AM. As a secondary player in this drama, I was enlisted to help set up the party, chips, soft drinks, and other snacks. I arrived early, just in time to hear the stern admonition from *Chérie's* mother to "take care with the couch. It's brand new, and I don't want to see a spill or a smudge on my new white couch." Having witnessed *Chérie's* mother's temper with my own eyes, we both promised, and we meant it. Off Mom and Dad went to their celebration.

Soon friends began to arrive. Before long, cars full of partiers were disgorging Princesses and Princes from their winter chariots. Soon the driveway and even the gravel road out front were lined with internal combustion pumpkins. The party was swelling rapidly. With a mere 200 hundred students in our high school, it seemed to me like a majority were here to revel in the New Year. All of the guests were well behaved. The music was loud, and the conversations louder. Dancing, laughing, and there was drinking to be sure. No few cans of beer were passed around along with bottles of hootch tipped into cans of pop. But still, the merrymaking was not out of hand. Yet.

Then it happened.

What were the chances? I was standing in just the right place to observe the calamity unfold like a slow-motion train wreck. Here's how it went down: two girls passing each other in the living room, both a bit tipsy, and neither paying attention to the other. As they pass, they bump shoulders, laugh, then move on. The cigarette ash went unnoticed at first, then, "oh my God!" The glowing ash had, of course, landed on one of the cushions of the new white couch. Smack in the middle. Now, here is where it gets interesting. Someone grabbed the cushion and flicked off the ash. But that wasn't enough as the fiery ash had already burned into the cloth. A poke at the hole, then flip the cushion over to hide the damage. Problem solved, or so we thought. Fifteen minutes later, smoke began to drift out from under the couch into the room.

Everyone stood in a circle and pointed at the smoke. Having a least some sense of urgency, I grabbed the cushion and threw it into the snow on the stoop. A couple of guys picked up the couch and set it outside, just in case the fire was not entirely out. The formerly new white couch now sat on the back stoop, pathetic and lonely, illuminated by the light from the kitchen window and the winter moon. I must say the formerly new white couch was doing its best to blend in with the winter landscape, unsuccessfully I might add.

As if by some mysterious signal, the party immediately cleared out. Those kids left that house like rats on a sinking ship. In a few minutes, the only car left in the driveway was my little green Rambler. It looked terribly lonely sitting there in the cold moonlight. I confess if it had not been *Chérie*'s house, I too would have been like Kerouac, on the road and away from the scene of the crime. But… I thought about it and knew I could not abandon *ma Chérie* to the legendary wrath of her mother. There were no adequate words to console–no Hallmark card to make it better. There was only an empty place in the living room where a formerly new white couch had proudly sat, mere minutes ago. We waited in dejected silence for the ax to fall.

We did not have long to wait. When *Chérie*'s parents turned into their drive, the formerly new white couch pointed like an accusing finger, caught in the headlights of their car. By the time the parents parked and started up the steps of the stoop, the situation hardly needed an explanation. The burned cushion was a clue even a tenderfoot could decipher. We told our best story, and I stuck up for *ma Chérie* as much as possible.

Fortunately for *Chérie*, the formerly new white couch was not a total loss. Since the main part of the couch had not combusted, the damage meant merely a new cushion and a good cleaning. *Chérie*'s mother was not nearly as angry as I feared she would be and certainly had every right to be. I like to think her anger lessened in part because I stuck around to soften the blow. That coupled with the fact that Mom and Dad were somewhat merry after returning from a successful party. I'll tell you one thing, I indeed was sober.

It is true that what began as a fabulous holiday celebration had a semi-trag-ic ending. But on the positive side, I always felt that I gained a bit of respect from *Chérie*'s parents that night. However, doing the right thing by sticking around did not get me any accolades. But still, I had stuck. It can be no sur-prise that even though the party came to an abrupt end, life did not. Within a couple of months, like the formerly new white couch, I too was put out on the stoop. Young love, what can I say?

Grandpa (Fin) and Grandma (Lottie) Gray in Los Angeles in 1946. They drove their new Ford across the country to visit family.

The Fur Trade

I have always had a fascination with history, particularly Early American History. As a little boy, I exercised my imagination by making wooden swords, knives, pirate pistols, and rifles. I would read of Daniel Boone, Davy Crocket, Bowie, and a host of other early American frontiersmen. I would carefully study the pictures of their weapons, and then I would cut a pattern out of an old board and shape them with a pocketknife. I made Bowie knives, bows and arrows, swords, lances, and a Kentucky rifle paired with its' ubiquitous pistol. A discarded broom handle would serve as a barrel, bent nails as both trigger and hammer. It is safe to say my interest in antique weapons has yet to wane. Only today, my wooden toys are now the real thing, old firearms collected over a lifetime.

As a boy, one of the principal interests of my life was, and still is, with the American fur trade of the early 1800s. My fantasies of the old mountain men would run rampant while pretending to be a lone mountain man riding into the wilderness of the high Rocky Mountains, living among the Indians. Some days I would be fighting with the mighty Blackfoot nation, and other days I would be wintering amongst the Hidatsa or Crow.

In the 1960s, trapping fur-bearing animals, like the muskrat and mink, was still a viable way to make extra money. I knew two grown men who worked summer jobs, and, in the winter, they "ran" trap lines. These guys put out hundreds of traps covering many miles in a radius. Every day they hit the back roads and creeks checking traps in a different area, and if I knew these men, a couple of the nearest bars to boot. Back then, a muskrat pelt would bring $2.50 to $5 and a mink $20 to $40 per hide, depending on their condition and the open market. There were, of course, other animals that were saleable, the skunk, raccoon, fox, and coyote each had value.

My older brother decided to run some traps as the ponds, creeks, and ditches around our farm were teeming with muskrats—or 'rats—and the potential of earning the extra income of a few hundred dollars through the winter was good money for a young boy. By the time I was ten years old, I was following his lead. I bought several of his old muskrat traps and set out to become a fur trapper.

At first, I set my few traps in the ditches close to our house and had little luck. In time I began to range further from home and use the drainage ditches where I could see signs of 'rats. The muskrat is herbivorous, a plant eater, and builds its lodge out of plants and mud. If snow cover on the vegetation becomes too heavy in winter, they may even eat the inside of their house. When 'rats leave the water to eat or cut plants to build lodges, they leave a distinctive trail and wear down a path along the banks going to and from the water, a telling sign of where to place one's traps. With my traps better placed, I began catching 'rats, learned to skin them without making holes in the hide, and earned a few dollars for a lot of work.

The year I turned twelve, we moved a few miles west, and by that time, my older brother was near to graduation and no longer in the fur business. Our new farm had a substantial creek that flowed around the farm. It made a long loop from one-half mile south of the farm and one-quarter mile north, winding around like a huge snake—this, before most of our creeks were straightened to prevent spring flooding. There were no ponds, but plenty of 'rats, a few minks, and even a beaver or two populated the creek. The beaver I left alone, as there was no market for them. By then, I had a couple of dozen traps, which I set out along this long meandering path of the creek and a couple of others in some select ditches.

In the mornings, I would rise around 4:30, grab my rifle, knife, and billyclub, then walk south of the house until I hit the creek, and then follow along, checking each of my traps. If a trap held a 'rat, he would most likely be drowned. If not, I would smack it smartly on the head to avoid damaging the pelt. In the afternoon, when school let out, I would do the same thing along the north branch of the creek.

When I caught a 'rat, it took only a couple of cuts along the back legs, turn the skin inside out while pulling it off, then it was pulled onto a stretcher that kept the skin taut. The pelts went into our freezer, much to the dismay of my mother. When I had a good pile of skins, I would take them to town on a Saturday where I sold them to Mr. Swank. He would give me 20¢ for a 'possum skin, which I knew to be worthless, and market price for my 'rats. Once I caught a beautiful brown mink, which netted me $20. I left there richer and as proud as a peacock.

Trapping was far from exciting. It was a chore—work I did before my farm chores, breakfast, and then the bus to school. But, it was my work, and I did it on my own, and I got paid for the work I put in. Can you imagine the excitement of a boy turned loose on the land to roam free with knife, gun, and dog?

I did have a couple of exciting moments, though. I had set a trap in the middle of an animal run in a slough south of the house. I suppose thinking I might catch a coyote, as it was kind of far from water and unlikely to trap a 'rat.

This trap stayed empty until one afternoon. I went boppin' back along the path, and could see something in the trap. It was no coyote, it was a huge old yellow tomcat, and boy was he mad. Now back then, most farmers would simply shoot a stray cat and leave it for the coyotes, as cats were often chicken killers. But I didn't have the heart to kill something that had done me no harm, and I couldn't eat the meat or sell the skin—what was I to do?

Old Tom was wall-eyed, and every time I would make a move toward him, he would wallow around the trap to face me spitting and growling in a low mean rumble, needle-sharp claws extended ready to rake me. I moved off a safe distance and sat down, and we studied each other for a long few minutes. Suddenly I smiled. I knew the answer. I reached out with my rifle and dropped the barrel on him then stood on my gun. The startled cat was howl-

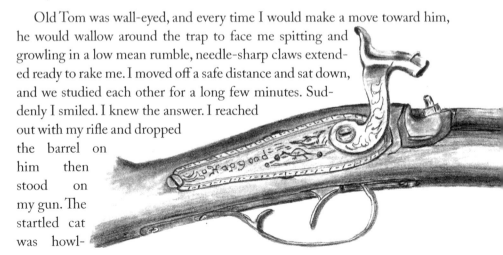

ing with pain and spitting with rage. With my other foot, I squirmed around until I could step on the trap mechanism and release him. I hopped off of my rifle, and old mad Tom tore off with an extremely indignant look back, and not even a "thank you very much" for his rescuer.

Another time, when I was fourteen, it was in the dead of winter, the temperatures were down to minus 20°. So, when the old fashion alarm clock jangled at 4:30 AM, I certainly did not want to leave my warm pile of homemade quilts for the cold, dark morning of my unheated bedroom. Grabbing my clothes, I tore down the stairs and dressed by the warmth of the gas stove that heated only the main rooms in the downstairs. I dressed in everything warm I had; long johns, extra shirts, thick coat, two pairs of gloves, and overboots.

It was still dark when I slipped from the house, but the waning moon reflecting off of the snow and my feeble flashlight gave enough light for my journey. The dead weeds along the fences threw long, eerie blue-black shadows from the light cast by the waning moon. There was no wind, just the vise grip of the extreme Iowa cold, the early morning silence broken only by the squeaky crunch of rubber boots on snow.

Trudging south, I headed through the farm lot opening and closing gates, followed the edge of a wide slough until I hit the neighbor's fence line, scaled the fence then followed the slough down to the creek. It had been a heavy winter. Snow piled against fences, and old weeds in places meant I had to wade through it up to my hips. Of course, I tried to stay where it was the shallowest, on the hillsides and cow paths. The creek and slough met up about one-half mile from home. The creek could be a tiny stream, which one could step across, but it also became much wider and deeper where the beavers had plied their trade and the water backed up into deep pools.

At 20° below, one would expect all water to be frozen solid, but I knew that was not the case. I had previously observed fish swimming around underneath the ice in the depth of winter. One day I even shot a few, and we had a fresh fish dinner in January.

As I walked the banks of the creek looking for my trap sets, I discovered one with the chain stretched out into the frigid water indicating there was a 'rat on the other end. I couldn't quite reach the end of the chain, where I staked it into the water, so I stepped out onto the ice to grasp the chain and pull it back. The ice cracked, and before I could step back, it broke. I plunged chest-deep into the creek. Instant cold. Instant trouble. The icy water hit my skin like an electric shock and needles of pain shot through my hands, legs, and arms, everywhere it touched below my shoulders. Fortunately, my rubber boots kept the water out, and my feet stayed dry.

There was no time to ponder the seriousness of my predicament. I scrambled out of the water and onto the bank, scooped up my rifle and ran, ran the half-mile back to the house. I knew if I stopped, my clothes would freeze to me in a minute, and I would never make it the rest of the way. As it was, even in motion, my coat, pants began to freeze into one solid block of ice. My soaked gloves froze around the shape of my rifle and made climbing fences very clumsy.

Fortune smiled on me, and I made it home with no more problem than getting very, very cold. Once inside the warm house, I shucked my frozen clothes and drank lots of hot coffee huddled by the stove in one of Grandma's old quilts, while my mother quietly clucked her disapproval and prepared hot oatmeal. After I could finally feel my fingers and the rest of me was getting warm, I dressed in dry clothes and headed outside to do my morning chores. On the farm, cattle and hogs don't give a whit about near-death experiences. They still must be fed and watered.

The next fall was the year I started high school. I broke my leg playing baseball early in the summer, so I was unable to play football in my freshman year. With no after-school commitments, my trapping continued. However, getting up at 4:30 AM caught up with me, and I would often nod off in my classes. The principal phoned my parents, and my trapping days came to an abrupt end.

Today, except for the rare trapper still out there in America, fur trapping seems quaint and distant, even barbaric to some. But back then, for me, it was a way of life. It was undoubtedly a way to assert my independence at a young age. My traps are long gone, but I have never lost my love of the lore of the American fur trapper, one man against a vast unknown wilderness. Today I even own some of the old rifles and knives that could have been used by these intrepid pioneers in the early days of our countries' history.

The Beaver Men are ancient history now, fur coats replaced by synthetics like Gore-Tex. Even the six to eight families per square mile of the hey-day of farming in are a thing of memory. Now, with so few farmers living on the land, the fox, raccoon, skunk, muskrat, coyote, and beaver have reclaimed their rightful place and once again populate the creeks and valleys of our Iowa farmland.

Rubarb Crisp

3 cups rubarb
2 tsp. orange juice
½ cup sugar
¼ tsp. cinnamon or allspice
1 Tbsp. butter
4 Tbsp. melted butter

1/3 cup brown sugar
2/3 cup sifted flour
1/8 tsp. salt
1/4 tsp. baking powder
2/3 cup quick oatmeal

Add sugar, butter, orange juice and spice to rubarb. Place in baking dish (greased). Mix dry ingredients and combine with butter and brown sugar and place on top.

When I Was Seventeen

The morning light streaming through my bedroom window wakes me. It is 6:00 a.m., and the chilled, damp air smells sweet and feels comfortable after the muggy heat of the night. My room is on the top floor of an old farmhouse whose roof is without benefit of insulation against heat or cold. It has no air-conditioning (few did back then) and little air movement through the single window. I slide out from under the damp, wrinkled sheets and slip into my well-worn jeans, pull on a long-sleeve chambray shirt, then step into tired work boots.

As I descend the rickety stairs, I push the long hair from my eyes. It is 1970, and most of my friends are growing our hair as long as we can before we are forced to cut it when school begins in the fall. In the kitchen, I pour a cup of coffee from the stained pot that has been bubbling for over half an hour. Dad is outside, taking care of the livestock. Mom is at the table drinking coffee and listening to the Farm Report on the radio. The radio is nearly always on; played so softly, it is almost an afterthought. It is tuned to KMA in Shenandoah, home of Farm Report and Frank Field, our link to current livestock and grain prices as well as weather and other interesting information.

I gulp down the first cup of coffee sleepily, kiss Mom on the forehead, and head outside to help feed and water the livestock. I distribute a couple of buckets of shelled corn to the chickens, check their water and fill if needed. The hogs are on auto feeders and waterers. I just check to make sure all are working. One feeder is nearly empty, so I shoulder two fifty-pound bags of feed and refill it. In the lower barn lot, I scoop out several shovels of feed into the bunks for our twenty head of cattle. I look down in the valley where they are grazing and shout "s'boss, s'boss." The heads of the cattle come up in unison, and they turn their faces to the sound. Slowly they begin an inexorable move toward the barn and their breakfast. I head back to the house for mine.

Stepping into the kitchen, I find on the table another cup of coffee and a large bowl of oatmeal. It is Friday morning, and when I finish, I tell Mom that I'll be home after work but am spending the night with Rod.

I smile in anticipation of the coming evening. Like all teenagers, I cherish my freedom, and I have a fair measure of it. At seventeen and a senior in high school, I have been working jobs outside the farm for three years. Mostly I hire out for farm work. Haying in the summer, tractor work in the spring, shelling corn, and any other jobs the farmers need in the winter. I also work as a handyman/janitor at the high school.

Since I turned sixteen a little over a year ago, I am expected to buy my own clothes and provide my own money for entertainment. I purchased a car, and I am the one who has to pay the gas and upkeep. I don't mind. As long as my grades are good and I stay out of trouble, I pretty much come and go as pleases me. I am required to do chores and attend church on Sunday. Wednesday also, during the school year, where all us Catholic kids attend CYO after mass.

My smile is prompted by the knowledge that I will spend my evening with Rod, Jay, and Mike. We are rarely apart. We'll meet in town by some unknown radar, climb into someone's car, and cruise around. We'll probably sit in the park and talk with friends, boys and girls. Later we will drink beer, lots of beer. We'll wind up at Wilson's Lake, talking into the early morning, smoking and drinking until we give up and go to sleep in my car or on a blanket on a picnic table or on the grass.

Breakfast finished, I grab my old floppy felt hat on the way out the door. It is gray from dirt, black in places from oils stains and sweat. I stuff a pair of leather gloves in my back pocket and retrieve my favorite hay hook from the porch. Jumping into my car, I fire it up, head out the drive and throw gravel for a quarter of a mile as I tear down the road. Radio blasting, I flip down the visor and catch my pack of Old Gold cigarettes. Lighting up, I settle in for the drive. Ol' Man Robinson called a few days ago and asked me to put together a crew to do his haying, a two-day job for four young men. There is some small badge of honor in being the one asked to pick the crew, and usually, you get paid a little more. Also, if your guys are hard workers, you get invited back, and other farmers hear about your ability to put good kids to work, so they hire you.

I enjoy calling friends but had only a few that I would ask to work with me. It had happened in the past that I'd worked on mixed crews, kids I'd hired, and ones the farmer called. A couple were lazier than sin, which made the rest of us work harder. Today I'd hired the crew. Bob Robinson was over eighty years old and wasn't going to be much help, so we were pretty much on our own. I'd called Chris, Danny, and Dick, guys with whom I played football. They were all farm boys. They needed no instructions on what to do.

It was a ten-minute drive to Robinson's, and at 7:00 a.m., the burning orange orb was already over the horizon. I parked my car under an ancient elm for shade and greeted my boss. The others drifted in, and we were ready to work by 7:30. Bob and his seventy-eight-year-old brother, Frank, would drive the tractors pulling the lowboys, flatbed trailers. Us "boys" would pair off, walking on each side of the trailers, taking four rows at a time.

Today promised to be and delivered a typical August day in Iowa. The temperature flirted with 100°, and the humidity was nearing 90. The long open rolling fields of hay had only shade for the mice and rabbits. Each man saw to his personal outfit as we rode the trailers out to the field, dangling our legs and smoking. Some wore only t-shirts, jeans, and sneakers. Others, like me, had on long sleeve loose shirts and leather boots. I was allergic to the scratches the hay made on my bare arms. The long sleeves kept me from itching, and the leather gloves protected my hands from blisters. Most farmers wore baseball caps with various feed/seed logos. Me? I liked my old floppy hat. Everyone carried his favorite hay hook, the one they felt fit their hand. I guess you could say we were, at least, semi-pro at this haying business.

It was a short eight minutes to the field. Cigarettes were flipped away, hats firmly planted on heads, and gloves tugged on. Casually, four young men stepped off the moving trailers and ambled over to the object of the day, the round bale.

Most farmers used round bales because they weathered better than square bales. Some liked the square bales, but still, the round ones reigned supreme

back
then. To-
day they are pretty
much a thing of the past be-
ing replaced by giant round bales that
weather in the field and no longer need strong
young men to help store them. Nearly in unison, as if
choreographed, each of us reached down and hooked a bale of
hay. Hoisting it up using the fulcrum of a thigh, we pitched
it onto the front of the slowly moving lowboy. One bale at
a time laid head-to-head, we filled the lowboy from front
to back. When one layer was done, another got added. If
you knew what you were doing, each layer settled into
the one below, and the load won't shift or fall, even on
a hill. At seven layers, the lowboy was pretty well filled.
On one job, Danny and I threw as high as nine layers. We were showing off
for the fifteen-year-old farmer's daughter, who was driving the tractor and
wearing very short shorts. Throwing bales that high is akin to shot-putting a
forty-pound weight high over your head with precision. This day is too hot
to show off, and seven high will do.

Each guy scrambles to the top of the load for the ride back. With each
lowboy fully loaded, we go slowly. There is a slight breeze on top of the hay.
For a few minutes, we can relax. Usually, we talk, lie about girls, how's the ball
team going to be this year, and pick on each other. We have gone to school
together from grade school. We've played football together for five years.
Farm boys all, we grew up together, choring, playing on teams, drinking, and
often chasing the same girls. We are a team on and off the field, in and out
of school. It is after 8:00 a.m., and already it is hot, not nearly as hot as it will
get, however. But we know this by instinct. Movements are conserved. When
we are at work, it is fluid; all muscles are straining. At our age and given the
work we do, each of us is rock hard. However, when we rest, it is complete
rest. Jugs filled with ice water get passed around. I can speak with absolute
authority on the fact that there is no better elixir in this world than ice water
drawn from a deep well and drunk on a hot summer day.

Back in the barnyard, the tractors are stopped one behind the other. Today
we are working with an elevator. Hooked up to a power take-off, the long

narrow machine has a never-ending chain with periodic catches that will haul each bale up into the hayloft and drop it. One of us will pull the hay off the load a bale at a time and fill the elevator. The other three will be inside the loft "catching" the bales and stacking them. Working inside the barn is hot, dusty, and dirty work, so we trade off jobs from time to time. Our two loads unloaded, and stacked we knock off the dust and reach for our cigarettes. Like Automatons, we climb back on the trailers for our ride back to the field.

Averaging between 50-70 bales per load with 1,000-1,200 bales in the fields it will take 14-20 loads to complete this job. The more we work, the quicker we are done. This task is a day, day and one-half job. It is now beastly hot, and as the heat increases, we get slower. We get six loads in by noon, however, and it is looking good. Mrs. Robinson makes the lunch. A lifelong farm woman, she is experienced cooking for a crew, and the food is plentiful and tasty–roast beef, mashed potatoes, green beans, and homemade bread and butter. Later there are pies and a cake with lots of ice tea and coffee. Full nearly to a painful state, we lay under a shade tree and compare plans for the night. Those with steady girls will be with them. Us bachelor bulls will be milling around with the herd. I've had a couple of girls I liked. We played slap and tickle in the backseat. Others I've dated and enjoyed but none serious. I didn't know it at the time, but that was about to change.

The afternoon is more of the same, only hotter. By 4:00 p.m., we are ready to finish for the day. Tomorrow, Saturday, we'll wind up this job by noon. Moving slowly, Bob writes our checks for the day's work. The heat is hard on him. Over eighty, I don't know this, but he will die in his sleep a few days later. His wife and brother will both follow within the year.

The others take off at intervals to avoid choking on each other's dust as they roar down the dry gravel roads. I linger a few minutes to visit. I want to make sure everything went right today, and Bob was pleased with the job. These are people I have known since I was a little boy. I like them, and they like me. After a few minutes, they've inquired about Mom and Dad, my older brother in the army. Soon I take my leave, headed to town to the swimming pool. In the trunk of my car is a fishing pole and tackle, a rifle, clean clothes, and a swimming suit rolled in a towel. I tear down the road at high speed, hit the highway on two wheels, and roll into town.

At the pool, along with a few other friends, is my crew. I shower, and we lounge around outside talking to and ogling the lifeguards, all local school-girls in bikinis. After a little while, I head for home, where I'll have dinner with the folks and my baby sister. I change clothes, pack my work clothes in the trunk of the car, and head back to town. As expected, Rod, Jay, and Mike show up in turn. We act as if each was a surprise and long-missed when in actuality, we saw each other last night. We ride around telling stories, lounge around the park, and at some point, we head toward Clearfield, looking for new girls. We pick up a couple, and they ride with us for a while. Eventually, their boyfriends show, so we lose their company. By midnight we've wound up at Wilson's Lake sitting under the stars drinking beer.

Then suddenly, it's Monday, and we start two-a-day summer football practices. On the field at 6:30 a.m., run for two hours, shower, then I'm off to work at the grade school. At 4:30, we are back at football practice, on the field, and running again. By the end of our workout, my muscles are screaming. Too tired to play with my friends tonight, I go home exhausted and sleep until 5:30 a.m.

This week I get a couple of afternoons off from work at the school, so I hire out to pick up hay until 4:30 p.m. then drive to ball practice. By the end of two weeks and the start of school, us football players are all in top shape. The coach likes his boys. We've played together for years and last year had a great season losing only two games and winning our conference. We expect this year to be better.

Coach believes in being in shape, so we run. I sing, and it drives him crazy. I sing badly. He runs us harder. I sing more. We run carrying a teammate on our backs up a short incline. I sing. Coach laughs. He likes this kind of crazy dedication and toughness. I am small, 5 feet 4 inches, and 140 lbs. But I am quick and muscular. I can hit hard. I have been playing offensive guard for a couple of years. Tom is 5 feet 6 inches and 140 lbs. He is the Left guard. We look like midgets next to our tackles. No one makes fun, however. Tom will be All-Conference this year. We will lose one game this season. As I said, Coach likes this kind of devotion, this drive. He tells a newspaper reporter who asks about my size that I am "dynamite."

During the second week of practice, I am walking back from the field to the gym. I spot a cute girl, Kim, and she is standing with another girl. I am sweaty, stinky, and I don't have my front teeth in. I have a partial plate for my two upper front teeth. I'm not looking too cute. I like Kim—she's a cheerleader in football and wrestling. Her friend is just back from Europe. Really. We talk. I like her. We haven't stopped talking yet. 🏠

Just in Case

Writing a memory piece often gets the writer accused of rampant nostalgia. As if recalling the past is, in fact, a longing for that same past. Sometimes it is, but mostly it is committing the sin of aging, being that writer who is recalling how the world of their youth was, in contrast to the world today. Well, if such is a sin, then I am a sinner.

I am brought to this story by something that was in the news not long ago–the story concerned the parents of two young girls. The girl's parents were arrested and charged with Child Endangerment because they routinely allowed their girls to walk to school and go to a nearby park without supervision. Well, I'll let that stand on its own. But the very essence of that story started me thinking of my young life on our small Iowa farm.

I was born in 1953. My sister tells me that until 1948 my father and grandfather farmed with horses. Yes, the original horsepower. I do recall Grandpa Gray had a corner of his barnyard filled with old threshers and other horse-drawn equipment. When I was very young, that old equipment was a place for me to play. I would climb and scramble over the rusty hulks replete with sharp tines and chains. There was never any admonition from either parent or grandparent to "be careful."

Every farm kid I knew was required to take on varying and increasing responsibilities from choring to handling large equipment. Most of us nearly as soon as we could walk. My mom worked in town at the Produce, and when my older sisters moved away, I spent much of my free time with my dad. In the spring and summer, this meant riding on the tractor or playing alongside the field as he worked. In the fall, it was not unusual to be in the wagon while he picked corn, hanging onto the sides and dodging tumbling golden missiles.

Harvest time on the farm. Corn. Up until the late 1960s, ear corn was pretty much the only way to harvest that crop. Farmers had in succession one-row, two-row, and even four-row pickers. The harvested ears were stored in bins, to be shelled later, or hauled by the wagon load into the Elevator in town and sold right away. My jobs were… well, I'll get to that in a minute.

At a time before I can recall, Grandpa Gray acquired a Case tractor, a 1949 D perhaps. Ever since I could remember he no longer used the old tractor for fieldwork, but the little Case did serve multiple purposes. Its most important reason for existing on Grandpa's farm was to keep his hand in the business of farming. My dad, often with the help of Uncle Don, farmed our grandparent's 160 and our own 80 acres, nine miles south. The Case tractor kept Grandpa involved in the farm and gave him access to the furthest reaches of the acreage. He liked to take his tractor out into the pasture to watch his small herd of fat-cattle. On the side of the tractor hung a bucket of salt and a spade. When Grandpa saw a Russian Thistle, he'd stop, spade it out of the ground and sprinkle salt in the hole. That alone kept him busy. When we worked in the fields and needed a water break, or were called in for a meal, there would be Grandpa Gray rolling out to meet us driving his Case.

That brings me to my harvesting jobs. By the time I was nine years old, I was driving our tractors, moving equipment between our two farms. One of my tasks for corn and beans was to haul the grain-filled wagons into town to the grain elevator, where the grain got weighed and dumped. I always pulled two full wagons behind the tractor. My second job, the one that would undoubtedly get my parents arrested today, was to kick the corn out of the wagon into a running farm elevator. This job was also a secondary but vital one for Grandpa's old Case tractor. You see, on this model, the power take-off (PTO), was a large spinning drum located just under the right wheel. When engaged, the drum turned a wide belt, which in turn ran the never-ending chain of the elevator to lift corn, beans, oats, or hay bales into their storage buildings. The tractor was backed up beside the rear of the elevator and the belt attached to both drums. Then carefully, the tractor eased forward to create tension on the belt. Once the PTO lever was engaged, the belt drove the elevator with, as I recall, a God-awful noise.

Now, here is where I was repeatedly admonished by Dad and Grandpa to have caution, as getting too close to that belt with loose clothing could get you snatched right into the moving equipment. Growing up in farm country, I knew of men who had only part of a hand or lost an arm, even had been killed in farm accidents. I lost a classmate when the tractor he was racing flipped over and pinned him underneath, killing him. I never thought about it much then, but it was a dangerous job, especially for a young child. When we brought in a wagon load of corn to store, the wagon backed up to the hopper on the elevator. The end gate pulled up, so whole ears spilled into the hopper and began its short journey up the pipe and unceremoniously dumped into storage. Dad would be in the granary running the movable nose of the elevator so that the bin filled up evenly. Now the first part of the corn fell right out of the wagon just from gravity, but as the end became cleared of loose ears, it was Grandpa's duty to jack up the front of the wagon bed periodically. My job was inside the wagon, where I would kick corn down into the hopper. Of course, as the back of the wagon rose, I was at an increasingly perilous angle so that when all the corn, at last, slid out, I was clinging onto the sideboards of the wagon, kicking corn and making sure I did not fall into the hopper myself.

Are there yet children on farms and other occupations doing dangerous jobs? I have no doubt. And, in all seriousness, I never felt frightened or threatened. This type of task was just the work that needed doing. Of course, I am sure my old friends from long ago can attest that this story is but one of the many potential dangers that were a way of life on the farm at that time. But the courage I gained from those days, the freedom I found in shouldering responsibilities change me for good. Today farming, for the most part, is a far different way of life than in the 1950-60s. And more's the better. But it always pays to be safe. Just in case.

Grandpa Gray, (right) and a neighbor, unloading corn, posing with his Case tractor. (1958)

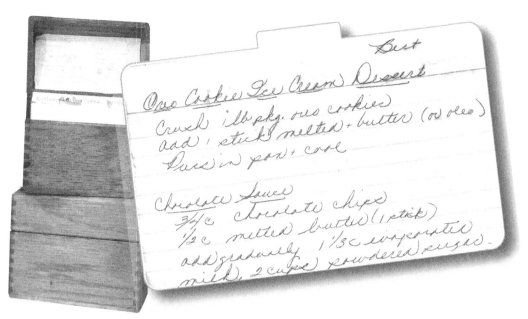

A Dog in Fog

I grew up with a gun in my hand. From practically as soon as I could walk I would accompany my father and brother into the field in pursuit of small game. By the age of five, I owned a BB gun and was allowed to carry it in the field, strict gun rules prevailing, of course. By age nine, I was the proud owner of a single-shot .22 rifle and became an avid squirrel hunter. I still have that gun and could not list the number of squirrels, rabbits, and even pheasants I've put in the pot with it. When I was eleven, Dad handed me a single-barrel .16-gauge shotgun, and I joined the ranks of the pheasant hunters. The scattergun was an old Montgomery Wards with a straight stock. For a skinny little eleven-year-old, I practically needed to back up to a tree to let it off without taking a few steps backward, but it was mine, and I wasn't giving up for anything or anybody.

Back in the 1960s, there were only a few counties in Iowa that had a significant pheasant population, and Taylor County was one. The opening of pheasant season was an event. Stores ran hunter specials, one of the bars gave away a brand-new shotgun to the person who brought in the longest tail feather. Even the churches held special hunter services and potluck dinners. Our tiny town was so crowded with hunters for the first two weekends of the season it was a traffic jam. Long-lost relatives appeared in pickup trucks and campers. The typically lonely gravel and dirt roads of the countryside became lined with cars and pickups, cruising for a place to hunt.

At the age of 15, I was already a seasoned hunter. I would pick up shotgun or rifle and hit the outdoors at any free moment during the season. Dennis, a classmate and friend and I would often stop out-of-state cars and ask them if they needed a guide and a place to hunt. In this fashion, we met new people, hunted behind good dogs, and traveled further from home than we could have on shanks mare.

When opening day of 1968 rolled around, I was more than usually excited for the hunt. The previous year I had acquired a Labrador pup I'd intelligently christened "Lab," and I spent the spring and summer training him. Dad and I were going to open the season together, and I was eager to discover if my training of the dog was worth a damned. Training a bird dog is always a tricky proposition. Mostly the hunting stuff comes naturally to a bird dog with a pedigree, but you never find out what they can do until the first time you get them on live game. Will he have a good nose? Will he be gun shy? Will he come on command and fetch a downed bird? Well, tomorrow was the day to answer those questions.

We woke in the morning to a world entirely blanketed in fog. You could not see more than a few yards, and it was akin to walking through a steam bath, only cooler. Undaunted Dad and I loaded up the guns and dog and drove the truck a few miles north. In actual fact, all we needed to do was walk out back of the house on our own farm, but this year an old friend of Dad's had invited us to hunt on his place. Bill said his backyard was alive with roosters. That sounded good to me. Bill and his wife lived on a good-sized farm in a dilapidated old house, and the acre or so around the house was grown up with horseweeds at least seven–eight feet tall. While Bill didn't seem to believe in using a mower, his lassitude made for perfect cover to shelter all kinds of wild game.

After making our polite greetings, we retrieved our shotguns and scooted behind the house following Lab along one of the several fallen fences. The area around the house was originally a series of feedlots for hogs and cattle and consisted of several fenced-in rectangles in places connected to old buildings. All of this was nearly an unbroken jungle of grasses and tall weeds. Hidden in random places were pieces of abandoned farm equipment. With the thick weeds and dense fog, it was hard to keep from barking a shin or turning an ankle on old iron. Hidden boards and random lengths of loose wire also kept the walk interesting.

With such thick fog, the birds would not want to fly unless pushed off the ground by the dog. In this dense cover, they would slip and run, then sit. Flight was their last resort. It was evident from the dog's body language that Lab was onto something immediately, the question was it pheasant or rabbit? Rooster or hen? Anyway, we knew he had a nose. Dad and I were on either side of a fence that ended at an open tractor road, and as we approached the opening, mister rooster launched out of the fog. *Bang!* Rooster down. Lab ran over to inspect this thing that his nose had been seeking. I knew then he was going to get the hang of his new job.

We each took one side of another fence and two minutes later, same thing, same result–two birds up, two birds down, not bad. I had a bird, and Dad had a bird, Lab knew his job.

As we worked deeper into the weeds, it became a surreal world. The jungle of plants was nearly impenetrable, and the soft damp fog surrounded us. Only a short distance apart, we had to talk to each other to discern locations. Lab would appear and disappear like a black apparition. Pushing through the thick weeds my heart would stop when a hen pheasant burst from underneath your foot. "Hen!

My sketch of a Ring-neck rooster pheasant.

Hen!" was the call not to fire. Before your heart could stop racing, the bird would vanish, the fog swallowing up even the sound of her wing beats.

We walked into the densest patch of cover, hoping to push another rooster to the outside and onto open ground. We could not see the dog. It wouldn't have made any difference if we could have. It was so thick in the tall weeds I could not have put a gun up to my shoulder if twenty roosters flushed at once. Walking carefully and expecting a flush at any moment, Dad and I broke through to open ground at the same time. Lab popped out just behind us, his tongue lolling and looking as happy as a dog can look. He barely glanced our way when he turned and stuck his nose back into the cover. Another rooster blasted out of the weeds. I led him and swung with his rise. *Boom!* Bird number three was in the bag. We worked that patch a while longer but only heard a few old boys cackling away in the fog. We decided to change locations and walk along the gravel road across from the house. There was an unpicked field of corn across the road. The grassy ditch would be an ideal place for a rooster to be napping on this damp morning.

Now I don't know if the reader has ever seen a country gravel road, but for the uninitiated, let me try to explain. In the spring, the County drops loads of gravel onto the winter-damaged roads and grades the rock level. As the roads get used, the gravel tends to wander over to the outside edges. At the same time, spring and summer see a lot of weeds and grass growing along the edges. Periodically the County will cut the weeds and grade the gravel back into place. This grading tends to leave mounds of plant detritus along the roadsides. As we walked, guns at port arms along the edge of the road, I stepped on one of these mounds. No one was more surprised than I when Mr. Cottontail burst out of the pile of gravel. I was surprised, but I rolled him anyway.

Hey, we thought that was fun, wonder if there are more? So, we spent the next 30 minutes in the dense fog stomping on gravel mounds along the roadside. All told we shot four rabbits, and we already had the three pheasants. We decided to call it a morning. As we walked along the roadside toward the truck Lab was working the ditch next to the cornfield. Well, you know it, he stuck his nose into a clump of grass and up comes a cackling rooster. He got about 20 yards out into the field when Dad dropped him with such a pretty shot. He folded right up.

"Good shot," I yelled.

"Yeah, I hope I can find that rooster in all that corn," was Dad's laconic response.

I stayed on the road to mark the spot, and my father scrambled over the barbed wire fence and plunged into the standing corn. I guided him to the likely place, and he kicked around for a few minutes. Pretty soon, I was getting some "damn its" and "I'll be go to hells." Dad hated to lose a bird.

It became pretty apparent we were not going to find that bird, so Dad grudgingly trudged back to the fence. Just as he got ready to boost himself over, Lab popped out of the corn. "Hey," I yelled, "were you looking for that?" I pointed at Lab, who was proudly bearing a mouthful of decidedly dead pheasant. "Well, I'll be damned, I guess he'll make a hunting dog after all," said Dad, taking the proffered bird.

I remember it was a good day, a very good day.

Pistachio Bread
1 pkg yellow cake mix (not with pudding)
1 sm pkg pistachio pudding (instant)
4 eggs
1/4 cup oil
1 cup sour cream
1/2 c. chopped walnuts
1/8 c. water
3/4 c. maraschino cherries (halved)

Topping:
1/4 c. sugar
cinnamon

Combine ingredients; Mix with a spoon

The Letter Jacket–
Be True to Your School

Not long ago, I found myself rummaging through old photo albums look-ing for pictures to use for a birthday party. In my search, I came across my old scrapbook. After the birth of each grandchild, my Grandma Gray would start an album for that new grandbaby. After a time, it was up to the child to add to it and keep it going. Along with baby pictures and school activities, my book contains a record of my athletic accomplishments through high school. Carefully preserved under plastic, taped to the inside back cover, are my wrestling medals. I smiled when I rediscovered them and became trans-ported back to a time when one of my most prized possessions was my letter jacket.

The antecedents of the letter jacket go back to 1865 and Harvard College. In need of an identifier for the football team, the letter H was sewn onto gray sweatshirts, and a uniform was born. If a player put in enough time each season, they kept their jersey. By 1891 the H was being sewn onto sweaters that "letter winners" could sport on and off-campus.

Fast-forward many years and through countless college and high school teams, in 1968 you would find me at Dale's Clothing proudly buying my black and gold letter jacket in preparation for entering Lenox High. Of course, as a freshman, I was just over five-foot and barely weighed 112 lbs. Hardly an auspicious physique for an aspiring athlete, but I was determined to hang an L on my new jacket. And over the next four years, I did, along with letters in football, wrestling, track, and–of all things–music. Our footballers were especially proud of the "Conference Champs" patches we sported both our junior and senior years. At that time, a first in the school's history.

I was quick to discover that the letter jacket was not only a great identifier of status in one's hometown, but it told an instant story when one went to a gathering of teenagers from other towns. From across the room, one could rapidly identify what school, what sport, and how good the wearer was in that sport. This detail is especially true for wrestlers because wrestlers and those who ran track traditionally sewed their medals onto their letters. A champion wrestler would "clink" when he walked. The more medals, the more he clinked. I desperately wanted to clink.

By my junior year, I was beginning to hang medals on my L. I placed in wrestling tournaments at Mt. Ayer, Leon, and Sectionals. I would add a couple more in my senior year. That first lonely medal was getting company. Of course, I hedged my bets by sewing them close enough together to clink (at least a little) when I walked. I still recall there is no sight quite like seeing a wrestler who never loses, wearing his letter jacket. After a while, a wrestler may run out of room to sew on his vast array of gold medals. Whew! The burden must be heavy. It always reminded me what a minor player I really was. The thing is, that unless the medals are all gold, even though each one represents a triumph, they also represent a heartbreaking loss. Still, I was proud of my medals.

Like any school anywhere, our prettiest girls were cheerleaders. Of course, for the football cheerleaders, the Fall Friday nights could get pretty chilly. I was often asked to loan my jacket to one of the girls to help them stay warm during the football games. My only stipulation was that they count my medals after each cheer. Those sweet girls never lost one.

For four years, I proudly wore my jacket. In the fall, it kept the chill off. In the deep winter, I would wear it over a yellow Tiger hoodie, and of course, it warded off the spring rains. When I traveled to other towns, it was my status symbol, letting all know that I was a Lenox Tiger, and at Lenox, we were pretty good at a lot of sports.

Of course, after four years as a Tiger, the administration finally kicked me out of school by actually graduating me. That fall, I was off to Graceland College, and of course, I wore my high school letter jacket.

In the last half of my senior year, I was at a party. In the crowd, someone stumbled and threw a glass of bourbon all over my jacket. I had it cleaned, and all seemed well enough. Walking across campus at Graceland with friends, it began to rain. Instantly I started to smell like a highball. If you could have added ice cubes, I could have done Halloween as a drink. My beloved jacket had to be retired. For years it hung upstairs in my closet at my folks' house. I don't know when it got discarded, but it certainly served me well.

Last year I found myself sitting next to a young athlete who was about to graduate from high school. I congratulated him on his successes and asked if students still wore letter jackets or if they were no longer cool? He assured me that the letter jacket is still going strong. Looking back, it may seem silly to some to have attached so much importance on awards, games, medals, and prestige. I am always aware that one can fall into the "old man" trap of remembering being much better than I truly was. Truth is, I was able to compete on a very limited stage. But I didn't need to wrestle at Iowa or aspire to the NFL. No, what I needed, what I used, was the opportunity to parley my little successes at Lenox High into the idea that I could go to college. And I did. Eventually, they kicked me out of Drake University by graduating me. Who knew if you hung around long enough, they gave you a diploma and booted you out? At last I had my hall pass to the adult world. Yet, my letter jacket lives on in my heart.

The letters I proudly wore on my jacket for six years.
I lettered in Football, Wrestling, Track, and Chorus.

91

Lemon Pie
1 cup water
3/4 cup sugar
1 tsp. grated lemon rind
4 Tblsp. flour
2 Tblsp. cornstarch

1/2 cup cold water
3 egg yolks, beaten
1 Tblsp. butter
4 Tblsp. lemon juice
1/4 tsp. salt

Boil 1 cup water, sugar, salt, lemon rind; add flour and cornstarch mixed with 1/2 cup water. Cook slowly 5 to 10 minutes, stirring constantly. Add beaten yolks; cook 2 min. Remove from heat, add butter and lemon juice separately; stir well. Cool slightly

Of Hogs and Hope

When I was a young man, one of my favorite things was to watch baby pigs come into the world. From the age of sixteen to eighteen, one of my jobs was to sit with farrowing sows in the spring, a job I did happily. When a mother pig, a sow, gives birth, it is referred to as *farrowing*. In the normal cycle of farm life, a boar is let loose into the pen with the sows in the early fall. Then, by spring, the little ones are ready to pop into the world.

In the upper mid-west, Old Man Winter often retains his loosening grip on the world into late spring, so it stays cold at night, much too cold for little pink newborn baby pigs to survive. We farrowed from twelve to thirteen sows, and when the mothers-to-be were close to their birthing dates, we moved them into a farrowing house. The farrowing house was a long low building with a concrete floor and small, five-foot by seven-foot pens running down the outside walls with a door at either end. Each pen had, on either side, a two-by-four rail nailed about a foot off the ground running the length of the pen. The space in the pens was narrow, and each sow weighed between 300 to 500 pounds. When a sow lay down in her pen, there was a genuine possibility she could accidentally crush her babies. The rails were a simple, cheap, and ingenious answer to this problem. The small space created by these boards gave the piglets a place to scramble out of harm's way and avoid getting crushed by Momma.

We prepared the farrowing house by spreading clean straw on the floor. Because of the hog waste, the straw had to be scooped out and changed daily. Cleaning the pens was also one of my chores. Stacks of clean towels were placed on a shelf to prepare for the multiple births, and each pen had a low-hanging heat lamp turned on for added warmth. These lights would burn night and day until the new babies were big enough to create their own warmth, a couple of weeks after their birth.

Once the first pig began squealing its way into the world, they just kept coming day and night until the last sow delivered her last baby. This time was the time I liked. I would sit up with the hogs in the cold evenings after dinner and into the even colder nights to assist the mothers with the birthing process. If, as happened most of the time, the babies popped out with no problems, I would scoop up the grunting little newborn, wipe it down with a clean towel, tell it hello, and tuck it to mama's breast.

Each sow typically produced eight to twelve babies each year. It was not unusual for a baby to become stuck in the birth canal. This fact is the real reason we watched over the birthing process. If a baby was emerging back feet first or got sideways, then it was virtually certain all the other unborn piggies would die. Possibly even the mother. When I observed a sow in trouble, I would climb into the pen and calm her by talking to her quietly and stroking her head and back. Working my way down her body, I would reach into the birth canal and grasp the baby by the legs and gently tug until our newest porker popped out into the world.

I spent my nights in silence. I would smoke, and think, and plan. And wonder. I would wonder what was out there for me beyond that great dome of cold darkness surrounding this isolated farmstead. Beyond the great distance, both physical and mental, between my small world and the rest of the universe. I liked it here, however. I was safe and warm. My only immediate worry was right in front of me, and I had the power to affect that.

I remember, vividly, the smells of the new babies. Their fragrance is as fresh and clean and hopeful as any smell on earth. The combined aromas of fresh straw and old dust. The guttural grunts of the mothers and soft grunts of the babies as they slept and nursed and played with their new siblings. I loved the feel of being warmed by the heat lamps, even as I could feel the cold seep in around the walls. It felt to me like I imagined it would feel to be in a cocoon, warm and safe. I lived in this world so many years ago, and now I can only live there in my memories.

A few years after college I did several drawings and paintings of the old buildings on our farm. I knew they would only be standing for a few more years. I was correct.

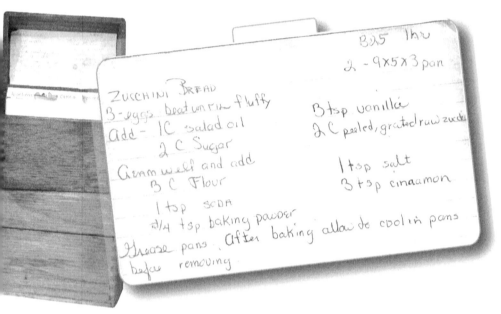

The Road Not Taken

The time is early spring. The year is 1971. Karen (my future wife) and I had been dating for six months. It was increasingly apparent that we liked each other and were going to continue to see, as much as we could, a future together. I don't think we'd imagined the future that was ahead, however.

This year I was a senior in high school, Karen, a junior. That week there were posters up advertising a Spring Fling dance in a nearby town. Karen agreed to go with me, so we were all set for Friday night. I can recall, after all these years, that it was spring because of the light clothes we wore to the dance. Spring in Iowa can be a glorious time of year. The nominal warmth of 50 to 70-degree days, while cool, can feel positively balmy compared to the freezing temps of a long Iowa winter. The prevailing fashion for young girls at the time were eye-popping short shorts. Karen had several pairs and the figure to wear them. They were so short and so tight that, as one man said, "you could count her assets."

We made it to the dance and proceeded to have a splendid time dancing with abandon to the most current music. I don't recall anyone else from our school being there, but we were so in tune with each other we didn't notice. Now it was not unusual for trouble to start if you were a strange boy from another town "intruding" at such a function. As a matter of fact, it was entirely routine for altercations to break out amongst teenaged Alpha males. Often from a boy, or boys, with no dates and usually drunk. But being fearless, strong, and dumb, I always felt like I could take care of myself. Truth? I had been fighting since I was a small boy. This was just the way my world was at that time. Still, since I had been dating Karen, I was attempting to become more genteel. And control my temper. She let me know that she didn't appreciate and would not tolerate that type of rowdy behavior.

So as the evening progressed, we were enjoying the music, the dancing, and each other. A particularly rockin' song came on, and it energized the dance floor. When Karen danced, she could be very expressive. She would lock eyes and give me a devilish look. Her pretty face framed by her long hair. Throwing back her shoulders, she would shake from side to side and make her breasts dance. Her dancing electrified the dance floor. And me. Just then, there they were, the wolf pack. Four boys who were obviously drunk came cruising through the dance floor, bumping couples out of the way. As they passed just behind Karen, one of the boys was smitten by her butt cheeks, which were tantalizingly close and seemed to have mesmerized him. He was medium height and heavy set. Small eyes set back into a round face, and the fact that he was plastered, gave him tunnel vision.

Anyway, he stopped and slowly contemplated Karen's gyrating posterior. I was instantly on alert and began a quick count of my most likely problems. I already had a scenario in mind, and it wasn't pretty. I figured my best bet was to get in fast and do as much damage as I could before the rest jumped on me. Drunk Boy weaved back and forth for a minute and came to a conclusion. He started to reach his hand out to grab at Karen. I stepped closer to get past Karen and hit him. She was dancing in complete oblivion when she saw the expression on my face. Just as the boy reached out, he dropped his hand, spun around, and lurched away. I recovered, smiled at Karen, and a short while later, we left the dance.

The next morning, we awoke to a tragic story. A boy at that dance was so drunk he'd gone outside and passed out on the hood of a car. Later, he rolled off into the street and was hit by a passing car and killed. It was, of course, our Drunk Boy– the same boy. All my life, I have wondered what the outcome of that night might have been if I had hit him?

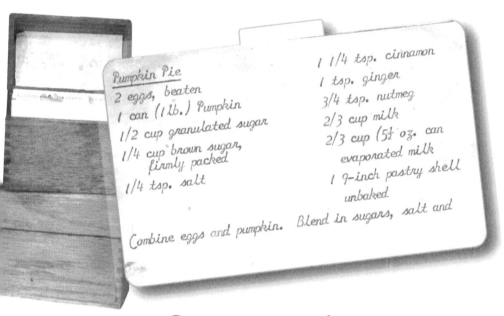

Pumpkin Pie
2 eggs, beaten
1 can (1 lb.) Pumpkin
1/2 cup granulated sugar
1/4 cup brown sugar,
    firmly packed
1/4 tsp. salt

1 1/4 tsp. cinnamon
1 tsp. ginger
3/4 tsp. nutmeg
2/3 cup milk
2/3 cup (5¼ oz. can
    evaporated milk
1 9-inch pastry shell
    unbaked

Combine eggs and pumpkin. Blend in sugars, salt and

Summertime, and the Livin' is...

I was seventeen in 1970, the summer between my junior and senior years in high school. 1970 was the summer I grew up. Always accustomed to taking on responsibility this summer would prove to be a test. One of my parents had to be in Omaha for a two-week stay. I now forget which parent, but I am ahead of myself. That summer, as I had the previous summer, found me working at the school on a government program. Tom Christensen and I were employed 40 hours a week to paint walls, refinish desks, and any other maintenance required in preparing the school for the fall session. For a boy used to heavy farm work, it wasn't too strenuous. Often, I would also hire out to pick up hay for local farmers. I had cash for clothes (which I was expected to buy), gas, and a little fun. Girls were always on my mind, and I was currently sparking Linda. Linda was five-foot-eleven to my five-foot-four. We sat down a lot. Our relationship was never serious, but it was fun.

Along with my other work, I helped my father on our farm. Daily chores were a fact of life, feed and water the cattle, hogs, and chickens, among other duties. By this time, my mother's health was failing, and she was unable to work.

My best friend, Rod, and his family were going away on vacation for two weeks. Now, it is a fact that Rod's family practically adopted me. He and I spent nearly every free minute together, either at his home or mine. It was not unusual for us to sleep in our cars. Camping out, we called it. As it happened, Kenny, his dad, was a prosperous farmer with a lot of farmland. The Millers lived about ten miles north and east of Lenox. Our farm was two miles south and three and one-half miles west. So, we lived some distance apart. Since I spent so much time at Rod's, it was unspoken but expected that I would pitch in and help with Rod's work. Kenny would hire me for jobs like tractor work during the spring planting season or haying in the summer. Kenny inquired, "would you be interested in watching the farm in our absence?" My duties would include making sure the livestock were fed and watered, and no one stole equipment off the farm. I would get the house to live in, the truck to drive (free gas!), and food in the fridge. Plus, I'd get paid. Of course, I said, "yes."

As it happened, my farm duties coincided with my parent's two-week absence at the hospital in Omaha. So, my days proceeded something like this: early in the morning, I would rise, feed and water Kenny's livestock, drive 15 miles, repeat same at the home farm, then motor back to Lenox where I would arrive for work, on time. At 4:30 P.M., I'd do the livestock tango backward, finishing my work at Kenny's early enough in the evening to eat, bathe, and drive into town for some fun. Oh yeah, I forgot to mention I got Kenny's liquor cabinet as well. After more than a week of this, Linda offered to fix me dinner. I accepted. She was in the kitchen preparing something. I was in the tub, soaking away the day's grit. She came in matter-of-factly and brought me a drink. For some reason, this familiarity made me feel mature.

My two weeks passed. Mom and Dad came back, and all was well on the home farm. Rod and family returned to a well-run operation, and all was satisfactory. I resumed only 40-hour weeks, plus chores and extra jobs. Linda? Well, Linda found another guy, her future husband. But that is another story. I believe, for me, those two weeks signaled the beginning of me becoming an adult.

Russian Thistle

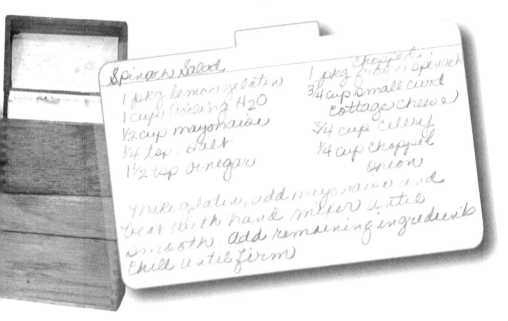

My Alphabet Youth

The NAACP, KKK, NFO, CYO, & Rustlers (!?)

The late 1960s and first few years of the 1970s were a turbulent time in America. The war in Vietnam, protests, and the growing disaffection of America's youth dominated the national news. Speaking for myself, born in the early 1950s, by 1968, I was just coming into my teens. I suppose this is when most of us become aware that there is a whole 'nother world outside of our immediate families. The war touched us, of course, many of our young men had served and even died. The pictures of the struggle came into our homes each night through the news programs. But, the national protests and general dissatisfaction of the young populace would be years away from finding our small town in any serious way. This fact didn't mean, even as a young teen, that I was unaware. It's just all of that was someplace else. I, and most boys like me, were concerned with girls, sports, and hunting.

There were anomalies that niggled in my brain, however. Of course, I realize that one is born where they are, and that fact often colors the world around them. Born in a small town in southern Iowa, I never much questioned the lack of diversity, nor the loose language I often heard from many adults and kids too, for all that. Our town was so lacking in any difference that there was not a single person of another race other than white to be found inside the city limits. The same with religion—no individuals of the Jewish, Muslim, or Buddhist faiths could be found worshiping in our town. In fact, the only group considered a minority then were the Catholics. And I was one. More on that later.

The NAACP in small-town Iowa. I'm not sure when the realization dawned on me how forward and courageous these men of color who drove around to small Iowa towns collecting for the NAACP must have been. I do remember it was an annual occurrence to view a black man (two usually) walking our streets. I distinctly recall though one day, I stood staring, as these two gentlemen parked on Main and climbed out of their car. The language that we used to describe people of color came into my head. Yes, I said *we*, and as a young boy, I was no stranger to passing on the jokes and other racial epitaphs. But what struck me full-on was what was said by us bore no resemblance to who I could see walking our Main street.

I lived in a poor farming community; success was the banker, doctor, lawyer, and large landowner. Most others vacillated between middle class and poverty, and in some cases, extreme poverty. Yet, here I was, looking at two very handsome men with apparent poise.

These men, these dark skinned strangers, sported expensive suits, diamond rings, and drove a well-appointed late model car. That started me to wonder if perhaps much of what I heard from the locals might not have been hyperbole based on ignorance. And, maybe it came from a deeper place than I knew? I would eventually put a two with a two.

The KKK and its long reach. In the 1920s, the Ku Klux Klan had what came to be known as the Second Resurgence. The KKK fever swept through the Midwestern states, including Iowa, where previously it was moribund or even relatively unknown. For a time, membership in the Klan swelled to 5 million members. History tells me that in our town, the KKK held parades, men covered in the traditional garb of white sheets riding horses down Main Street. Of course, the humorous thing (if one can find humor here) is that they were virtually all recognized by the horses they rode and their boots. On a sadder note, there were threats of violence against Catholics and exclusion by some from the greater community. I'm happy to say that even though this happened, the Kluckers were by no means a majority. Gradually the Second Klan began its decline until the advent of World War II saw a precipitous decline in the Midwest and a falling back into the southern states. The Klan directed their hatred at people of color, Jews, and Catholics, and as I previously noted, I was reared a Catholic. Now, just because the Klan faded did not mean some of the attitudes of the people who were former Klan members suddenly went away.

By the time I reached the age of ten years old in 1963, I had started to sense some of those feelings directed at the Catholics in our community. There are examples but mostly a general "feeling." However, I can relate two such instances, the first when I invited a close friend to the church for a party. He informed me his dad would not let him set foot in our church, as "we would capture him and make him a Catholic." Another a few years later, after I thought much of this had faded, I asked a girl to a dance. After checking with her father, she informed me that "no, she could not see me socially as I was a Catholic, and she a Baptist." It would seem that by the time I graduated from high school in 1971 and off to college and marriage in 1973, that all of those sentiments were history in our town. Boy, I was mistaken. My new Methodist in-laws were recipients of KKK-type hate mail after their daughter married a Catholic. Sigh. This stuff dies hard.

The NFO, farmers on strike? The National Farmer's Organization (NFO) was officially founded on 22 September 1955 in Bedford, Iowa, and headquartered in Corning, Iowa. Early on it reached a membership of 149,000 members. The NFO established as a highly militant protest group, and was bent on highlighting the low pay and plight of the American farmer. With their 1967 general strike, the NFO achieved national notoriety. Even as a young boy, I was curious how any organization could unite individual farmers who had readily chosen a solitary lifestyle? But unite they did, up to a point. The '67 strike called for withholding certain commodities from the market, namely milk and hogs.

As a part of their more militant action, the NFO and Corning, Iowa, made the national news when thousands of gallons of milk were poured onto the street and flowed down Main. In other "actions," hogs were slaughtered but not butchered. Tempers and violence flared in the Midwestern states. By no means, not all farmers were members of, or friends to, the NFO. There was intimidation on both sides, barns threaten with burning, fires set, shots fired, fences cut, tires flattened, windows broken. But the most tragic result of the strike was when a group of NFO farmers tried to prevent a truck from driving into a stockyard, and two men (NFO members) were struck and killed. For many, this was way too close to home.

I was a witness to the violent emotions from both sides. One afternoon I was standing in what was then the pool hall listening to my father and a friend talking about the NFO. Dad's friend had some very loud and negative opinions about the organization. One of the more prominent NFO members overheard the remarks. Well, almost everyone within earshot had heard. The NFO rep got right up into the other man's face and pointing his finger said, "you know your barn could just burn?"

Now, Dad's friend was a big man and not one to back down. His face became red, and he leaped to his feet, pointed his finger back, "You listen, you SOB! Your barn will burn as easily as mine." There was no more talk of barn burning after that. The NFO is still very much in existence and through new leadership has morphed into a collective bargaining group for farmers.

CYO every Wednesday, or else. It would seem that organizations, primarily known by their initials, influenced much of my youth. CYO stands for Catholic Youth Organization. As with most religion-affiliated groups, CYO existed to show Catholic teens the path to living a good religious life while following the tenants of the church. It was both instructional and social. CYO, in my youth, was on Wednesday nights. The evening would begin with a Mass and then a gathering in the basement of the church. That meant, of course, that during the school year, I was attending Mass twice a week. I didn't really mind–many of my friends, classmates, and teammates were in CYO. We periodically held dances and parties, but there was no question in my house whether I would be there, or not. I would. Well, as it sometimes comes to pass with young boys, I was smitten by a girl. Eventually, we became just friends. However, through a quirk of fate, she was sent to The Mount, a convent in Maryville, Missouri, to study. Yes, I said *convent*. The Mount is where she met and introduced me to a young woman from Panama in Latin America. A beautiful girl–I was entranced–but really, I knew this was just a passing fancy. But I pursued the girl with as much vigor as a 16-year-old boy could muster.

One particular Wednesday, a friend convinced me that we could make the hour drive down to The Mount and back arriving in time for Mass. "Well, let's go," sez I. And we were off. After a flying trip down to northern Missouri, I confidently walked into the all-girls school only to be met by Mother Superior and summarily ejected from the premises. I'll probably never get thrown out of a better place than a convent. The reverse trip was even faster. Thankfully no police were there to mar our great jet-like journey. However, I was deposited at the church just as Mass finished. Thinking to sneak in the back door and pretend as if I had been at Mass, I slipped through the door. I stood up straight when I came face to face with my father, I was instructed to apologize to our priest. Was it worth it? Oh, heck, yes. The next year The Mount closed its doors, the beautiful object of my affection went back to Panama, and my friend returned to finish her senior year at home.

Rustlers, *the wild west ain't dead yet.* Anyone even remotely familiar with my writing knows what an influence Westerns and the Old West had on my life. But, of course, the stuff of TV and the movies were fiction. Right? Horse chases and gunfire. Hang 'em from the nearest tree, and all that. In the late 1960s and early 1970s, prices for livestock, notably beef cattle, were at a high. The area where I lived was described as "rural," but that doesn't quite do it justice. *Rural and isolated* might be a better description. Farmers and townspeople who live in communities like ours rely on the common decency of their neighbors. As it is in all of mankind, there are always those few who will take advantage. This human failing is how Wild West rustling reared an ugly head in the latter part of the 20th century in southwest Iowa. I recall vividly in the late 50s and early 60s on our first farm how my father had to protect against chicken thieves and those who would drain gas tanks. From time to time, we would hear a ruckus in the night, and he would venture outside to fire his old Montgomery Ward single-shot .16 gauge into the sky.

One time, while having a few beers uptown, and knowing his man was within hearing, he mused that he knew who the chicken thief was, and the next time he was shooting for real. That was the end of the chicken thefts. But jump forward ten years, and suddenly there were reports of groups of cattle and hogs gone missing. Rustlers? Rustlers! It seems that some enterprising individuals figured out that in the wee hours of the morning, it was easy work to drive a truck into an unguarded pasture, load up a few head, and drive them to a distant market while faking up papers. We, too, were the sad victims of the crime spree. We kept 13 brood sows, and each Spring, they would yield in the neighborhood of 130 babies. The Spring of 1970 was no exception. One day we made a count and discovered that we now had only 90 pigs in the pen. Poof, just gone, along with much of our profits. Time has dimmed my memory of the outcome. I do remember that the rustlers of southwest Iowa were eventually apprehended. One (or maybe two) were from local families. Most given 18-month sentences. And so, this closed that strange chapter of local lore.

And, also, the musings on My Alphabet Youth.

Five-Cent Beer
in a Ten-Cent Bar

When I walked into the bar, it felt like a trip back in time. Technically, a half-century ago, it was referred to as "the Pool Hall" for the prosaic reason that one could get up a game of pool there even if one were not old enough to drink alcohol. The polished walnut bar on the left as I came through the front door was long and heavy; booths were on the right along the wall. A flimsy faux fence separated the pool players in the back from the earnest drinkers in the bar. These were the days when old men and boys also haunted the place along with the more practiced drinkers up front.

The entrance from the street into the bar remained ajar during open hours; propped open as I recall by the makeshift doorstop of concrete block. The outside world kept at bay by a heavy screen door that banged with authority each time an eager patron lunged through on his way to imbibe. Stools lined the broad bar, a wild west style mirror hung above a shelf of liquors, and a well-stocked cooler advertised drinkers' preferred brews, then mostly Schlitz, Budweiser, PBR, and a few other outlying brands. Posters of semi-clad babes hawked the favorite thirst quencher, or perhaps a poster of a flushing pheasant to remind us that we lived in God's country where real men drank the advertised beer. The proof that we were patronizing a back-water bar, however, showed in the rack of counter checks (blank checks that could be made out for cash written on any of a dozen banks in the vicinity) and over-large jars containing pig's feet, hardboiled eggs, and sausages each floating in their own pickling juices.

From a very early age, this saloon and its denizens became as familiar to me as my living room or any of the fields that I roamed with rifle and dog. I'd been gracing this establishment since before I could read or count. Most Saturdays you could find all of the male members of my family patronizing the pool hall. My brother and I in back shooting pool. My grandfather, who never imbibed, sitting on a backbench visiting with old friends, and my father up front heartily drinking with fellow farmers.

On the other side of the partial wall, the establishment had straight pool tables, snooker, and billiards. If I recall, straight pool (usually eight ball) was ten-cents a game and billiards/snooker 20 cents, though I could be mis-remembering. The most unusual thing was that there was an attendant to rack the games for you. When one finished a game and wanted another, you pounded the fat end of your stick on the well-worn wooden floor, and a new game would be set up. I believe this job allowed the man to earn pocket change. When he was gone so was that job. After that, the loser racked the next game.

Saturday was the day farmers paused in their work and drove wives and children to town. The men bought items at the hardware or feed store, got haircuts, wives shopped for groceries and clothing, the children turned loose to play with friends and terrorize the Five and Dime buying penny candy and perhaps a twenty-cent movie at Elsie's theater. While it seemed that the pool hall was caught in a time warp, of course, changes came, albeit slowly, but changes never-the-less. The old wall disappeared and an oven that could heat sandwiches in minutes appeared. Limited food choices now served at the bar. The jars of pickled foods went away, never to reappear. I surmise that those pickle jars were reincarnated as slowly turning hotdog ovens in truck stop convenience stores across America.

For the farmers and merchants in farm country, other changes arrived that would in a few short years alter the landscape. New machinery allowed for farming larger and larger farms more efficiently. Small farms were absorbed by more successful farmers eager to add to their holdings. No longer were they picking ear corn and storing the ears in bins to be shelled later, the picker-sheller ended that practice. Sadly, fewer farmers meant fewer merchants; eventually, clothing stores, barbers, restaurants would close. Occasionally, someone would reopen a business only to see it to go the way of the previous owners. I too changed from small boy to high school age, where I attended classes, played sports and worked at the school part-time as janitorial help. Summers, full-time and winters I would work for an hour before school and all-day Saturday unless I was wrestling in a tournament.

What does any of this have to do with a five-cent beer you may be asking yourself? Very little, and kind of a lot. As I described, the bar had been a hangout of mine for years, and that is where I met the man I'll call Mark. Mark and I met one Saturday while I was in the bar eating one of those new quick-heat sandwiches. He seemed to crave a bit of conversation, so we struck up an acquaintance that lasted until he quit coming. You see, Mark was a retired railroad engineer, and he would tell me, or anyone who would listen, about his years on the railroad. I enjoyed knowing the man and hearing his stories of railroading. Tall and yet straight, I suspected he was in his seventies at the time. The kick was that his wife would only let him have beer on Saturdays. Picture this: Mark would walk downtown dressed in his best railroad engineer clothes, striped overalls, striped engineer cap, watch fob attached to

his old-time pocket watch, and a bright red bandana tied around his throat. Every inch a railroad man. A man dressed for what he considered a solemn event, his attire a well-earned uniform, the watch his badge of authority.

At that time in the pool hall, a beer drinker could buy either a large, ten-cent beer or a small half-beer for five cents. Mark always arrived with two nickels, one for each of the beers his wife allowed him. Mark would seat himself perching on a bar stool next to me and signal the bartender he was ready. A small beer would appear on the bar in front of Mark, who would reach into his pocket, extract a nickel, and with a forefinger push the coin across the bar. Then, out came the pocket watch to mark the time. He would visit with me for long minutes before even touching his glass. Then checking his watch, waiting for some signal only he could fathom. Thinking this odd, I asked him about his beer drinking habits. Mark explained that he detested cold beer, so he waited patiently until the brew became more or less room temperature. Once Mark took a sip and was satisfied it was drinkable another draft materialized in front of him to begin its warming. The second, and last, nickel was carefully and deliberately pushed across the board, plucked up by a smiling bartender then disappeared into the till. In this fashion, Mark would while away the better part of a Saturday slowly, slowly enjoying his two five-cent beers and pleasant conversation happily recalling his life's passion, the railroad.

Many years have passed since the five-cent beers, but the bar remains rooted in the same building. The pool tables are long gone, replaced by tables and more booths, and the bar is now a full-sized restaurant. Today, when I drop in for a drink, I might visit with as many women as men or find families with small children eating their dinners. Pleasant enough, but for me the walls yet reverberate with a banging door, clink of beer bottles, and clack of pool balls. Fond recollections of a day gone by and my tale of a five-cent beer in a ten-cent tavern.

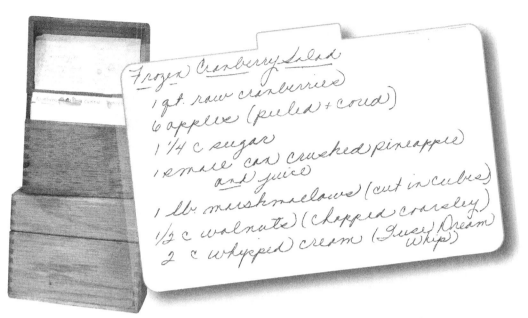

Frozen Cranberry Salad
1 qt. raw cranberries
6 apples (peeled + cored)
1 1/4 c sugar
1 small can crushed pineapple
   and juice
1 lb. marshmallows (cut in cubes)
1/2 c walnuts (chopped coarsley)
2 c whipped cream (Juse Dream
   Whip)

Mr. Rat and the Quick Draw Kid

From their origins in Asia over 2,000 years ago, the common Brown Rat has made its way to every continent in the world except the Arctic and Antarctica. The Brown Rat goes by many other names: sewer rat, Hanover rat, Norway rat, or wharf rat. As every old farmer can attest, they certainly made their way to the Iowa farmsteads. Definitely, they made themselves at home on our farm south of town. As a small boy, one of our favorite games was rat killing. Often, we would venture out in the evening with a .22 rifle and a flashlight. We would spy the critters up against the buildings or when we would move a pile of old lumber. Our farmhouse had no indoor bathroom, so the facilities were a double-holer outhouse. Our dogs were rat crazy, and when we tilted the outhouse, the dogs would jump underneath and pull out any rat that had taken up residence. Grabbing the unfortunate rodent by the back of the neck, the dog would shake the furball until they broke its little neck and crushed its skull.

Growing up on a farm in Iowa in the 1950s until the mid-1970s, buildings for storing grain were a common sight on any farmstead throughout the Midwest. Back then, most farmers raised livestock, so grain was stored in large quantities for feeding purposes or to sell when the market looked good. Granaries filled with oats or corn, both shelled and on the cob, were a common sight in any farmyard. Until the mid-1960s, corn was picked on the cob and shelled later. It wasn't until around 1970 that the picker-sheller had virtually replaced the old corn pickers.

Back in my childhood, it was not uncommon for a farmer to fill a corn-crib with ears of corn and not shell it until needed, often for several years. I recall, in about 1969, Harry Freeman asked my dad if he would help shell corn, and would he bring me along? Frank Stanger contracted to drive his old truck-mounted sheller to do the job. Harry's son Gary, Dennis Hayworth, Dan Hewitt, and I were the muscle. I don't remember who all was there but the usual suspects for sure; Harry, Dad, Edgar Weese, and Russ Wurster. The adult's job seemed to be to sit on overturned buckets, drink beer, and direct us kids to do the work.

That day the kids' job was to empty a very large corncrib of some hoary ear corn. I'm not sure how long the corn had been stored in that crib, but it was many years. It had been there so long that the passageway built to leave space to push the sheller's links into the crib had collapsed. Years of dust had settled into the loose ears of corn. As an added bonus there were rats and mice in droves. It was a corncrib high-rise of nasty vermin. We tied t-shirts over our mouths to be able to breathe through the thick dust. We would shove our scoops into the pickup-sticks pile of ear corn and when we pulled back the scoop, little creatures would scamper in all directions. After a short time of trying, and mostly failing to whack the quick little fuzz balls with corn scoops, each boy found a weapon. Then, as we scooped corn, we killed rodents with impunity. I picked up a part of an old horse collar that had a brass ball

on its end. When a rat ran by, I'd whack him with my improvised club. There were so many mice we just grabbed them behind the head and pinched. Everyone wore leather gloves to protect our hands. The gloves worked to our advantage, as the mice could not bite our fingers. Though sometimes the little critters would get a hunk of leather and sink their sharp teeth in far enough that we had to shake them off after being squished. To this day, I have never seen so many rats and mice in one place.

By the time I was twelve, we had moved to a different farm a few miles away. This old homestead had been there for a hundred years. Along with the house, there was a summer kitchen built in the days when meals were cooked over wood stoves. We also had the luxury of indoor plumbing. There were no more outhouses to overturn where rats could hide. However, we still had plenty of rats in the outbuildings. My mother raised chickens and liked to keep some shelled corn for their feed. Dad purchased a small granary that sat near the road, where along with the shelled corn, we stored cattle and hog food in 50 lb. bags. The building was built with two 2" x 14" boards in a large X to support either end. It was not slatted, but the rats had managed to chew through the wooden floor and had built quite a subterranean village underneath the granary.

Ever since I was old enough to chore, I always hung my work jeans on the back of the bathroom door. I had a Cub Scout hunting knife hanging from my belt, and, unless they were in the wash, my jeans were always ready-to-wear. When I was seventeen, I added a small .22 revolver to my armament. I liked to carry the pistol, in the event I surprised old Mr. Rat on my rounds while doing chores in the mornings and evenings. I was prepared for all-out war.

Since I was a small boy, I had always fancied myself as a cowboy, albeit one without a horse. I never let that little detail stand in my way. From the time I could hold a toy gun, I practiced my quick draw. When I eventually graduated to a real pistol, I was shooting at clods, tin cans, and other stationary objects. If the enemy were to ever come "over the hill," I was ready. I even had my trusty companion, "Boots the Wonder Dog."

One afternoon I headed to the granary to get a bucket of corn to feed the chickens. When I swung open the door, there sat Mr. Rat on one of the crossbars, just staring at me. As surprised as I was, Mr. Rat froze. I slipped out my little pistol, took aim, and fired. He jumped like he was stung, then charged down the crossbar directly at me. He was coming like a wounded lion. That rat came down that crossbar so fast he charged right underneath Boots. I back peddled about five feet, and Mr. Rat, at last, collapsed in a death rattle. He lay there looking at me, sides heaving, snapping his nasty yellow teeth, and then he died. Some help the wonder dog was.

After that, I felt it was time to declare war on the rodent population on our farm. I dug out my old muskrat traps and set a few inside the granary. I stapled the chains to the floor so any trapped rat could not drag them down their holes, then covered the traps with old feed sacks to give the creatures a feeling of safety. My plan was a success as I caught several of the nasty critters over the next few weeks.

One bright spring morning, I opened the granary door to see the chain on one trap taut underneath a feed sack. I stepped into the building to move the bag when Boots charged by me, stuck his head underneath the covering, and with a horrible Yelp! pulled back. As he frantically backed away, I saw that Mr. Rat was firmly attached to the end of Boot's nose. Boots retreated as far as the chain length would permit. Mr. Rat stretched out as far as he could stretch, one leg in the trap and the other three clawing air. As quick as a blink, I jerked my pistol and shot the rat right off the end of Boot's nose. I'm not sure what made

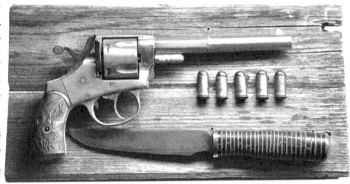

The surviving remnant of the old granary. On it I have mounted Great Grandpa Gray's knife and one of my antique pistols.

me do it, but I am certain I could never do it twice. Boots was no worse the wear for his rodent encounter. Once Wonder Dog was free from the angry rat, he mauled his tiny attacker with doggy zeal.

Within a few weeks of the rat incident, I graduated from high school. The day after graduation, I was painting houses and working road construction. My farm chore days were over. The rats, rat dogs, and other such adventures are now only the memories of a long-ago youth. It seems odd that these memories are the things that stick in my mind, not the home-cooked meals of my mother, or the bright sunny mornings and beautiful red sunsets of the Iowa prairies. Go figure. But… even today in my gunroom there's an antique pistol and knife; both hang on a small board. That short piece of board is all that's left of that same old granary where Boots the Wonder Dog and I waged war upon the rat population on the Callahan farm. 🏠

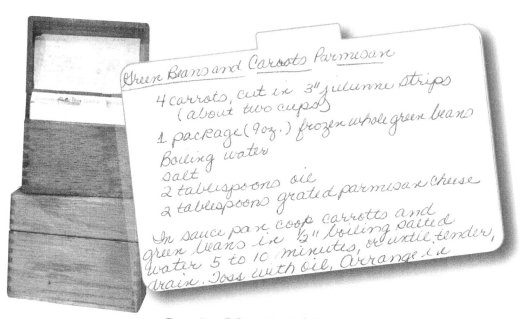

Green Beans and Carrots Parmesan

4 carrots, cut in 3" julienne strips
(about two cups)
1 package (9 oz.) frozen whole green beans
Boiling water
salt
2 tablespoons oil
2 tablespoons grated parmesan cheese

In saucepan coop carrots and
green beans in 1/2" boiling salted
water 5 to 10 minutes, or until tender,
drain. Toss with oil, Arrange in

3 1/2 Miles-
A Story for Karen

It was late afternoon when I turned my steaming car off of the paved highway and onto the muddy gravel road that would take me the final 3 1/2 miles to the farm. It was Friday, and I was making the sixty-mile trip home from college just as I had every weekend of my freshman year. This weekend was special because it was Senior Prom night, and Karen, my girlfriend, would soon graduate from high school. This night was to be the last prom of our lives.

The weather was unusually poor for this time of year. I always recall spring being beautiful in Iowa, especially in early May, around my birthday, which was just one week before. Typically temperatures are mild, and the grass is greening up in preparation for the plowing and planting of the soil. Growing up, I had come to expect balmy days in May as a sort of birthday present from God. Not this year, however–Spring had been frigid and rainy, the rain unrelenting. Today it was bone-chilling, damp and cold. The rain had fallen for days and had finally worn down to a snivel. The clouds hung low like a gray blanket over the earth, and water dripped from every surface. It had rained steadily since late March. The gravel roadbeds were saturated.

Gravel roads web the entire rural portion of the state of Iowa. Cars, trucks, and tractors traveling on the road to our farm had worn tenuous two-rutted paths more-or-less down the middle. When two vehicles coming toward each other would meet, each would wait until the last possible moment to swerve off the ruts where the road became soft and mushy. Invariably, struggling to keep one set of wheels on a stable path, their back ends would fishtail and churn up mud the consistency of fresh concrete. In one heart-pounding, nail-biting moment, they would slide past each other like two ships at sea. Once they passed, each would ease back into the center ruts where it was relatively dry except in those places where the water settled in potholes and formed muddy pools.

Easing off the firm footing of the concrete, I pointed my '64 Chevy Impala down the gray gauntlet and prayed that the chewing gum I'd stuck on my radiator hadn't yet completely melted. Months ago, the radiator in my dilapidated car sprung a leak, and as a poor struggling college student, I couldn't afford an expensive repair. Each Friday, before I set off toward home, I filled the tank with gas while chewing several sticks of gum, which I then jammed on the radiator to plug the leak. It ordinarily took it about the 60 miles to get hot enough to melt the gum wad. A comically effective solution to my problem.

My freshman year of college, all but completed, I was looking forward to the summer. Only a year and a half ago, the mere idea of my going to college had been beyond my comprehension. Karen changed that. I began dating Karen just before Thanksgiving in my senior year of high school. Growing up together in a small town, we knew each other, of course, but we couldn't have had more opposite backgrounds if one of us had been from the Arctic Circle. Karen's father was a physician, one of two in our town, while my father was a farmer, who after thirty years of farming, still lived below the poverty level. Tall and pretty, Karen was a bookworm who never dated. Until me. Short and athletic, I was somewhat of a tough. I was also a football player. In my senior year, after our football team won the conference championship for the second year in a row, Karen and I were thrown together while celebrating. I saw a friend in a car and jumped, howling, through the window, beer in one hand, cigar in the other. I landed in Karen's lap. Later that night, we drove around aimlessly, like teenagers will, and talked. I can't recall what we talked about all these years later. I do remember I found talking to her incredibly easy. I couldn't for the life of me fathom while this sweet, beautiful girl from a prominent family would give me the time of day. I asked her out. She accepted.

Showing up at her house literally scared the hell out of me and would every time I walked in the door for a very long time. Today schools and psychologists talk about giving children self-esteem, but back then, such a thing was unfathomable. You grew up. You were expected to cope. Looking back, I can see now what Karen gave me was my self-esteem. In our small town, we were, each of us, treated by others consciously and unconsciously according to our parents',–and by default–our own station in life. Which, in no small degree, determined ones' community standing. By treating me exactly as she would anyone else, Karen gave me something few others had and in such a way that made me aspire to more. Karen was the only person I can remember who had ever asked what I wanted to do with my life, then encouraged me to go out and do it.

Where was I? Oh yes, college. One day, in a matter of fact way, Karen asked which college I planned to attend. I looked at her with the most stupid, blank look imaginable. (A look I've perfected over the years I might add.) Stupid and blank, because, as I said before, the thought of college had never entered my head. People in my family didn't go to college. No one had. Ever. There was no money and no prospects, and until my junior year, my grades had been diffident. And that's putting it kindly.

Well, Karen's question rattled around inside my noggin for a few days then I made an appointment with our guidance counselor. Wally failed to mask his shock when I asked for college applications, but he dutifully helped with petitions to four schools. I chose small colleges that had wrestling teams. I played football for eight years but was not nearly good enough to continue in college. Wrestling had been a passion since I discovered it in eighth grade, and I had done better than all right in my last two years of high school. Even so, I wasn't sure any colleges would want me. As it turned out, I got invitations from three schools, and in March, my mother and I went to visit Graceland College.

Graceland had a good wrestling team, and after a campus tour and a workout with their All American 118 pounder, I was pleasantly surprised when they offered me a tiny scholarship and set me up with enough aid and loans to pay for tuition, room, and board, and books. I was off to college!

Karen and I continued our budding romance separated by only sixty miles and the four long days between Monday and Friday. This separation, of course, was the reason for my regular weekend trips back. Or as Karen would later put it: she couldn't get rid of me. However, I remember too that when her family went on vacation, she pitched a fit because she was forced to leave me behind for two weeks.

Our growing bond alarmed Karen's father immensely, so in an inspired attempt to loosen it, he had arranged for Karen to attend Drake University. Drake was only one hundred miles from our hometown, but as a cost- ly private school, it seemed far above anything I could hope to attain. However, in March, I cut classes and made a secret journey to Des Moines and applied to attend Drake. I talked to their financial aid people, and Drake, as it turned out, had money earmarked for a few under-advan- taged students. I qualified. We hadn't yet told anyone that we would be off to Drake together in the fall. That domestic discord was still several months in our future, and we kept the secret right until my car, with Karen in it, headed for college at summer's end.

Tonight, was prom night. There would be dinner, dancing (it was the Age of Aquarius), a midnight movie, a little necking, and back to Karen's house for breakfast.

The ancient Impala shivered and rocked as I tore down the slippery grav- el, fishtailing at every soft spot, rear-end wagging like an NFL halfback. I was at the farm in less than five minutes. Our farm was over 100 years old and had once been prosperous, boasting a comfortable house with summer kitchen, two hen houses, two large barns, hog house, corncrib, garage, and a scale house. Sometime in the not-distant past, a sizeable modern machine shed appeared. Time and the ministrations of the various tenants and owners (including–no, especially–my father) had not been kind to the buildings and fences.

Most farms, even prosperous farms, aren't very attractive and were made less so by this day's dreary, muddy conditions. Even so, I always thought our farm looked like something I'd read about in the books *Tobacco Road* or *God's Little Acre*. In the seven years our family had lived here, all of the buildings, including the house, had become dilapidated. One year the older of the two barns and the corncrib had simply collapsed. Fatigue and neglect being the twin catalysts of their demise.

Sliding to a stop, I hopped out of the mud-encrusted car eager to begin preparations for my evening. The ground past our driveway sloped downward to the surviving barn. Beyond the barn, the land rose uphill away from the road to the distant pastures. Exiting my car, I could see my father on the hill one hundred yards distant, waving at me and shouting. I couldn't understand him, but I could tell he was frantic; so, I grabbed my jacket and trotted down the muddy gravel drive, through the barn, and out the back. Emerging from the back door of the barn, I picked my way through the mud and around the fresher cow piles. I looked up in time to witness the most woeful and comic sight I believe I've ever seen before or since.

Now you must understand I'm short Yet, at five-foot-four I'm still two inches taller than my Dad, who walked with a rolling gait even when he was sober, which wasn't all the time, by any means. So, here's the picture: running crossways of the hill was a huge Holstein cow in the process of giving birth. Her work should have been completed, but halfway out and halfway in was her calf, head, and one leg protruding from her vulva and the other leg, along with the rest of its body, firmly wedged down inside the mother. Attached to the calf's free leg was a rope dragging twenty feet behind. Following in his peculiar rolling gait, like a punt tossed on an angry sea, was my father, vainly trying to catch hold of the rope.

I was incredulous and wanted to laugh, but the emergency was too appalling. It was immediately apparent that when Dad found the cow in mid-birth, he saw the problem. Attaching the rope to the calf, he tried to pull the calf without going for help. The mother spooked, leapt to her feet and ran in fear of this interruption of the natural birthing process. Now it was life or death for both the calf and the mother.

I hurried up the hill to reach my father. He ceased chasing the cow, realizing he was doing more harm than good. He suggested I get in front of her and head her off. I didn't feel we could control her out in the open. My idea was to drive the entire herd into the barn and then let them back out, one-by-one until we had the mother corralled in a confined space.

Within a few minutes, we had the herd headed for the barn. Moving them gently along as I hollered "s' boss, s' boss" the call that mornings and evenings brought them in to feed. They came eagerly, and our mother-to-be followed docilely. Once inside, I pushed and coaxed her into the far corner away from the door. As Dad worked the massive sliding door, I drove the rest of the herd back out, one-by-one, until our nascent mother was the only bovine left in the barn.

The heavy Holstein was nervous and wall-eyed by this time, and to avoid sending her into shock, we understood we must move fast. Dad was cursing softly, convinced by now that the calf was dead. Strangled by his mother's vulva, the calf's eyes rolled back inside its head, and its tongue lolled out the side of its mouth. It didn't look good.

The barn, divided into three parts, had holding pens on each side of a haymow. That mow was nearly empty at winter's end. The ancient barn had been built using the straight trunks of pine trees as support poles to hold up the structure. The old pines still had chunks of bark on them. Between the poles ran a fence that separated the pens but allowed the cows to put their heads over and eat hay.

Dad moved the cow closer to the haymow. I grabbed the rope and vaulted the fence. Quickly, I looped the rope around one of the center posts, and as Momma pulled away, I planted a foot firmly on the pole and leaned back on the rope. Desperate and frightened, she began to dig in with all four feet and strain. There was a real and immediate danger of her rupturing herself. Dad stepped up behind her, thrust his hand down inside and tugged on the trapped leg. In an instant, the calf slipped out and plopped to the ground where it lay motionless. Climbing back over the fence, I grabbed an old gun-nysack and wiped off the mucus and blood from the newborn, clearing the air passages. After that, I removed the rope and flexed the baby bull's legs to revive circulation. Nothing.

"Dead," growled Dad, "damn it all. Well, we saved the mother anyway."

"Not so fast," I said, "he's moving."

Sure enough, the calf began to move listlessly. Then the newborn wiggled about and soon struggled to his feet, commencing a wobbly-legged search for his mother and her udder. It was a great feeling as we slapped each other on our backs in congratulations. We watched the bovine Pieta for a minute to make sure they were alright, then headed to the house.

Suddenly I realized I was wet to the bone, muddy, and cold, and in my haste to revive the newborn, I had gotten blood on my only jacket. No matter, the cow and calf were both alive and healthy. By now, it was full dark, and my plans for leisurely prom preparations had evaporated. As I passed through the outer porch into the kitchen, I hung my jacket on a peg. Once inside, I sat shivering at the kitchen table while Dad regaled Mom with the details of our heroics. Going to the cabinet, Dad pulled out a bottle of Seagram's Seven, whiskey. He unscrewed the cap and set the bottle before me.

Now I'd like to tell you that alcohol had rarely passed my lips, but that would be far from the truth, strong spirits being something of a family weakness. But it was unheard of for my father to offer me any, especially in our home where my mother could glare her disapproval. I hefted the bottle and took a healthy swig and passed it across the table.

As we shared the bottle, we talked of the cow and calf, and school. Soon conversation shifted to my relationship with Karen. My father had made no secret of the fact that he thought I was overreaching my station in life, and even though he was fiercely proud of me, he wanted, at the same time, to drag me back and have me share his life. I demurred, refusing to be drawn into a never-ending argument. I assured him that it wasn't serious. Serious was his Catholic language for sex. A concept that frightened him, if possible, even more than status and money. Don't misunderstand, I love my father very much, and, as I'm sure is the case with most parents, we had a complicated relationship. I had always been my father's favorite and had traded on his good graces my entire life. When I got older, our relationship would get much more complicated, but I was naive enough then not to comprehend this fact.

I didn't realize it then, and in fact, I would not realize it for many years, but that night, at that moment, my father and I were as close as we had ever been. And as close as we would ever be the rest of his long life. Sometimes I think about that night, how it was, sitting across the table from Dad. How tired and happy we were. I wish in some way we could have recaptured that feeling again, but we never would. But I understand. Really. The direction and choreography of my future were up to me. I wouldn't be diverted. Not by my father, or anyone else.

By now, I was running late, and I hurried to bathe, my head spinning from the whiskey and still shivering from the cold. No tuxedo this year as it was the Centennial of our small town, and all social activities revolved around our hundred years. I owned a blue pinstriped, three-piece suit that looked vaguely old-fashioned. To accessorize it, I had purchased a cheap bowler hat for costume effect. It was 1972, and in the fashion of the day, my hair hung over my ears, nearly to my shoulders. I had attempted to grow a mustache that resembled nothing more than sweat on my upper lip. I can still look back on pictures of Karen and me posing at the door, ready to depart. Her radiant in her pink gown, hair piled on her head with two tendrils curled around her ears, holding her corsage. And me smiling with smug self-importance, holding that silly hat.

Bath completed, fully dressed, at last, I was ready to leave. Flower in hand, I headed for the car, avoiding the mud and deeper puddles. I brought a change of clothes for later and grabbed my jacket off the porch. I looked at the blood and paused, then shrugged and decided to take it, having no other choice. Take it, or do without, my life had been exactly like that for nineteen years. Either use what you had or do without. Poverty teaches one many immutable lessons. Anyway, I reasoned, it wasn't that unusual in our farming community for nature to make her presence known in our lives, even during our most civilized occasions.

Once in the car, I hit the gas, barely missing the mailbox on the way out of the driveway. I floored the pedal and with a shower of mud and rock shooting from the churning tires. I sloughed down the sodden gravel road with the reckless abandon and insouciance of a nineteen-year-old who was positive he could never be hurt. Skidding to a stop at the highway, I turned my car onto the smooth, solid concrete ribbon that would take me to Karen. Then, leaving one world behind, I slipped into another.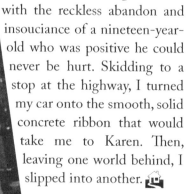

Prom (1972) with Karen in her parent's dining room.

119

Whole Strawberry Pie

1quart strawberries
1 cup water
1/2 cup sugar
1 1/2 tablespoon cornstarch

Few drops red coloring
Baked pastry shell
sweetened whipped cream

Hull and wash berries and crush about 8 of them. Combine sugar and cornstarch in little saucepan and add water and crushed berries. Cook until thick and clear and add red coloring.

Pour hot mixture over whole berries. Turn quickly coating each berry with glaze. Turn into baked shell and chill. At serving time top with sweetened whipped cream.

Pig Headed

It was late in the afternoon when I pulled my steaming 1964 Chevy Impala into our farmyard. About 5:00 PM most likely. As usual, after my last Friday class, I gassed up and sealed my leaking radiator with a wad of chewing gum and hit the highway for the 60-mile drive to the farm. I rushed home every weekend since the beginning of fall classes at college. I did this not out of homesickness, but from a desire to see my girlfriend.

It was the spring of 1972, and I was nearing the end of my freshman year. This year was the only year of my life after I turned 14 that I had not worked at a job. For those nine months, my job was to go to school. I repaid myself by achieving an A average. A factoid that would surely come as a shock to most of my former teachers who saw me as problematic at best.

When I was in my final two years of high school, I had been pretty independent–expected to buy my clothes, pay for my car and expenses, and entertainment. So, it shouldn't be a surprise that when Dad wanted fieldwork done, I charged him as I would any other farmer. Paying me did not make him happy, but I pointed out that if another farmer called, I would be missing a paid day. He saw the logic in my argument. I hasten to add that this debate did not include routine chores but applied to walking beans and picking up hay. But now I was in college and working summers on road construction, I had no compunction about pitching in around the farm, without pay.

It had been a cold, wet spring in Iowa. As I slowed for our drive and eased off of the muddy gravel road into our farm's drive, my mind was not on the weather. I was anticipating dropping my bags at the house and getting a cup of Mom's been-perking-all-day coffee while I let my car cool enough to reapply some new gum to the leaking radiator then head directly to see my girl. As soon as I opened my car door, I could hear Dad cussing back behind the machine shed.

Curious, I walked down the drive toward the barn, and as I rounded the corner, I saw Dad attempting to herd a young pig back through an open gate. As I watched, he would get the hog turned and moved right up to the entrance, and then the hog would whip around and shoot right by his leg. If the little fellow made it up the drive, he'd have the whole world to run in, and

then it would be hell catching him. Dad was flushed, angry, and his cap was a quarter turn to the left. The set of dad's hat was a clear indicator that he had a few beers in him.

"Hold up," I called. "I'm coming."

I turned the little porker and headed him back toward the open gate. Dad swung in behind him, and again, just as the pig got inside the gate, he spun around and made his charge for freedom. Quick as an old western gunfighter, Dad whipped his hammer from his overalls and, with an underhanded swing, caught Porky right between the eyes.

"There, you little son of a bitch! That'll teach you."

I stopped slack-jawed as I stared at the now lifeless pig on the ground. The porker had been dropped in his tracks and was now

121

bleeding profusely from ears and nose. His eyes were rolled back into his head. He had to be dead–I thought–deader n' dead. The loss of any livestock on the farm through sickness or theft was an expensive proposition, so I couldn't believe that my father had intentionally killed what amounted to walking money.

Finding my voice, I stammered. "Jeezus Christ! What the hell?"

"Well, God damn it. He made me mad," was Dad's only response.

Dad bent down and picked up the forty pounds of ham and bacon and tossed him through the gate into the lot. As we closed the gate and walked toward the house, I looked back over my shoulder. Mr. Piggy struggled to his feet, shook his head, and trotted off to find his friends. I don't think my father ever gave it a second thought. That was life on our farm.

On a summer visit home in 2001, I spent an afternoon doing watercolors of my former neighbor's dilapidated barn and his ancient corn sheller. In my youth I spent many hours shoveling ear corn into the hopper of this beast.

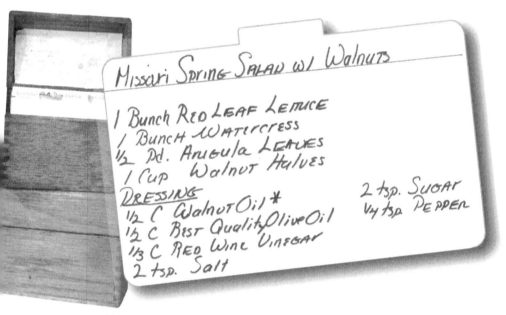

Missouri Spring Salad w/ Walnuts

1 Bunch Red Leaf Lettuce
1 Bunch Watercress
1/2 Pd. Arugula Leaves
1 Cup Walnut Halves
DRESSING
1/2 C Walnut Oil *
1/2 C Best Quality Olive Oil
1/3 C Red Wine Vinegar
2 tsp. Salt
2 tsp. Sugar
1/4 tsp. Pepper

A Lamb in A House of Characters

Late in the summer of 1972, I moved into new digs in Des Moines. I recently transferred to Drake University from Graceland College, where I spent my freshman year. The drive from our rural farm to Lamoni was a short 60 miles. Graceland's campus had roughly 2,500 students, or about two and one-half times larger than my hometown. Drake University, 100 miles from my hometown, is not a large campus by college standards, but it is five times the size of my entire hometown and located in the heart of a city of 250,000 people. Back then, it seemed like a huge city to this country-boy.

My girlfriend was also set to attend Drake as a freshman. In an effort by her parents to keep us far apart, they'd encouraged her to enroll in a different college than Graceland. Consequently, that spring, I found myself sitting in the Financial Aid office of Drake applying to a school that I couldn't afford and had no business attending. I was accepted. In the summer, I went back to my old job on road construction, moving shovels full of wet cement from one place to another. For the first part of the summer, I lived outside the city with my sister and her family. Then I rented a bed in the attic of an old house just off Drake's campus. The old three-story house was home to eight men, and the cost of my bed for the month was $25. Just before classes were to begin, I rented a room in another house about a block from the Drake's Computer Center where I would be working in the fall semester. The room I rented was also close to the Drake Art Center, a then-new edifice where I would spend much of the next three years of my life. My job at the Computer Center allowed me to pay for books, art supplies, rent, and food. Rent was $65 a month.

In my new digs, I found myself a lamb in a house of characters. I was accustomed to small-town behaviors and leery of the big city. The room was in a house that was once beautiful but had deteriorated over the years. It was one of many single-family dwellings in the area inexorably being swallowed by Drake as the campus grew. The owners were a retired couple named if I remember, Florence and Albert. Flo and Al. Albert was a corpulent man who spent virtually all his time ensconced in his lounge chair attired in dun-colored slacks and a dingy white wife-beater while continuously watching TV. Balding and nearly blind Al wore thick horn-rimmed glasses that gave him the appearance of a bewildered owl. Florence was mousy and dumpy with a face that wore a permanently anxious look. Her mouth turned into a frown much more often than a smile. Flo's everyday attire was a print house dress so ancient it had less shape than she did. The wash-worn dress covered a thin white slip, no bra. When she moved, imagine a bag of potatoes, continually shifting inside of a bag.

Flo and Al were tired people, both cranky and suspicious of a changing, out of control world. They were wary of renting one of their rooms to a young college-age boy fearing in no particular order, sex, drugs, alcohol, loud music, and radicals with long hair. I was given to understand that while they would rent to me, they were keeping an eye on my activities. I believe it was Flo who said, "well, okay, but I'll keep my eye on you," an inauspicious beginning to any relationship.

Flo and Al rented the entire top floor of their home, four large bedrooms, and a single bathroom. A wide staircase took a half turn to the top floor. My room was just to the left at the head of the stairs next to the bathroom. It was, in fact, a lovely room for so little money. It contained a full-sized bed, a dresser, a spacious closet (wasted on my meager wardrobe of three chambray shirts, two pairs of jeans, and one old suit), one small table with chair, and a refrigerator. For the money, the room was spacious and clean. One wall facing the back of the house had a large window. Through that window was a landing for a wooden fire escape. It made a dandy back door. When Flo and Al began to let rooms, they were forced to add the appendage at their expense, a constant source of irritation for them. The second outside wall in my room also had a window, which had a scenic view of an alley.

I had three neighbors, almost like roommates with such close confines. Across from me was Jerry, down the hall Raymond, and next to him, Bill. Before I begin describing these men, I must preface my remarks. These, each, all, were wounded individuals whose lives had dealt them a lousy hand of cards. Even so, they lived with as much dignity as their circumstances allowed. At the time, I thought myself impoverished, I had no money, and I had to scrape together rent and food, month by month. But these men thought of me as a young and an already successful college student. To them, they could only see an upside for me. They were men capable of great kindness, living in a society that was not kind to them. But the simple truth is they were odd. As the Patti Smith song goes, they were Outside Society.

Raymond: Ray was the most conventional of the three men but very damaged in so many ways. You see, Ray had lived the American dream. Family, home in the burbs, executive position, then he drank it all away. Ray's face carried the lean hunted look of a drinker. He was about five foot eight and thin as a toothpick, his longish hair oiled and slicked straight back. Ray would go out of his way to talk to me and do me any kindness. I think in some way, I reminded him of his children. Children estranged from his life. One time Ray asked me to drive him to a neighborhood in West Des Moines. We sat outside of a lovely suburban ranch, which Ray informed me used to be his. His wife and children still lived there. He was allowed no contact with them.

Because of his business experience, Ray had the ability to manage people. As such, he'd found a job as crew boss of a cleaning crew that serviced a large insurance company headquartered in West Des Moines. For a few months, both Karen and I worked for Raymond. Each evening after classes, we cleaned bathrooms, vacuumed offices, and emptied the trash. In his life, Raymond had faced his demons and survived, but it was a fragile peace he'd made with himself. With Ray, every day felt like looking into a cracked mirror.

Then there was Bill. Bill was a little man in every sense of the word except his heart. He stood barely five feet tall with a body shaped like a pear. He was not smart, probably operating with something under a 100 IQ. Bill bussed tables at a restaurant a couple of blocks away in what was known as Dog

Town, so named because it was on the edge of the Drake Bulldog's campus. In addition to busing tables at the restaurant, Bill sometimes washed dishes and occasionally cooked. Bill could have been 40, but I would guess 60. Bill was dying. Bill was dying piece by piece from emphysema and a lifetime of chain-smoking. In the long hours, when Bill was not working, he sat in his room with the door open, smoking and coughing. The coughing persisted 24 hours a day and sounded as if he were bringing up a piece of his lung, which I suppose he was. Bill was pleasant and seemed to enjoy having me come down and visit with him. He rarely put two words together but would laugh at the things Ray and I would say. In the end, Bill had no upside. Life had not treated him well, and death was not being any kinder.

And finally, Jerry. Jerry was, through the misfortune of a bad birth, the most damaged and by a long distance, the saddest. Jerry was borderline mentally disabled. He was physically damaged as well. One arm was shorter, and one leg dragged as he lurched forward in a stumbling walk. His face was misshapen, and his mouth was overflowing with a hideous looking tangle of damaged teeth. Because of his malformed jaw, his speech was guttural and difficult to understand. Through no fault of his own, Jerry carried this burden through his entire life. With looks like a monster and a lurching walk, people were not kind to him. Jerry eased his pain with alcohol. I tried to be as helpful as I could to Jerry, but really, he was just plain weird and difficult to be around. As much compassion as I had for Jerry, interaction made me exceedingly uncomfortable. One evening a knock on my door was Jerry asking to borrow my toothbrush. I politely declined. Looking back, I see that I should have given one to him, but at the time, I had so little myself that a new toothbrush seemed a luxury.

Jerry worked in the same restaurant with Bill, busing tables. The only jobs within walking distance that either could do. Early that fall, it was announced that the restaurant would close due to lack of business. Bill sat in his room smoking and coughing saying nothing. Jerry was beside himself. With no options left to him, he became like a cornered animal. He drank even more than usual. Late one night I heard the most wrenching sound coming from the alley. Looking out my window I could see Jerry, drunk and shouting gibberish to himself and anyone else within earshot. He moaned, he howled, he cried. He was wailing and, in trying to walk, falling. Soon I heard him crawling up the steps. Then I could hear him sobbing on the landing, too drunk to walk, or even crawl further. I helped him up the stairs to his room. I'm sorry to say that's all the help I ever had for poor Jerry.

My time in The House of Characters was coming to an end. Shortly after the drunken incident with Jerry, I rented a one-bedroom apartment farther off-campus. Karen was uncomfortable with the looks and insinuations from Flo and Al when she came to my room. Flo and Al were even more crazy with the thought that there might be booze, sex, drugs, rock music, and visitors at all hours tramping up and down their fire escape. My presence in their home was too much a clash of cultures for all of us. I relocated to an attic apartment a few blocks away, across University and down 22nd street. My contact with Flo, Al, Raymond, Bill, and Jerry ceased the day I left. I would never learn what fates befell my former housemates. But honestly, I could never conjure up a happy ending.

GAMMA PHI BETA
Barn Party
April 6, 1973

At the Gamma Phi Barn dance, my first ever sorority party. That's me dancing with Sherry Friedman, still a life-long friend. In the background is Debra (Mewhirter) Straw, another life long friend. I am an honorary Gamma Phi Beta.

The Wedding of the Century

As I write this, I am thinking of the Wedding of Prince William. The media has already dubbed it the "Wedding of the Century" early in the second decade of the 21st century. All this frenzy is most likely new to those who were not yet born when the Prince's mother and father, Prince Charles and the lovely Diana, were dubbed the Wedding of the Century in 1981. Of course, their union did not last, and Diana's life ended in a tragic car accident on a rainy night in Paris. Even Charlie and Diana did not lead the Wedding of the Century pack. In 1937 Charlie's great-uncle, the Duke of Windsor, famously renounced his seat on the throne as King of England to (gasp!) marry an American divorcee.

Of course, merely-famous weddings have been coming down the pike for many, many years. Most notably, Hollywood stars and their famous couplings, which often do not last more than an extended news cycle. But I am not thinking of them. And I am certainly not dwelling on the Royals and their unions. No, my real thoughts are about my nuptials nearly four decades ago—what our family has dubbed the Wedding of the Century—not for its beauty and splendor, but, for the utter ridiculousness of the day.

128

It all began in an ordinary enough way. Karen, my wife, and I grew up together in Lenox one year apart in school. We started dating in high school, and by my second year in college, we were attending Drake University, still a couple. I don't know if we just wore them down, but Karen's parents decided to accept me into the family. We became engaged to be married at the beginning of the fall semester in 1973. Plans were underway for a mid-November wedding.

There were probably more than a few who might have wondered, "What's the hurry?" The truth is we were madly in love and wanted to begin our life together. I recall a sorority sister of my wife's who lived with her boyfriend instead of the sorority house, through four years of college. When her parents would call the house, they were informed that she was "in the shower." She would return their calls later. These parents must have thought they had the cleanest daughter in the whole Midwest. Shortly after her graduation, the woman and her boyfriend married. They divorced within six months.

At any rate, the plans for our wedding needed to proceed pretty quickly. At the same time, we had to keep our classes up. No small feat, but this was before the days of mega-weddings for ordinary people, which made the planning process somewhat more straightforward.

Back in the early 1970s, our union presented a couple of problems that today will, to many, seem quaint. First, was religion. I was reared Catholic and Karen Methodist. In 1973 there were still remnants of the old Ku Klux Klan residing in our town. As a child growing up, I heard and saw evidence of the Klan attitudes that still lurked in some corners. My in-laws held no such prejudices about religion or race, but I am afraid they did get some uninvited "literature" in the mail that cast aspersions on the Catholic faith. Also, one of my groomsmen was very dark-skinned with an Afro haircut. I heard some buzz around town that we had a Negro in town. Why anyone should care I'll never know, but true never the less. John "Brillo" Laccari was 100% Italian from the east coast. Ah, well, different times.

The second thing was more subtle but perhaps more challenging. Karen and I were from wildly different financial backgrounds. Being from such diverse backgrounds was cause for concern on both sides of the aisle. My parents had a fear that I would abandon them and become "something else." What that something was, was never specified, but it was real to them. Karen's father had a fear that I would quit college, go to farming, and move his daughter and a couple of kids out to the farm. Happily, both sets of parents were proven wrong.

The families discussed the logistics of the wedding and agreed on the essential details. First, the marriage would be in the Catholic Church. In an unusual twist, a Catholic priest and a Methodist minister would conduct the ceremony concurrently. At that time, our church had no priest in residence, so I had to petition the Bishop in Des Moines to assign a priest to perform the ceremony. They were happy to accommodate.

One point was contentious. It was when my father learned we did not plan to have a full Mass during the ceremony, only the actual wedding vows. I got an emotional, angry call during which Dad expressed his feelings that he would not attend our wedding without a Mass, Catholic Church, or not. I was intractable; he could come or not; it was all the same to me. The big day was soon upon us, and my father relented and decided to attend. But as would soon be seen, I had underestimated my father's emotional state of mind.

Karen's folks were following tradition and graciously agreed to pick up the tab. Then I discovered that the groom was expected to rent the tuxes. As a flat-broke college student, this was a problem for me. Once again, they agreed to pay for the my soon to be brother-in-law, Clark, who was a groomsman. I sold my car to pay for the other tuxes. Karen's Aunt Maggie, a skilled seamstress, volunteered to make the wedding gown. Maggie spent countless hours sewing on hundreds of tiny seed pearls. The finished dress was a work of art.

The night before the wedding, the various members of the nuptial party were ensconced in different homes around Lenox. The guys thought to try on our tuxes and discovered a couple that would not fit. My dear Grandmother ripped seams and re-sewed well into the night. Problem solved. We gathered at Big John's Tavern for a pre-wedding celebration. What I remember most about the early part of the evening is a couple of Karen's sorority sisters, both girls reared in upper-class Jewish families in Chicago and Peoria. Entering the bar, they caught a look at the stuffed coyote over the bar and the intoxicated cowboy hat and booted patron dancing (stomping really) with equal enthusiasm to both Rock and Country Western; they darn near turned around to go back to the city.

Friday, rehearsal day, the furnace in the church broke, and the cold froze the keys inside the organ. That night when our vocal soloist tried to practice her songs, she could barely sing as her face became frozen. That, plus the fact that she was Jewish and from New York, she did NOT know the words to

The Lord's Prayer and kept asking, "What the hell kind of word is *Hollowed?*" She did learn the song, and we left rehearsal with a promise of restored heat in time for the nuptials. The morning of the wedding dawned bright and cold. But thank goodness, the heat was back on at the church.

The wedding party had instructions to be at the church early for our wedding pictures. As the time approached, everyone was present, except my parents. Fearing the worst, I jumped in the car and headed uptown to the bar. "Seen my dad?"

"Yeah, he left a while ago, but he was here all morning drinking boilermakers, beer and whiskey shots."

Oh great, I thought to myself. I headed back. Mom was in the church, her face a black cloud. "Where's Dad?"

"He's in the truck drinking with your future Grandfather-in-law."

"Oh jeez," I groaned then went to fetch Dad and Grandpa Howland.

When the wedding party was at last fully formed, we began the picture taking. The groom and parents, bride and parents, all the various combinations posed. At last, it was time for the group portrait. As we lined up in front of the altar, the photographer requested that my father move forward a little. He shuffled. "More please." Shuffled again. "A little more, please." My father stepped off of the top step and rolled unceremoniously down the steps. At that moment, if any family member had been armed, I would have feared for Dad's life.

The big event was close at hand. Guests began to arrive and find their places. My father, the regular bell-ringer for our church, took it upon himself to ring the bells. No joyful noise, he tolled the funeral dirge. That could have been funny, but he was earnest in his grief.

The church was filling up, and most of our guests were in the pews. There was a minor commotion in the narthex of the church. A gaggle of Karen's sorority sisters had arrived en masse. Debby Klitsky, a football cheerleader, came directly from the game in Des Moines wearing her cheer leading outfit. Right there in the back of the church, the girls formed a circle enveloping her, and in a long minute, she emerged in a dress and heels, peeled the band from her ponytail, and shook her hair out. A few giggles and waves and the congregation was fully seated.

Much to our delight, when the priest and minister arrived, they discovered, quite by accident, that one had on a black robe and the other a white robe. They looked like salt-and-pepper shakers. All was now ready. With the usual nervousness, the groomsmen and I filed out to take our places. Sitting in the front pew, a mere three feet away, my father bawled in great wracking sobs.

I heard his raspy whisper, "It's not too late. You can still back out."

I was incredulous. I half-turned, and in a stage whisper, I urged him, "Shut up, old man."

With the organ fully thawed, *The Wedding March* commenced, and my lovely nineteen-year-old bride-to-be was gliding down the aisle escorted by her father. My mother-in-law, following instructions, stood, and the congregation rose with her. The entire wedding took only fifteen minutes, which included prayers by each minister, beautiful songs, and the actual exchange of vows. The brevity of the ceremony was good because my mother-in-law forgot to sit, so everyone stood for the whole shebang.

Fifteen minutes may seem a short time for two people who intend to spend their entire life together, but there it was, we were married and headed down the aisle for cake and coffee. But wait, we had to spend fifteen minutes getting my father to stop sobbing so we could have a reception line. Finally, the handshakes were underway. When Mrs. Miller, my former English teacher, came through the line, I latched on to her immediately.

I had been arguing with Karen's Aunt Maggie about the pronunciation of a particular word. I don't even recall now which word, but convinced I was right (not merely correct, but *right*) I put the question to an expert. Pauline got a most confused look on her face, and my new wife shot me a *look*.

"Well, Pauline opined, I believe you are both correct." So, I was merely correct, but not right. This moment was probably not the best time to pursue such a disagreement.

In what I could only feel was God's little joke, the temperature in the church had gone from freezing and miserable to way hot and even more miserable. The reception area in the church was like an oven. The beautifully decorated tables included candelabra with long elegant candles. It had become so hot that during the ceremony, all of the candles lopped over to resemble dripping commas or single quotation marks. They looked sorrowful indeed. It made my new mother-in-law giggle, though.

We did the coffee and *cut the cake thing* that newlyweds do. Once we finished at the church, we were having a second reception at the Country Club with light food and an open bar. Throughout the day, the temperature had been dropping. Iowa in November can be very pleasant, but in some years, winter comes early. This year was a cold year. Of course, my friends thought it would be fun to decorate our car. They poured hot molasses over the windows and sprinkled them liberally with Cheerios and toilet paper.

When Karen and I exited the church into the late afternoon gloom of an early winter, the town policeman, Clark Moore was waiting to give us a siren escort to the Country Club. This courtesy was a quaint practice Clark did for newlyweds in town as they left their church, either on their way to a reception or leaving town. Because of the brown coating of hardening molasses, I could not see out of the windows, so I tried to wipe off the solidified goo with TP that was fluttering off of the antenna. Not even a smudge would come off. Of course, Karen brushed the car in her wedding dress, getting some of the goo on her in the process, precipitating our first married fight. Once in the car, Karen yelled at me for my boorish friends. What was I to say?

In order to see where I was going, I needed to roll down my window and drive with my head out, which was pretty uncomfortable in the winter air. As I pulled out of the parking place, Officer Moore hit his siren for a couple of blocks but then quickly shut it down when he realized I was driving directly to the car wash. Once there, Officer Moore proceeded to take my picture while I tried to wash off the molasses and not ruin my rented tux and shoes in the process. From the car wash, we got our siren escort to the Country Club.

The second reception went well, aided by booze, food, and music. Well almost. My newly minted parents had severely underestimated what a gaggle of college kids can eat and drink. I shudder to think what the bar bill was that night. My father proceeded to get even more gloriously drunk than he was before the wedding. He danced with several women and had a bang-up time. Karen's second cousin Bernard tipped a few as well. When he backed his Caddy out to leave, he backed it squarely into the lake. It required a wrecker to extricate the car from the lake.

My sister-in-law attended alone, my brother being stationed overseas at the time. So, my new brother-in-law, Clark, offered to drive her home. She was most certainly unable to drive herself. On the 10-mile drive, she proceeded to decorate the inside of his car with the results of her good time.

Soon enough, it was time for us to depart on our honeymoon. We were heading to Des Moines for a night in our new apartment at the married student's dorm. The next day we were going to have lunch in Amish country, then drive up to Decorah to spend the week at Karen's grandparent's house while they were in Lenox. It was a honeymoon designed for a college student's budget.

Unbeknown to us, Big John's Tavern had been saving beer cans for a week. They wired four tails onto the car that must have each been twenty feet long. When I turned the car around to leave, the cans trailed back so far that I ran over the strings of cans. At my new in law's, I unhooked the wires and tossed the lines of beer cans onto the front yard. Later, my mother-in-law, Martha, told me that the neighbor kids played with beer cans for days.

Suitcases in the trunk, we pointed our car north into the arctic cold of the Iowa night. Our "Wedding of the Century" was over, and our new life begun.

Coda: In the years to follow, Martha would hear other mothers waxing poetic about the beauty and splendor of their children's weddings; a few who were already on their second spouses. She would chuckle and say, "Well, Karen's wedding was not beautiful or lavish, it was crazy and funny, and it took."

Our wedding day
November 17, 1973.

Pork Chops with Amber Rice
6 pork chops, 3/4 inch thick
Salt and pepper
1 1/3 cups packaged pre-cooked rice
1 cup orange juice
1 can condensed chicken and rice soup
Brown pork chops in heavy skillet; season with salt
and pepper. Place rice in 12 x 10 x 2 inch baking
dish; pour orange juice over rice. Arrange browned
pork chops on rice. Pour chicken soup over all.
Cover and bake in moderate oven 350° for 45 minutes.

Layla–How Eric Clapton Helped Me Graduate from College

"Layla, you've got me on my knees.

Layla, I'm begging, darling please.

Layla, darling won't you ease my worried mind."

Spring 1975 in Iowa was particularly beautiful. I remember distinctly so many details from that time as it was my final semester in college. It had been a struggle to be sure, but Karen kept me on the straight and narrow after one disastrous semester just before we tied the knot. I took a full load of classes, worked on campus at the computer center, and on weekends I stocked shelves all night at Dahl's grocery in Beaverdale. In the evenings after I clocked out of the Computer Center, I would head to the library to study. At the start of my senior year, Karen dropped out of school to work at the university and take a couple of free classes. It was on me to finish my degree so that Karen could finish hers.

I registered for classes with some confidence in my senior year. I had several class credits transfer in from my time in the Reserve Officers Candidate (ROC) program with the US Navy. I spent the summer of '74 in Newport, RI in Officer's Candidate School and those classes were going to put me over my limit for graduation. Or so I thought. My advisor pulled me aside and pointed out that I would need more than a full-course load. That, and the fact that I worked, he said, would make it difficult to graduate. I guess, as an art professor, he was unfamiliar with the principle of physics that states: a body in motion stays in motion. I was not about to be stopped at this critical juncture.

The first semester went by, and we toiled on and off campus through a severe Iowa winter. At last, spring arrived. That year Eric Clapton released his milestone album, *Layla, and Other Assorted Love Songs*. It seems he had fallen in love with his best friend's wife, Patty. His best friend was none other than George Harrison of the Beatles fame. To assuage his passion and guilt, he fled to America, consumed lots of drugs and alcohol, and cut an album based on the ancient tale of Leda and the Swan. Thus, Layla as the object of the love-struck singer.

"What'll you do when you get lonely

And nobody's waiting by your side?"

That spring, if you were a young person on campus, you could not escape *Layla*. I am sure I heard the song (or snatches thereof) at least six times a day for many months. I loved the song, and every time I heard it, it lifted my spirits. While walking across campus, the song could be heard floating out of the doors of the art studios, the student lounge, and on car radios. It was utterly ubiquitous. Believe me, I needed all the lift I could get.

When I showed up to register for classes for my final semester of college, I received a surprise. If I wanted to graduate with my class in May, I would have to take a nineteen-hour course load. Groan. Now for those who think art classes are just drawing pretty pictures, let me dispel you of that notion. Not only would I have nineteen hours of courses, but four of those were also studio classes. Each studio class is three hours per session, graphic design (my major), painting (advanced), sculpture, and printmaking (a second minor and also an advanced class). In addition to my class schedule, I still worked at the computer center and continued to work the all-nighters on Friday and Saturday nights at Dahl's. It seems that sleep for me was not going to be an option.

Now, before you all get to thinking that I am whining, and this was the worst thing in the world that could happen to me, it certainly was not. I was in a place in my life where my job was to learn and create. I loved it. I found it much more satisfying than farm work or construction.

March inevitably gave way to April, and I had to address some weighty things as graduation day approached. My entire grade in Graphic Design was based on my portfolio presentation at the end of the semester. I *had* to make a good grade in Art History to complete the required twelve hours. The JC Penny Student Art Show was approaching, and I wanted to enter a painting and an intaglio print, for competition. If that were not enough, my sculpture instructor Doug Hendrickson announced that Drake would be the host of the ten-state Flatlands Sculpture Show, and we (sculpture students) would be preparing the space downtown on our own free (!?) time. Also, each sculpture student was to present at least one sculpture to a jury of art professors and our student peers. A requirement for work to be accepted into the show.

Heading into the final month of the semester, coffee, cigarettes, and No-Doz were constant companions. After class, after work, after the library, I would head to my tiny studio in our two-bedroom apartment and work on drawings for my portfolio. Keep in mind this was the Dark Ages when we drew on paper. It was many years before personal computers and digital art. I would fall into bed around two or three in the morning. Karen would rouse me for my eight a.m. Journalism class, where attendance was mandatory. As Journalism was one of my two minors, I had to be in class. Ugh!

One Friday night in early May, Karen made a dinner date with married friends. We were to attend before I was off to my night job. I was exhausted. I excused myself to the bathroom and took a five-minute nap (ten?). When I came back to the table, I rejoined the conversation. The next thing I knew, my face was in the mashed potatoes, and I was snoring.

"Like a fool, I fell in love with you,

Turned my whole world upside down."

It was nearing the end of May, and graduation was approaching. I could see my goal in sight. Everywhere I went Eric's epic love for Patty played on and on. And each time I heard it, my spirits soared a bit. Damn, I loved that song and the sentiments that went with it. I was in an emotional place to be sure.

In the days before the opening of the Flatlands Sculpture Show approached, I would head downtown to put in my time sweeping out rooms and picking up trash. The venue for the show was the second floor of an empty office building owned by the Hubbell family, one of the wealthy families in Des Moines and major supporters of Drake. It was hard not to know the Hubbell name, as one of our buildings on campus was Hubbell Hall. Hubbell Hall was the dining hall, so it was near and dear to most student's hearts and stomachs.

One morning I had just finished sweeping a pile of dust into a bin. In one hand, I held a cigarette and the other a bright orange ceramic coffee cup. The garish colored cup came from home, and I liked to drink out of it as it reminded me of my mother. I was standing in the middle of the room, contemplating my work when I went sound asleep on my feet. The empty cup slipped from my fingers, shattering on the floor, and the cigarette burned my fingers. For a minute, I was wide-awake. After cleaning up my broken cup, I crawled into a corner, curled up, and went fast asleep. I was nearly at the end of my rope.

That weekend the show opened to large crowds–room after room filled with original, imaginative sculptures created by students across the Midwest. My sculpture, a small carved wooden piece entitled *The Tower of Orthanc at Isengard*, was accepted into the show. My first real art in any show! Karen and I dressed in our student best and headed downtown to see the exhibit. As we entered the venue, I spied Doug, my professor, talking with another couple. He saw us and motioned us over. To my surprise, he introduced us to Mr. and Mrs. Hubbell, our very wealthy patrons.

Doug was a large bearish man who towered over me. With a sly smile and a twinkle in his eye, Doug put his arm around my shoulders. He turned me toward the Mr. and Mrs. Hubbell and announced, "See this boy? Underneath those shoes and socks, this boy is barefoot." Then he laughed. I guess after four years at university, I was still a hillbilly from the sticks. Ah, well.

The next night Karen and I were relaxing at our apartment when the phone rang. It was one of my art teachers; she wanted to know if I planned to attend the JC Penny Art Show opening in a couple of days?

"Well, yes," I replied. My painting was not in the show, but my intaglio etching was accepted.

"Okay, be sure and be there," and she hung up. Imagine my absolute shock to discover that I had been named co-winner of the printmaking division of the show? And, bonus, the honor came with a cash prize. Believe me, as impoverished college students, we needed the money.

"Please don't say we'll never find a way

And tell me all my love's in vain."

Suddenly, it was a beautiful day in May in the state of Iowa. My portfolio, paintings, prints, and sculptures completed. I had a paper for my journalism class to write and finals to take. It was all of a sudden, a downhill slide to the finish line. Then those tasks too were behind me. Graduation day arrived.

On the Saturday of graduation, our families gathered in Des Moines for a family first, a college graduate in the Callahan family. When I got in the car to drive to Vets Auditorium, Eric Clapton's *Layla* was playing on the radio. I smiled. My old friend had brought me through to complete my goal. Now it was on to the next chapter of my life. And, the next Clapton song: *(You Look) Wonderful Tonight*, which would help guide my marriage for many years to come.

A college graduate! Drake University, 1975.

The handwritten recipe card reads:

Spanish Pork Chops   serves 4
4 loin pork chops, 1 inch thick
salt, pepper
4 slices onion
4 tablespoons ketcup
½ cup diluted vinegar
1. Place chops in shallow baking pan.
2. Sprinkle with salt, pepper
3. Place slice of onion on each chop top with Ketchup.
4. Pour vinegar around chops
5. Bake 1 hour at 350°

Lookin' Out
My Back Door

I knew Donny as a boy, and I knew him as a man. It is impossible to tell Donny's story without telling at least some of mine. We grew up in the same small town. In reality, I grew up like a weed between the fence rows on a farm several miles from town. Donny was six years older than me, and as such, he traveled life's paths somewhat ahead of me. The thing about a small town is that in one way or another, most people's lives become inextricably intertwined. This fact was brought home to me as a young boy on a summer Saturday night. My father, who bowed to no man in his capacity to drink and disremember his obligations, was part of a loosely knit group of running buddies who all shared similar traits. More about them, shortly.

I was eight years old in 1961. Farming in the Midwest was near its economic height for the small family farm. Then, nearly every square mile supported from four to six families, unlike today, where you are lucky to see one family per square mile. In our town on Saturday nights, the stores stayed open to accommodate the farmers, and they, in turn, would bring their families to shop and visit. In the mind of this young boy, it was an idyllic time. We lived miles from town, so Saturday night was an opportunity for me to see other children my age and experience the freedom of exploring the nooks and crannies of civilization, unencumbered by authority. On any typical Saturday, my mother would be working her job at the Produce, my grandfather would sit and visit with old friends while Grandma shopped and my father would dole out allowance and head directly to the bar. My money and I made a beeline immediately to the 5&10 to stock up on penny candies. I would spend the next several hours running the streets with friends and sitting in the back of the tavern watching the men and high school boys play pool while my father and his cronies sat up front and drank beer.

This night it was just dark, and all my friends had headed home. I was entering the tavern to find Dad when out of the front door burst a woman with one of my father's friends seized by his ear and firmly in tow. Walking on tiptoes, she had a vise-grip on the ear and was wagging her finger in his face and cursing him furiously. Mrs. Reynolds was a short, round woman and mother of two kids close to my age. I knew her as a church-going, strict woman who treated all the kids in town as if they were hers. She told us all how to behave in no uncertain terms. In truth, I thought she was an old bitty, but really she couldn't have been older than her early thirties. She had a death grip on Mr. Wurster's ear, and she was telling him he had no business spending all his money drinking while his wife and kids sat at home waiting. Furthermore, she wasn't about to put up with it either.

I just stood and stared as she and her prey went babbling off into the night. This scene was a sight that set my world upside down. It didn't make sense to me and was not in the natural order of things as I understood them. Later, when I could ask my dad about it, he looked at me as if I were the most ignorant child God had seen fit to saddle him with. "Why that woman is his sister," he chuckled. A light, as they say, shone down on me. Then and there, I developed a keen understanding of the interrelationships that invariably exist between people in small towns and the idea that siblings from the same nest could find such divergent paths while living within a mile of each other. Such a lesson teaches one to be cautious about how you talk about others. You could very well be speaking to a cousin, brother, grandchild, or in-law. Such is life in a fish bowl. Much like when young people fall madly in love, break up, and marry others from the same locale; years later, people still remember. In many ways, we are who we were in high school, to our dying day. When I say I knew Donny, this is the context in which I knew him. That, and I got to watch up close as he spiraled out of control with the assistance of my father and his unruly friends.

Donny was an ordinary boy, no better or worse than many who came before or since. He had two brothers, one a stolid boy who grew into a stolid man and the younger, a happy-go-lucky kid who stayed that way as well. Donny's only sister was as pretty as she was nice. She was ten years older than me, so all I remember is that she was a beautiful young girl. Donny's father always had a ready smile for kids and a friendly word. When I was in high school, I trapped fur-bearing animals, and he would buy my skins. Often he gave me two dimes for hides I knew to be worthless.

Donny was a big boy, built like a sack of cement. In high school, he was six-foot tall and weighed in over 200 pounds and was a pretty good football player. He was like countless other kids in that he was not much of a student and was merely biding his time until he could graduate and leave home. In our small town, if you didn't farm and your father couldn't put you into a family business, there wasn't much reason to stay. When Donny graduated, he headed off to the Army for a two-year stint.

My life went forward, and soon I was a junior in high school. By then, Donny was discharged from the Army and had returned. He arrived back to the same place he'd left, only to take up a spot at the bar where he could be found drinking beer between odd jobs. This period is when he fell in with my father's crowd. It all started naturally enough. Donny just wanted to kick back for a little vacation after his tour of duty. The thing is he kicked back and never left.

Donny liked our hometown, and no wonder. It's a good place to live. He told me he'd seen a lot of the world, especially the Aleutians, one very long winter, and he had no desire to go anywhere else. But with little education and no special skills, there was nothing for him to do except work odd jobs and eventually try a hand at farming. And farming, well, it took a rich man to start up from scratch and make it pay. Even then, you had to dedicate your life to the work. Farming doesn't leave much time for doing your plowing uptown at the bar. And this was during the good times for farmers.

My father was reared in a much larger town sixty miles away. A boxer, he came to town to train back in the late 1930s, which is when he met my mom, and they married. My grandfather was a successful farmer, and he gave my parents 80 acres of land that included all the necessary outbuildings and a barn along with a house. The house was originally an old one-room cabin that was added on to haphazardly. It had cold running water and an outhouse. My parents and five kids lived there until 1965 when we moved five miles away to another 80-acre farm.

By dint of an unfortunate birth and his prodigious ability to plow uptown, my father never lived above the poverty level his entire life. He didn't work alone, however. Oh no, he had a group of cronies who, when they weren't drinking at a bar, would get together to do various farm tasks. Things like shell corn, move cattle, castrate hogs, pick up hay, any group activity where they could drink beer all day and still have a good excuse for the wives when they got home. These weren't bad men.

On the contrary, they were lots of fun and, in most respects, good fathers. Having these guys around while I was growing up was akin to having five dads. But the other truth is, and I knew it even as a boy, is that their way of life was hard on wives and children. Things undone, and money spent on beer meant less for the family. All this fun came with a price.

With no direction or prospects, and being an easy guy to get along with, Donny began joining Dad's gang in their watering holes and on their work details. He was still young at this time and just having fun with a bunch of guys, mostly old enough to be his father.

I played football, and by my senior year, we had a championship team and were looking to repeat. Our coach got the idea of having men who had played in school come out and scrimmage against the team to give us some serious competition. This, back in the day before insurance worries would not permit such a thing. Well, Donny was one of several *old guys* who suited up. Most of these men were twenty to fifty pounds over their playing days, and many smoked like chimneys. I thought then (and still do) that it's a wonder there were no severe injuries or any heart attacks during our scrimmages. The coach managed to scrape up just enough veterans to complete a team, so he filled in with some second-string guys, and the game was on.

Most of these guys would play for ten to fifteen minutes and then collapse on the sidelines gasping for water and sneaking smokes. By this time, Donny, who showed up for the scrimmage, was way over 200 pounds and could barely get a practice jersey over his protruding gut. To tell the truth, at first, these guys scared the hell out of us, but we soon figured out we could outrun them, and they wore out quickly. As I said, it's a wonder we didn't kill them.

Life, as it does, went on. Donny became just another of the guys hanging with my father and his crew. From the time I was three, I spent a lot of time with my father, so I knew my dad and his friends well. At least from the per-

143

spective of a young man. Donny was much closer to my age, so I gravitated to him. He was always kind to me and a very funny guy. Somewhere along the line, Donny had developed an odd way of talking. He spoke in colloquialisms. Asked if it was still raining, he'd observe that it was "raining like a cow pissing on a flat rock." Or, he might opine that someone was "dumbern' a box of rocks" Or, "he was so surprised, his eyeballs swapped sockets." Donny could go on like that for an entire conversation. Sometimes he'd leave you scratching your head, trying to understand what he'd just said. But he always left you smiling.

One Saturday in the spring of my senior year, Dad decided he needed help castrating and vaccinating his hogs. Enter the crew. By this time, it was often the teenagers who did much of the work. Our fathers would usually sit around drinking beer and telling us what we were doing wrong. This day it was the crew and me. For those who aren't farming savvy, boy pigs, raised for meat, are castrated at about 30 pounds, and at the same time, they, along with the girls, are vaccinated against several diseases. Castration causes the males to gain weight faster and ensure that the girls won't have litters until you want them to. As the men herded the pigs into a small pen, my job was to grab a pig by the back legs and throw it over a waist-high gate. I would secure the kicking, squealing porker on its back spreading its legs while the veterinarian gave it shots and if it was a male with two quick strokes with a razor, a poke, pull, and slash, castrated it. I would drop the indignant and squealing porker into a different pen and fetch up another. It was a rainy spring, and the mud level in the hog lot was knee-deep. By the end of the day, everyone, except the Vet, got covered in thick, smelly mud.

By mid-afternoon, all the little porkers were back roaming free, if somewhat indignant. The Vet pocketed his check and waved so-long. As the only kid present that day, I was also the one person (other than the recently departed Vet) who was drawing a sober breath. Dad said, "c'mon in," so everyone trooped into the kitchen, mud, and all. We sat around the table, and I listened as they told stories. Boy, could those guys tell stories, usually about some mischief they got up to when they were drinking, but mostly just to tease each other. Sometimes, if you went unnoticed, you might hear stories about older folks and their sexual escapades.

Now, we raised several hundred chickens on our farm, so there were always eggs around. In the corner sat a five-gallon bucket full of fresh eggs. Someone, I forget who, remarked that an egg in your beer was good for you. Donny looked a little green and said that he couldn't stomach the idea of a raw egg. Well, the fun was on. Edgar W. reached over, grabbed an egg, cracked it on the edge of the table, and glurped it down, tossing the shell in the sink. Donny took one look at him and started to throw up. He managed not to heave, but they all thought it was so funny each began grabbing raw eggs and sucking them down. Donny was cursing and calling them "dirty rotten bastards" between retching and swallowing. They, of course, were laughing uproariously and, excuse me, egging him on.

Broken shells were flying in the general direction of the sink; some got there. Finally, Donny's aversion therapy successful; he decided to give it a try. In the space of an hour, they had emptied that five-gallon bucket, and there was egg, beer, and mud on the floor, walls, table, even the ceiling. When the beer was gone, so were the crew. They departed just before my mother came home. Mom, of course, was fit to be tied, but once she determined that I had not been drinking she reserved her ire for the old man.

I graduated from high school that spring and was off to college in the fall. I came home most weekends and frequently saw Donny uptown at the bar. Often we'd shoot a game of pool together. By then, he had married, but his habits were only getting worse. I learned that he was drinking a case of beer a day. I believed it. The funny thing was that the drunker he became, the better he shot pool. It was best to take Donny's money early.

Within another year, I was married and attending college two hours away. I happened to be home one day during the week and stopped uptown for a beer. I was the only other patron there, except Donny. It was mid-afternoon, and Donny was nearly comatose. Credence Clearwater was on the jukebox, Donny capering awkwardly to the music and singing, "do, do, do lookin' out my back door." Over and over. To himself. It was a hilarious and sorrowful sight. When I try to describe this, I find I am at a loss for words. Donny wasn't performing for the room— it was grotesque. He was merely lost inside himself. This image has stuck with me always.

The thing I believe that affected me most was that clearly, Donny had retreated into a separate world where only he and a single happy thought existed together. It disturbed me to see someone I knew and liked change into this caricature of a man. I was no stranger to drunks or aberrant behavior, for that matter. I had a lifetime of experience there. This was that, of course. But that and more. I couldn't equate this specter with the same happy boy I'd known a few short years ago. The smiling man standing on the sidelines cheering on the team. The nice guy who told jokes and treated me, a young kid, as an equal. He wasn't funny anymore.

That was one of the last times I saw Donny. I was married and only got home a few weekends a year. I didn't spend much of my own time plowing uptown. One evening a few months after the day I saw Donny in the bar, I got a phone call. They'd found Donny dead the previous morning. He'd driven his car off the road and into a water-filled ditch. At first, they thought he'd had a heart attack. He wasn't driving fast and was unhurt in the wreck; his car had just rolled off the road into the ditch. If he had gone off the road anywhere else, they'd have found him sleeping it off behind the wheel. This ditch was next to a lake, and the ditch, typically dry, was full of water from recent rains. Donny's car rolled nose-first into the water and filled quickly. Donny was so drunk he couldn't get out of the car. Probably never even woke up. He drowned.

Early morning, coming into Iowa after a storm. (2009).

For me, this is all ancient history, but I've thought about it for years. For some reason, it just won't leave my mind. My children believe that anything that happened before they were five is beyond the scope of understanding. But in their time, I'm sure they too will remember critical events of their lives. All of these men from the bar are dead. Amazingly, most died of old age—one from blood poisoning. An infection his liver couldn't fight as a result of his heavy drinking. But Donny was different. He was a many-years-long train wreck. I've always felt that he could see the train coming, he just couldn't, or wouldn't, get out of the way. Sometimes when I think back on my childhood, I remember my father and his friends. Or I'll hear an old Credence song, and I think of Donny. I always remember him capering and singing... *doo, doo, doo, lookin' out my back door.*

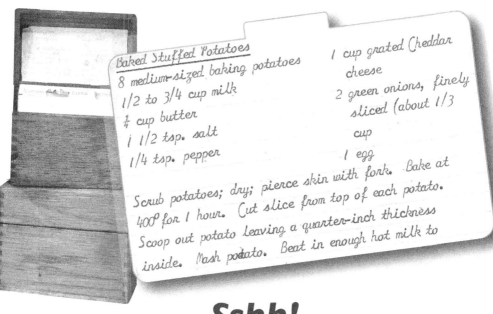

Baked Stuffed Potatoes
8 medium-sized baking potatoes
1/2 to 3/4 cup milk
¼ cup butter
1 1/2 tsp. salt
1/4 tsp. pepper

1 cup grated Cheddar cheese
2 green onions, finely sliced (about 1/3 cup
1 egg

Scrub potatoes; dry; pierce skin with fork. Bake at 400° for 1 hour. Cut slice from top of each potato. Scoop out potato leaving a quarter-inch thickness inside. Mash potato. Beat in enough hot milk to

Sshh!
I'm Hunting Wabbits

"It was the best shot I ever made and the dirtiest trick I ever played."–

Tom Horn, Apache Indian Scout, and Man Hunter, before being hung for murder.

In the winter of 1979, Karen and I decided to make a weekend trip home from Des Moines to Lenox. We brought along our close friend Cary, my oft-times pheasant hunting companion. It was mid-January, so pheasant season closed, but rabbits were still fair game. After work on Friday, we loaded our clothes and guns into the car and made the two-hour trip to Lenox to visit Karen's parents. Pleasantly ensconced in the Howland's warm home, we got a round of cocktails from Doc and a great meal from Martha.

The three of us were only a few years out of college and still felt the need to raise the roof whenever possible, so after dinner, we headed down to the bar to have a few and see if any of my high school buddies were extant. They were. Soon we were basking in the glow of old companions. Karen's brother showed, arriving from his job in Omaha. We pushed over and welcomed him with all the zeal of those with a good head start. The custom at this bar was, drink around the table, then you buy one round for the table. Pretty democratic for all that.

Several rounds went around, and Brother wasn't piping up. He looked sheepish and admitted that he had no cash, only his paycheck. "No problem," says I. "They'll cash it here." And so they did. The three of us thought it would be most clever to try and drink up brother-in law's proceeds for the week. A dirty trick I'll admit, but under the fog of hooch, that seemed like a grand idea at the time. The thing is, it was half-price drinks night at the bar, mixed drinks were 50¢, and beer was 20¢. The bulk of his check was very safe, even with a few extra bought for our friends. But by the time Last Call came around we were, all of us, very much the worse for wear.

The problem we suddenly realized was that we had forgotten the admonishment from our hosts. The former minister and his wife were visiting and spending the night. Martha warned, "Don't come in making a lot of noise and stinking drunk." Oops. We tried to sneak into the house undetected, but apparently, I made enough noise going upstairs to wake the dead, let alone the merely sleeping. The next morning was brutal.

I arose, almost literally from the dead. When I made my way down to breakfast, my mother-in-law's looks were lethal. I was trying to disguise my discomfort from the minister and his wife, who were present at the table. This reverend was the minister who married us, and I liked him very much. It seems that they had slept downstairs and were unaware of my noisy entrance. I perched miserably on the edge of a high stool, attempting to pull on my lace-up hunting boots. Every time I would bend over, I would get woozy. But Martha was certainly aware of my poor behavior and on the hunt. With a malicious smile, Martha inquired, "What's the matter? Are your boots too tight?" Ugh.

In spite of our obvious pain and discomfort, we managed to eat some food. Then Cary and I loaded up for our hunt and oozed our wounded carcasses into the car. We decided the best place to hunt would be on the way to my folk's farm where, I assured Cary my mother would give us some rocket-fuel grade coffee. Off we went. We headed south for two miles on the highway and then turned right towards the farm. At the top of the first hill, sitting in a fence line right next to the road, I spied a cottontail. Cary wanted to try out his new .357 pistol on the little bunny. He steadied for a shot, but the barrel kept weaving, a result of the previous night, no doubt. Bang! Miss. Bang! Miss. Of course, this happened six times before the bunny got bored and hopped off down the fence row. Great beginnings, as they say.

Out at the farm, we had a pleasant visit with Mom and lava-hot cups of coffee that would float that massive revolver Cary was toting. Soon we started to feel like at least a shadow of our old selves. We kissed Mom and hit the back roads, peering intently for rabbits sitting along the fence rows. We had, as our principle weapons, .22 rifles. Mine was a single-shot from Montgomery Wards, for which my dad paid a lordly $12.50 for it brand new and presented it to me on my ninth birthday. There was snow on the ground, the sun was out, and the

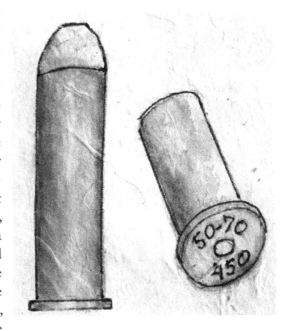

weather balmy for January in Iowa. The conditions were just right for finding cottontail along rural roads. Over the next few hours, a handful of bunnies were collected by each of us.

We were considering calling it a day when we topped a ridge, stopped, and could see several piles of trees bulldozed along either side of the road. I honed my hunting eyes along the jumble of trees, spying a bunny tucked up next to a tree limb. The rabbit looked to be pretty far; I guessed at least fifty yards. Along with my .22, the childhood gift from my father, I had with me an antique Remington .50 caliber rifle, made just after the Civil War. The trapdoor Springfield was supplied to our troops on the frontier to use to fight the fierce Apache tribes who were defending their homes and decimating homesteaders. The Army soon went to a .45-70 caliber rifle, and the .50-70s consigned to the Apache police. In fact, in many historical photos of these stalwarts, the Indian Scouts can be seen holding a rifle just like the one I acquired.

The .50-70 shoots a cartridge as big around as a man's finger and throws a chunk of lead large enough to kill a buffalo. I was hunting rabbits. After purchasing the old rifle from an antique shop in Arizona, I ordered some empty brass and bullet mold. I shot many hand loaded rounds through the old gun. It still shot straight. Of particular interest with this weapon is that most of a man's name is carved into the stock on one side, Fred Sh___, and FS, his initials on the other. I like to tell myself the Indians got him before he could carve his full name. Who knows? That's my story, and I'm sticking to it.

Anyway, today, my big game in the form of a fuzzy little bunny was basking contentedly in the sun, at what I am sure he thought of as a safe distance from danger. I rested the barrel on the window frame of the car, took a deep breath, and held the sights just a bit high and on his nose. "You'll never hit that rabbit from this distance." This reassuring quip came from my hunting companion. I slowly let my breath out and took up the creep in the trigger. The big gun boomed and set back into my shoulder. One count of the clock, and as I watched, mesmerized, the rabbit flipped three feet up into the air in a somersault, dead when it hit the ground. I just smiled at Cary.

From the car to the bunny, I paced off fifty-five long strides. Well, as long as my short legs can stretch. Not bad shootin'. But my surprise came when I picked up the rabbit to see if the massive slug left anything to eat. There was not a mark on the rabbit. The shot broke his front leg, and he was deaderin' dead. I looked where he had been sitting; the slug struck just under his chin, skimming off a hunk of frozen dirt. The shock wave made by the big bullet was what killed the rabbit.

Well, after my sharpshooting display, I figured I couldn't top it, so we headed back to town for some hangover medicine. The rabbits cleaned and the hunters too; I was happy to discover that I was no longer *persona non grata* with my mother in law. However, I was to be under the evil eye for quite a few years after the dirty trick we'd played on my brother in law. As I think back on this story today, I realize it has been longer than my memory since I have seen Last Call in a public tavern. These days last call for me means the TV News is over. Karen generally beats me to evening's end by a comfortable stretch. However, there were times, way back, many years ago when we thought we were setting the world on fire.

"Those were the days my friend, we thought they'd never end."–Mary Hopkins, 1968

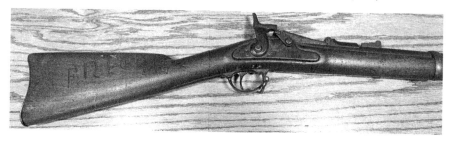

Beef and Rice Fiesta
1 lb. ground beef
1 medium onion, sliced
1½ cups water
1 can condensed golden
    mushroom soup
1 tsp salt

1 can (7oz) corn
1 tsp chili powder
1½ cups minute
    rice
1 medium tomato
1 green pepper

Brown beef in skillet, leaving meat in large chunks. Add onion and cook over medium heat until tender. Add water, soup, salt, corn, and chili powder. Bring to a boil. Stir in rice, add tomato and pepper. Cover and simmer 5 min. Makes about 5 servings

Come the Morning

The gods were having one hell of a party. They were bowling from the mountaintops, rolling massive boulders that crashed and bounced striking jagged sparks of fire that lit the night into day. The thunder came in seemingly endless waves. It was 1:00 am? 2? I couldn't be sure as the storm woke me from a sound sleep. I was in the back of my old Dodge truck inside the camper shell snuggled into a sleeping bag. I awoke to a storm so violent that the thunder quite literally shook the pickup, and lightning seemed to shoot right up through the camper. I lay awake, staring straight at the mere eighth-inch of aluminum that separated me from the wrath of Mother Nature. I knew this was going to be rough, and I lay trembling like a small child waiting for the worst to happen, while praying for the violence to abate.

My adventure came about when my friend Tim asked me if I wanted to use his property to go camping. He explained that he had a great little lake with lots of fish and plenty of room to camp. I could go out there anytime I wanted, and I really should take advantage. It was late in the summer of 1980 when we were living in our first house in Des Moines. Karen was traveling for the weekend, so I told Tim I'd take him up on his offer. "Only one thing," he said, "if you catch any bass, please throw them back so they can get bigger,"–understood and agreed.

Tim and I had gone to college together. More than that, we were in the same classes, both being Graphic Design majors. Same classes yes, but clearly not in the same *class*. Tim earned his way through school as a working graphic designer. By the time I graduated, I was pretty sure I knew how to spell graphic design. He went directly from graduation to the same studio where he'd been working for years. Within a couple of years, he went out on his own, where he rented a building a couple of blocks from the headquarters of *Better Homes and Gardens*, the magazine and book publishers. He shared the space with another designer, a young photographer, and, of all things, a custom knifemaker.

After graduation, I spent the better part of a year looking for a design job. I worked nights and slept a couple hours in the mornings then hit the bricks with my portfolio. I landed a production job, then on to a small local agency. From there, I went to *Better Homes and Gardens Real Estate*, and that's when I hooked up with Tim again. Tim is as affable as he is talented, so I always enjoyed sending any photo shoots his way. As a young artist, spending time directing shoots was a great learning experience for me as well.

Karen graduated from Drake in 1977 and went to work for Burroughs Wellcome as a pharmaceutical representative. She traveled southwest Iowa during the week, and some weekends were given over to sales meetings. As she was scheduled to be gone this particular weekend, I decided a little camping and fishing would be just the thing. In a conscious effort to recapture a small piece of my childhood, I dug out my old camping equipment, my fishing gear, and stocked up on pork'n beans and hotdogs.

Friday afternoon, I loaded up my gear and headed to Tim's property. Tim and four others purchased a large piece of land surrounding a small lake just south of Des Moines proper. There was a home built by one of our college professors, and the rest broken into plots for future houses. It was a pretty little lake, a couple of acres in size, and open grassy meadows on three sides. The eastern border was rimmed with trees and small coves and was very swamp-like as it was the low end of the water and it was stocked with largemouth bass and an old wooden rowboat available for use in fishing.

It was early evening when I pulled the Dodge off the highway into the lane leading to the lake. I wended my way to the back, toward the trees. I found a suitable flat spot with a downed tree trunk that made a comfy couch. It was late in the summer, but the weather had been merely warm, not the brutal heat one can get in August in Iowa. The sky was a bright blue, threatening to turn purple as the sun hung low in the western sky.

Once settled, I snagged my rod and reel and tackle box, jumped into the rowboat, and pulled into the middle of the lake. The evening rush, such as it is in Des Moines, was over, so the occasional car passing on the highway was far enough away that it could not be heard. The silence of the evening was a song unto itself. I reached into my tackle box and selected a small fly. After a couple of fruitless casts, I realized it was far too light for my rig. I changed up to a silver spinner, and that did the trick.

The only sounds were the whirring of the line as it left the spool followed by the hollow plop of the spinner entering the water. A slight swish of the line as I alternately took it up then let the spoon free fall through the water. Then wham! I could feel the sharp tug as a fish hit the needle-pointed tre-ble-hooks. *Set the line hard, and then begin to play with him, reel carefully, let him run, bring him in.* I caught several small bass of one-to-two pounds, gen-tly releasing each one after removing the hooks. It was getting on to full dark, and all this fun made me hungry. I rowed the boat back to its moorings. By now, the silence was replaced by a constant rise and fall of croaking peepers, cicadas, and the deep-throated *croak!* of bullfrogs.

The powder blue of the evening sky gradually became a deep blue-black blanket dotted with millions of stars hanging overhead so low I felt I could brush them away like so many grains of white sugar spilled on a dark table-cloth. I found my flashlight and gathered an armload of wood. I had already cleared a spot for the fire, rimming it with rocks and using a pan-sized flat stone for a cooktop. Within minutes I was sitting next to a cheery blaze reen-acting one of the most primitive actions of man, staring into a fire. Opening a can of beans with my pocketknife opener, I dumped them into an aluminum camp frying pan. I placed the pot on the rock to heat the beans then set about cutting a stick for my hotdogs. Reaching into my stash, I pulled out a jug of water and a flask of whiskey. I told myself, this is how Man is meant to live.

Later, with the last of the beans devoured and the uneaten 'dogs stored away, I cleaned my utensils and leaned back against the log with my latest book. I have always been an inveterate reader and feel quite put out if I don't read at least a little before I go to sleep. I remember my contentment as I sat by the fire, belly full, smoking my pipe, sipping a whiskey and water, and reading a Wild West novel. Soon my head started to hit my chest, and after several attempts to catch the meaning of the words that were swimming all over the page, I gave up and crawled into the back of my camper and snug-

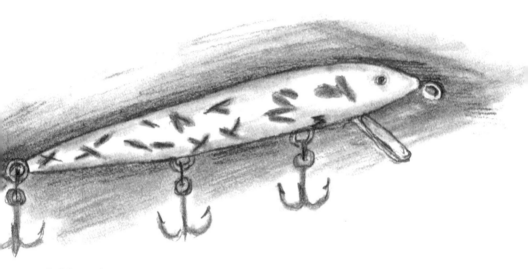

gled happily into my sleeping bag. I fell off the mountain into a deep, deep sleep.

That's when the storm woke me, leaving me shivering in terror. It began with earsplitting thunder and the sharp crack of lightning. It was all so close I knew I was in the heart of it. Then the wind kicked up. It came in gusts so powerful I feared it would flip over the truck. I worried that I was in a tornado or that a limb would fall on the fragile camper. I don't know how long the raging storm lasted but longer than I wanted it to for sure. The thunder rolled, the lightning crackled, the wind blew, and then the rain came. It slapped the camper shell in drops the size of small bird eggs. Dreading it, I waited for the hail to come pounding down, but fortunately, it never did. But the rain was sufficient to scare me silly. It rained in waves, buckets, deluges; it was Homeric in its intensity. And every single drop made a *gawd-awful* thumping on the roof of that camper a mere eighteen inches above my face. At last, the rain settled into a steady thrumming of small fingers on the ceiling. I drifted back to sleep.

I woke to sunshine and a different world. The previous night's rain washed away any vestiges of heat. The morning air was clean and soft. The insect serenade was replaced by the trilling of birds in the trees and the meadows. I managed to find some dry wood and get a fire going. I filled an old coffee can with water and set it on the flat rock to boil. As the water was heating, I took my morning ablutions and surveyed the surrounding area. It all seemed no worse for the wear, with not even a trace of the night's storm except for a few already drying puddles. With the water hot, I tossed in a handful of ground coffee and waited for it to roil itself into something worth drinking.

My morning coffee drunk, the fire out and stones dispersed, I grabbed my fishing gear. Settling into the boat, I took a deep breath. It was like drinking sweet air. It was just, simply, a magnificent morning. Rowing to the center of the lake I settled in, casting for my prey. I tried silver spoons. Nope. I tried plastic worms. Nope. I tried frogs. Nope. After a bit, the deep shadows of the trees along the water's edge caught my eye. *That's where I should be.* Turning the little boat, I rowed into the swampy area.

Maneuvering the boat around fallen logs and brush, I paused in an open spot under a canopy of small trees. It was a bowl-like area about twenty yards across with a submerged log on the far side. It was shallow, and the water so transparent after the rains, every detail of the bottom stood out with perfect clarity, including a couple of small fish and several active crawdads. *What a pretty little spot* I said to myself, *this is it.*

Rummaging in my tackle to find my newest lure, one I had just purchased, my hand found the Cotton Cordell Red-Fin. Five inches long with three treble-hooks, it had a plastic lip underneath the neck, and when you reeled, it dove, when you let up, it swam up to the surface with a tantalizing shimmy. I hooked it on and gave it a few tentative tries. It was an active little thing, and I liked the way it wiggled its hips like a seductive hula dancer or a cheap stripper.

I wasn't sure why I had chosen this spot. As I said, I could see every detail of the bottom, and there was no largemouth in sight. A couple more casts and then I'd head for home. Throwing overhand carefully to not catch the lure in the canopy of leaves just a few feet over my head, I let the line play out until the plug almost hit the log on the opposite side of the pool. At the last possible moment, I hit the brakes, and the lure plopped a few inches short of the log floating just under the surface.

I played Cotton reeling him down nearly to the bottom, then letting him swim toward the surface. Suddenly a big piece of the log broke off. But no, it wasn't part of the tree; it was a very large largemouth, and Mr. Bass was homing in on my lure. I still remember my surprised delight as I watched him materialize from beneath that log.

I slowed my turn of the reel, pulling the lure slowly down deep. Just as the bass got near, I let up a bit, so Cotton seemed to swim away, then I pulled him down again. Mr. Largemouth hit that lure like a heavyweight boxer. He came in from the side, and shaking his head, he hit Cotton Cordell, sucking in half of the five inches before he realized his mistake.

I half-lifted off the seat when I set the hooks on the old boy. He tossed and flopped, but he was caught for fair. Those trebles were not about to be thrown off. I wrestled him around and got him up to the boat when he ran for his log. I set the reel again and horsed him back. This time he ran under the boat. I worked the line around the prow, and we wrestled some more.

At last, the old man stopped fighting. I pulled him into the boat. This boy would go a good four pounds–a long way from a monster, but, in my mind, he was just as much fun to catch as a record-sized fish.

I got him disentangled from the hooks and took a good look so that I would retain his picture in my mind. And I have. I still have the Cotton Cordell, but I get out fishing rarely. I believe that night was the last time I slept out of doors—except the nights when I drive cross-country on my annual hunts and sometimes sleep in my car. But the memory of that weekend, like countless others, I keep in my pocket like so many small, smooth stones. My memories make a soft clicking sound that is always with me. Sometimes I pull them out one by one and roll them around to feel their time-smoothed edges. No matter the storms that pass in the night, one never knows what one will find, come the morning.

Gone fishin'. Me, brother Mike, cousin Jim, and cousin Donnie, 1960.

Hard Targets

"Here, this present is for Uncle Kevin."

It was Christmas at my in-laws, and as usual, the pile of presents sprawled willy-nilly from under the tree to fill up fully half of the large living room. Margaret Ann was our Santa, a position she held since she was hardly more than a toddler. At my in-law's house, as I am sure in many others, Christmas has a script. The script here is strictly followed year to year. Early in the evening, we gather in the dining room dressed for church. Dinner is served, then dishes done in time to make it to the candlelight service at the Methodist church a crisp two-block walk.

At church, we greet those old friends and neighbors we have not seen for a year or more. Hymns are sung, and the candles lit. Soon we are struggling back into winter coats while refreshing old acquaintances. After church and the appropriate hymns, we gather back at the house, in the living room. Jackets and ties removed, belts loosened, and comfortable seats found by all. Glasses get passed around and for the adults, bottles of champagne opened, with soft drinks for the young ones. The tree stands in the corner window entertaining all of the residents who drive or walk up and down the main street. The room is always half-filled with a mountain of gifts from those present and also from the various relatives in distant cities. The act of opening

Christmas presents is at minimum a three-to four-hour celebration of family. Each gift is selected, passed, then opened, and commented upon. One. At. A. Time. No exceptions, ever.

My package made its careful way around the room hand-to-hand. It was wrapped in plain white and just about the size of a shirt box. But as I closed my hand on the package, instantly, I knew this was no shirt. I began to tear up, and emotion clouded my face. Karen's smile turned to a look of concern.

"Are you OK? What is it?"

Now, of course, the whole room was staring blankly at me.

Holding back a sob, I was able to rasp, "I know what it is. It's your Grand-father's old pistol. The one Art had before he died."

Karen's grandfather died many years before I came into the family picture, but at some time he'd owned two guns, a double-barreled shotgun that had gone to Karen's Uncle Jerry in Minneapolis, and a single shot shotgun pistol that went to her Uncle Art. Art neither hunted nor shot, so he had the little gun mounted into a shadow box. I had been very close to Art and his wife, Maggie since I came into the family years before. Sadly, Art had died only a couple of years ago. He passed just at the age of retirement, and it had hit the entire family hard.

When we lived in Des Moines, we bought a house only a couple of miles from Art and Maggie. One time at their house Art brought out the shadow box with the old pistol. After that, I never missed an opportunity to examine it. The pistol is a rarity, and of course, I slobbered over that antique so much it's a wonder it didn't rust. Now with Art gone, Maggie had gifted it to me. I was simply speechless.

The gun is a slim little Stevens Offhand Tip-Up, and it shot a single 2.5" .410 shotshell. Originally, they were sold for controlling varmints in the barnyard, things like rats and blackbirds. These little guns had not been man-ufactured for many years. They were rare to find in any condition, let alone practically brand new.

Well, of course, Christmas came and went. We packed our plunder and headed back to Kansas. We'd moved to Kansas in late 1980 where we pur-chased a beautiful piece of land a few miles outside of Lawrence. The house sat off the road on five-and-a-half acres, three-and-a-half of that hay ground. A little creek bisected the hayfield. I gave the crop to a neighboring farmer who lived just around the corner. The beautiful thing for me was there was plenty of room to shoot without endangering or irritating my neighbors. I set up a post at the edge of the backyard where I could mount my automatic trap thrower, and on weekends I could be found shooting trap, alone or with friends.

Even though we lived a far piece out in the country, 30 miles from the nearest burbs in Kansas City, we were often busy entertaining, giving dinner parties in the winter months. And in the summer, barbecues and weenie roasts. Shooting contests often accompanied our summer parties. Well, you can imagine that just as soon as the winter cleared out, I had that little pistol out of its shadow box and in the backyard banging away. To my dismay, I quickly discovered how difficult hitting a flying target with a short-barreled handgun could be, even for the experienced shooter.

Pulling the heavy, spring-loaded arm of the automatic thrower down until it clicked into the locking mechanism I would place a brightly colored orange or yellow clay disk in the grooved arm. The pull-string in my left hand and the pistol in my right, a short tug, and the heavy spring would unlatch the arm, launching the clay pigeon into the air at high speed. I would swing my extended gun arm tracking the sailing target, trying to hold in front and above. *Bang!* Nothing. I repeated this many, many times. I went through two boxes of shells and became seriously discouraged. At last! I launched one out, and a single pellet chipped the edge of the clay bird! Not much to brag about, but now I had the formula. After that, I began to hit the targets steadily. Solid hits to boot.

The summer passed into fall, and the annual hunting cycle was here again. My new hunting buddy Scott and I, along with my Springer Droopy had a good fall hunt. Our little farm in Kansas was a mere three hours from the home farm in Iowa. This fact meant that I could get out hunting at least every other weekend if we did not have other plans. Then, of course, there was always Thanksgiving and the long holiday weekends, which gave me at least three days of uninterrupted hunts. On the weekends I did not make it up to Iowa, Droopy and I often chased the covey of quail that nested just across the road from our house in Kansas. Life was good.

The crisp air of fall and the gold, red, and brown landscape turned cold and snowy. The year had come and gone once again in the usual way these years do, and soon we found ourselves packing for our trip up the interstate, over the river and through the cornfields to Grandma and Grandpa's for Christmas. This year was a brutally cold year, and as we started north for Iowa, the temperatures were plummeting and an Arctic wind was gaining strength. We had both boys–Brad was just a baby–Droopy the dog, and we were pulling an old open trailer containing our luggage and bags of Christmas presents.

We left Kansas just after work and were due to arrive in Lenox around seven in the evening. It was warm and safe inside the car; ice crystals played around the edges of the windows in spite of the fact that the fan was blowing on high. Never the less our holiday spirits were soaring as we rocketed north through the cold darkening night singing Christmas Carols to the boys. We were an hour off the interstate in northern Missouri on a dark, two-lane highway at least one-half hour away from the next town when my joy turned to concern.

When I glanced down at the heat gauge, I was dismayed to see it begin a steady and alarming descent towards cold. If the radiator froze up out here so far from civilization, we could be in real trouble. No phones, no cover from the elements, and still over an hour from home. Even if I could flag down a passing car I would be forced to leave all of our presents, guns, and possibly even the dog here along the open highway while the family got someplace safe and warm. I pulled the car into an abandoned gas station and let the car idle in the hope it would gain some heat. If the car froze it would have to be towed, and it would be at least a day before it would thaw enough to restart it. Then I had an idea! I remembered a manila folder stuck in the pocket behind the driver's seat. I reached back and grabbed the folder, exited the car and was met by the bone-numbing cold. Lowering my head, I faced north and pushed into the wind. Opening the hood, I placed the folder in between the grill and in front of the radiator. The fan sucked it up tight, and we were delighted when the heat gauge immediately began climbing back towards warm. We were back on our way to celebrate our Christmas.

Christmas once again followed the usual script, which meant lots of family, food, and laughter. The next morning I was up early to head out to hunt with Droopy. Imagine my dismay when the temperature dropped to an actual 30 degrees below with a minus 60-wind chill. There was plenty of snow on the ground and more blowing with the frigid wind. What was I thinking? What kind of fool hunts in such weather? Me, of course.

Well, what the hell? I thought. I came here to hunt, so I just bundled up and headed out. Not having taken total leave of my senses, I planned only short walks from the car, which I left idling at each stop. The day called for short forays, not long walks away from the roads, which I made into the harshest environment I have ever hunted before or since. I discovered several things that day. First, that Droopy did not even notice that it was cold. He bounded around with his usual enthusiasm breaking through the snow and sticking his nose into every hummock. Second, in this cold, my movements were exaggerated and much slower. My extra clothes added nearly an inch to my reach, and my triple gloves made the trigger cumbersome. Third, my 1911 semi-automatic became a single-shot, as it was so cold the oil froze in the chamber and would not allow the gun to cycle. But, you can find game even under the harshest of conditions. I did shoot one rooster and a couple of rabbits. In the end, I decided it was unquestionably a day to be inside with the family.

The day after Christmas it was a balmy zero outside with a light wind and a middling sun. I loaded up Droopy and decided to cruise the road for a while. I am often able to see Mr. Ringneck crouching in a ditch hiding next to one of the many small fir trees that grow along the roads or leaning against a fence protected by a bunch of winter-dead grass. If I do spot a bird, I drive past slowly and stop about twenty yards past him. If I am very quiet and very lucky, I can load my shotgun and unload the dog in time to push back to the bird before he runs or flushes.

This morning I decided to drive out toward our farm using a different road than usual. Now road hunting can't rightly be called hunting at all. But if you have a little time to kill, and you'd like to merely entertain the possibility of finding a bird, and you would like to stay comfortable while still pretending to hunt, it has its place. Once the vehicle is nice and warm, you can put the radio down low, crank down a window and slowly, slowly creep along an old gravel road at a leisurely pace. It gives one time to think and ponder the important things in life.

I was barely a mile out of town on the road that goes past Barker Implement and heads straight west. Approaching the stop sign I had one eye on
the road in front of me, and one eye on the ditch across from the driver's side
window. As I eased the car to a stop, my brain registered something I thought
I saw in a patch of ditch firs, back a few dozen yards.

In cold, snowy weather, a bird or a rabbit will seek shelter under these
little Christmas trees. Some are barely seedlings, and those left undisturbed
can grow to many feet high, their branches starting at the ground and
climbing to a point at the top. I dropped the car in reverse and slowly
backed up twenty yards. As bright as any sign marker there it was, Mr.
Rooster heard the tires crunch on the snowy gravel, and he'd ducked under
a fir. His problem was he'd left his tail sticking out and on top of the snow,
looking like a party invitation.

Well, I thought to myself, this is just about a perfect opportunity to try
the little Stevens Offhand and put my skills to the test. I reached into my
bag and slipped out the sliver-slim handgun and a single diminutive shell. I
knew I'd only get one shot so one shell would do, for better or worse. I shut
the engine down and removed the keys so that the door wouldn't ding-ding,
then eased quietly out of the car. My feet made a scrunch on the snow that
sounded overly loud to me, but Mr. Rooster thought he was invisible, so my
luck was holding.

Carefully pulling up the rear hatch I popped the lever on the door to
Droopy's dog box, and he boiled out into thin air, clearing the ground by six
feet. When he came around and glanced my way, I pointed toward the ditch
where my quarrie's cloak of invisibility was about to prove an illusion. Droopy
hit the edge of the ditch at full speed pitching right over and going directly
to the hidden bird. I quick-stepped across the road just as Droopy dived into
the base of the tree and Mr. Rooster ran out the opposite side launching into
the air just high enough to clear the barbed wire fence. I extended my arm,
pointed the pistol, and lead him like one of my clay pigeons back in Kansas.
Boom! Mister bird folded right up and Droopy scrambled through the fence
and made his usual grand retrieve.

My, my I smiled to myself. The old gun lives. Wouldn't Karen's grandfather have been proud of that? I felt Art smiling down at me. On that, I'm sure
he would have had another drink.

After stowing the dead bird in the truck and getting Droopy back into his
box, I resumed cruising down the road. I was so lost in thoughts of family,

and those who had departed before me that I kept only half an eye out. After all, how much better could the day be after a shot like that? Best not to tempt the fates, you know? I was just about to come to the momentous decision to turn left at the next mile then head for home when I passed the farmstead of an old friend.

Just off the road less than fifty yards and east of his barn he had a small stock pond. I noticed a steer milling around the shore of the frozen puddle. Then I saw it, about twenty feet from the edge–a second steer had broken through the ice up to his haunches and was scrambling for a foothold onto a sheet of solid ice, desperately trying to make it back to dry land.

The steer's frantic flailing could not break the thicker ice close to shore. He could not get close enough for his hind legs to touch solid ground. In this bitter cold weather, he would soon tire and drown. Slamming the car to a stop, I leaped, out and just as I was about to climb the fence, a neighbor and his young teenaged son stopped to see what I was doing. The situation was very evident, so we wasted little time talking.

The neighbor retrieved a rope from his truck, and we slid and scrambled down to the icy pond. We got a big loop on the rope and were able to lasso the struggling steer. The three of us put all we had into hauling that steer out of the water and over the ice. We slipped on the snow and wallowed in the freezing mud, but we finally got him on solid ground. Once the steer was safe, we pushed and prodded both steers up into the old barn. The inside of the barn was empty except for a couple of bunks set end to end where the cattle could feed out of the elements. We closed the doors to keep them inside and warm. After a few shivered greetings and self-congratulations, I said I would give our friend a call so he could have the Vet stop out to see to the steers.

A couple of days after Christmas I ran into my friend uptown. Feeling something of a kinship with the animals I had helped rescue, I inquired about his recalcitrant steer. He shook his head and laughed ruefully. It seems that when the Vet came out to check on his steers, he found the one who had been in the pond stone dead. For some unknown reason, the steer had crawled up on the feed bunk, stuck his head in a hole in the middle of it, and flipped over, breaking his neck. And so it goes.

It's Never Too Late

Chatting with friends the other night reminded me of a favorite story. It's one I have told many times, but I will be happy to recount it once more. The story is about my wife's grandmother, Iona.

Iona was in very real terms a woman ahead of her time. She was born and reared on the prairies in Nebraska but boasted a pedigree that included membership in the Daughters of the American Revolution (DAR). On my wall, I have a tintype of Iona's father as a young man. GK, Guerney Knowles Pittinger, is shown with a friend, circa 1880. They are young and headed off to work on the Union Pacific Railroad. So it's easy to imagine Iona born into a pioneering world.

When I met Iona, she was already "Grandma" with grown grandchildren. She stood under five feet was round of build and had snowy white hair. In short, the very embodiment of how a grandma should look. But in reality, she was so much more than that. As a young woman, she attended and graduated from Business College. Later Iona went on to teach at the same college. She was wickedly smart and fiercely independent in a day and age when those characteristics were indeed not encouraged in the workforce, let alone in women.

Truthfully, even with this level of success as a pioneer in her own right, she still felt the pressures of society. Nearing thirty years of age and unmarried, Iona had accepted the idea that she was, and would always be, an old maid. That's when she met Karen's grandfather. Gerhard Jonas (Gay) Howland was born in Iowa of Norwegian parents and in his first thirty years had been a farmer and teacher. He left for Des Moines to attend The College of Osteopathic Medicine, and at the age of thirty Gay became Dr. Howland. Gay and Iona were married when she was thirty and proceeded to have four children: Keigh (GK, Gordon Keigh), Tyke (Leland), Donna, and Helen. They reared their brood in Decorah, Iowa where GK attended high school and college. After two years in college GK headed to Des Moines to the same college (COMS) where his father earned his medical degree. GK too became an Osteopath. Now there were two Dr Howlands. He came home to Decorah to practice medicine with his father.

Of course, as these things happen, a lifetime went by, Gay and Iona's kids grew, and soon enough their children were raised. I came into the picture in 1970 and got to know Grandma and Grandpa, and I loved them. I learned a few things along the way, and they are: there was always something I could repair for Grandpa; you could not make his drinks strong enough; don't bet on sporting events with Grandma, and… don't plan to win if you challenge her to a game of Scrabble.

By'n by fifty years passed. Iona (the old maid) had been married for fifty years, Gay had practiced medicine for the same fifty years, and that year they both turned eighty. Time to retire. Karen's parents had moved to Lenox many years before, and their other three children were in Minnesota. After a few years in retirement, it became evident the old folks needed a helping hand. Karen's parents–Keigh and Martha–bought the little house next door and invited Gay and Iona to move downstate. Iona thought this such a grand idea that she immediately sold or gave away nearly everything they owned in Decorah so that she could purchase new things for the house in Lenox. Courtesy of Karen's parents, Iona completely refurnished their new home with washer, dryer, fridge, china, and more. Iona was like a newlywed. It was a last major shopping spree for her who, as we all knew, loved to shop.

A few more years went by, and Gay passed on at the age of eighty-four. Shortly after his death, Iona had her knee replaced and during the surgery suffered a mild stroke that affected her ability to swallow. By 1987 Iona was losing her battle with life. In her final weeks, she needed to leave the little house next door and go to the Care Center, two blocks down the street. After she had moved to the Care Center, Iona went downhill quickly. When it became apparent that her time was short, Tyke, Donna, and Helen were called and made the trek down from Minnesota to say their goodbyes to Mom.

Helen, always beautiful and stylish, walked into her mother's room, her heart heavy with sadness. Iona, barely able to talk, lifted her hand and signaled Helen to come closer. Helen crossed to Iona's bedside, thinking to hear words of love and wisdom from her dying mother. Tears filled her eyes as she made small, tentative steps across the room.

Leaning in close so she could hear the fading voice of her mother, Helen burst into laughter and joy upon hearing Iona's words. Iona inquired, "That purse, where did you get it? I've been looking for one just like it." Iona was indeed shopping to the very end.

This moment is how I choose to remember that dear lady. Shortly after her death in 1987, our second son Brad joined us in the world. Iona would have loved Brad's quick and gentle wit. I see lots of Iona in him. She would have liked that.

Karen's grandparents, Dr. GJ and Iona Howland in their home in Decorah, IA, 1976.

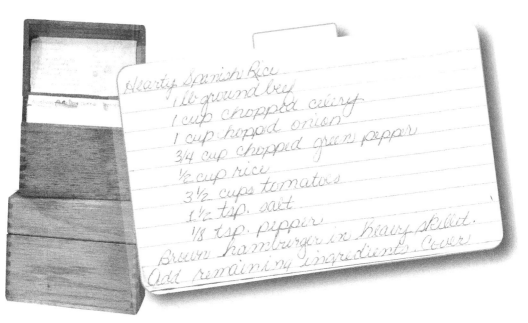

The Christmas Present

*Like most families, our family history is contained in stories passed down through the
generations. Of course, over time many of these stories get altered or disremembered.
Sadly, many get forgotten. In an attempt to chronicle some of our family histories
I keep a sketchbook/journal to record both the visual things around me and the
everyday happenings of our family. Births, deaths, graduations, birthdays, and holidays
are all in the books. Also, I jot down stories that highlight singularly remembered events.
This tale is one of those stories.*

Visitors to our home in San Diego often comment on three things. First,
the artwork that hangs in every room. The lovely atmosphere created by my
wife, one that makes everyone comfortable, is the second. The third generally takes a few minutes. In our front hall is a large basket, overflowing with
wine corks. You spy more cork-filled baskets as one wanders throughout the
kitchen, recreation room, and dining room. In truth, if you could see into the
baskets that line the top of the kitchen cupboards, they're also filled with...
wine corks. It then goes something like this, "Hmmm, you guys really like
wine. Don't you?" That's when I launch into my story.

My grandmother, Lottie was dear to me. She was not, however, what we
describe as warm and fuzzy. Born Charlotte Wheatley, in rural Iowa at the

beginning of the twentieth century, she had ten other siblings. I know little of her formative years, but I know a great deal about rural Iowa so I can make sound assumptions. Iowa in 1900 was a verdant garden for farming, but it required a strong hand to wrestle the bounty from the land. I too grew up there, within 25-miles of Grandma Lottie's birthplace. In Lottie's youth, horsepower was the primary method of locomotion. It wasn't until late in the first half of the Twentieth century that electricity came to many small towns, and indeed somewhat later for individual farms. Water pumped from wells either by wind or by hand. Livestock would have the benefit of the ubiquitous windmills that dotted the prairie landscape. People however generally pumped their water by hand and hauled it into their homes in buckets or had a hand pump installed in their kitchens.

At the age of twenty, Lottie married Alvin, A. I. "Fin" Gray. Fin was then thirty-seven years old and the first member of his family native-born to Iowa. His father, my great-grandfather, brought his family from Pennsylvania to Iowa in 1868 to claim $2-an-acre government land. This cheap land was located across the southern third of Iowa, which is bisected by Highway 34 from Illinois to Nebraska. Roughly following the old Mormon Trail, this is the route that Brigham Young and his followers took on their flight from Illinois to Utah. Much of the area south of this line was set aside and designated Indian Lands in the 1840s. By the close of the Civil War, there were few,

if any Native Americans still living in this vast area of grass and valuable land. Great-grandpa Gray became one of a hand full of hardy settlers to brave the empty expanse of land in Adams County. It would be four long years until the town of Lenox (in Taylor County) would come about and provide a nearby place to do business.

Grandpa Fin was born in 1883. By my calculation, he was too young to have fought in the Spanish-American War and too old for World War I. He was, however, the only one to stay on the land his father had settled. Fin was a handsome and athletic man. In his youth, he was a famous wrestler. Wrestlers came from all around the country to "throw" him. I have seen the posters. Somewhere I have one that states a Texas Ranger will "come north to do battle in two out of three falls with A. I. 'Fin' Gray." The Ranger did indeed come north and went back to Texas the loser. As a young man out in the world, I was often surprised to meet total strangers who knew my grandparents. The Gray's certainly made their marks upon their world.

I have a photo of the newly married Lottie and Fin. Fin is splitting wood and stands bare-chested, looking into the camera. Lottie standing in a long skirt in the style of the day is tiny and hauntingly beautiful. Soon enough two daughters arrived, my mother Ruby and my Aunt Dorothy. Lottie would often answer those who inquired about more children that "two was enough, she knew how they got there, and she was willing to sleep with a butcher knife if she had to." Lottie was (clearly) not warm and fuzzy.

Lottie's parents reared her as a strict Presbyterian, but in my youth, she and Grandpa attended the Methodist church. The list of things of which she did not approve was long. High up on the list were drinking, gambling, dancing, and cursing. This list went a very long way to explaining why she was less than fond of my father. Dad didn't gamble, but he hit the rest of the list and then some. There was always a tangible tug-of-war between Lottie and my father, Bob easing only when they were the only two family members still living in the same town. Even then it was a wary truce.

In their 49th year of marriage, my grandparents finally had an indoor bathroom installed in their home. For those of you reading this to whom this seems either backward or quaint, I had the benefit of an indoor bathroom for only three years at that time. For the first time in her sixty-nine years, my grandmother did not rise and make her way along the winding path to the little wooden house out back. Two days after Grandma and Grandpa's 50th wedding anniversary, Fin died of a massive stroke. He was in the field checking his cattle when he collapsed. I always felt this was his gift from God. He died doing what he loved at the end of a long, prosperous life.

I have another photo I keep in my office. From Easter 1962, the picture shows five generations, my great-grandmother, grandmother, mother, two of my sisters, and two grandchildren. Mary Pat, my sister, is holding Terry. Sitting in the middle is Jerry; Mary Pat's oldest. Jerry and Terry are one day apart by a year. My mother is holding my baby sister Stacy who at six-months is precisely between Jerry and Terry in age.

Within a year after my grandfather Fin died Lottie sold the farm to my

170

father and moved to town. A couple of years after that, I graduated from high school and was off to college. I was home many weekends and holidays and always made it a point to stop and visit with grandma. Time went by, and soon I was graduating from college. My sister Mary Pat had a wonderful celebration at her home where she served cake and champagne. Much to everyone's surprise, Lottie had a glass of champagne. As far as I know, this was the only time alcohol ever touched her lips in her long ninety years of life. It was done to honor me, an honor I will never forget.

The years followed, and I came home less often, but I still visited Lottie each time I was in town. In the late 70s Lottie had a severe stroke, but in some kind of miracle she had a complete recovery. As the years went by my family kept moving even further from our hometown, and our visits became infrequent. We stayed in touch through the mail and phone. On all the major holidays flowers were delivered to Lottie. The florist took special care with Lottie's flowers, and Grandma always seemed pleased. Eventually, the day came when Lottie felt she could no longer stay in her home. Many years after grandpa Fin's death Grandma moved into the nursing home.

Mary Pat phoned to ask if I would come back and help in distributing Grandma's household items. So, on a lovely Saturday my wife Karen, Mary Pat, Aunt Dorothy, Grandma, and I spent the day breaking up her house.

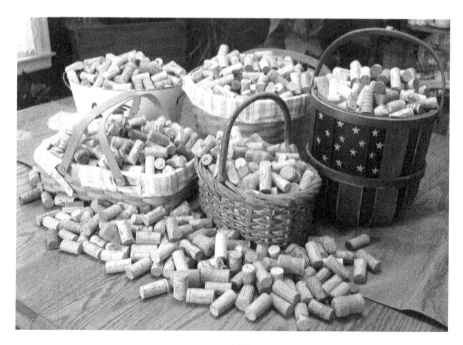

In anticipation of such a day, Lottie had written names on the bottom of specific items to be given to the cousins. It was a memorable day. We spent it talking about relatives and the antecedents of the old furniture. There was not a trace of sadness in the house that day. Grandma asked me to retrieve a box from the back room. A box filled with dozens of glass vases. Every bouquet sent over the years accounted for in this box of empty vases. Laughingly I said I would return them to the florist to be reused.

That October Grandma Gray turned ninety-years old and seemed to be in good health. She had all of her faculties and loved playing with her grand-sons, but by Christmas, she had lost much of her vitality. Lottie visited with my boys, thanking them for the basket of flowers, her Christmas present. But you could tell she was slipping away. I was out on our farm hunting when my father-in-law found me. Lottie had died. I was sad, of course, but I knew that after ninety-years on this earth she was tired and ready to rest. Over the years this beautiful, tough, little woman had become like the prairie where she spent her life. One thing I did know was that I would never have to miss her, as she would be with me each day of my life. Little did I know how the next few hours would make that so.

I hurried back to stow the dog, clean the birds I'd shot, and get myself cleaned up. I had barely accomplished all these tasks when looking out the window I saw Mary Pat, Aunt Dorothy, and Uncle Don climbing out of their car. As they headed up the walk to the front door, I could see an empty basket in Pat's hands. I instantly recognized it as the very basket that had contained Grandma's Christmas flowers. Grandma's last act before she died was to make sure Karen and I got the basket back. I laughed so hard I nearly started to cry. We visited a bit, and the basket was placed unceremoniously on top of the refrigerator in my mother-in-law's kitchen.

It was Christmas Eve. Christmas Eve at my in-laws is an experience. The gifts fill an entire room. We eat an early dinner, get dressed in our best clothes then herd the kids, grandkids, moms, and dads off to the Candlelight service at the aforementioned Methodist church. We make quite a show walking in a bunch the three blocks to church. After services, it's time to open packages. The kids, okay, and the adults, can barely contain their excitement. There is one other custom honored at Christmas; we drink champagne while opening gifts. There is laughter, oohing and awing until each person is nearly hidden from wrapping paper and stacks of gifts. This evening a prayer was offered for Lottie, and a toast made. We laughed at the thought of the many times she sat in this house while we drank our champagne or cocktails and never said a disapproving word.

Christmas came to a close about one in the morning. As we were cleaning up the mess, someone scooped up the champagne corks and tossed them into the flower basket on top of the fridge. We laughed and commented that Lottie probably wouldn't approve, but it was an excellent way to remember her. The basket went home with me, and whenever we opened a bottle of wine, the cork went into the basket. We have long since filled up that little basket and many others besides. I never open a bottle of wine that I don't think of that beautiful lady and the wonderful Christmas gift she gave to me on her final day. She gave me the gift of her memory.

And that, my friend, is the story you would hear if you ever come to my home and say, "Hmmm, you guys really like wine. Don't you?"

My dad's parents, Grandpa and Grandma Callahan in their kitchen in Imogene, IA.
August 1928.

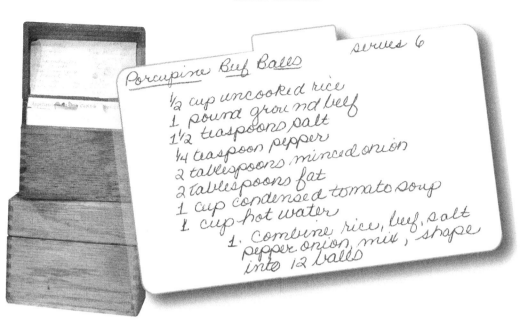

Porcupine Beef Balls — serves 6
½ cup uncooked rice
1 pound ground beef
1½ teaspoons salt
¼ teaspoon pepper
2 tablespoons minced onion
2 tablespoons fat
1 cup condensed tomato soup
1 cup hot water
1. Combine rice, beef, salt, pepper onion, milk, shape into 12 balls

Deciphering Dad

From my journal: June 26, 1997, Landenberg, Pennsylvania

My father died yesterday. Dad was 81 years old and sadly had been in a vegetative state for the last several years. We were all prepared for, and even on some level anticipating, his death. Still, I have not dealt with the loss just yet. I am on a plane to Des Moines to meet my sister Mary Pat and help with funeral arrangements. Dad had a long life although not an easy one. I began writing his obituary last night with limited success. It's amazing what we don't know about our parents.

Well, we are all gone from the farm; the area my Great-Grandfather homesteaded way back in 1868. Great-Grandpa Gray brought his family out to Iowa after the Civil War to purchase land sold by the government. The Grays came to Iowa from somewhere in Pennsylvania, and my Grandpa Alvin (Fin) Gray was the first child in the family born in Iowa. Strangely, Karen and I moved to Pennsylvania in 1991. In a way, I guess that means I went back home.

Dad married into the Gray family and spent the rest of his life farming, I think, because of my mother and the land available from my grandparents. Even though he did farm for many years, he was never much of a farmer. He probably would have been a good coach and teacher, but he couldn't afford to attend college.

Well, it's going to be a long few days. We've been in the air for a while, and an incident with my father just popped into my head, so I thought I'd write it down.

Shortly after Karen and I were married, we were living in what was called the Married Students dorm at Drake University in Des Moines. We drove home for the weekend, and I went hunting with my father. I'd grown up hunting with Dad and enjoyed it, but by this time in his life, "hunting" actually meant making a beeline to the Red Bull Tavern in Corning to drink and visit with his old cronies.

On the way to Corning, we wound up stopping off to see Al O'Dowd, one of Dad's oldest friends. Al knew I was interested in old guns, so he fetched out a relic from the back room, an antique-looking .12 gauge single-shot shotgun.

My first query was "How old is it?"

"Well… my brother bought it used in 1919."

So I supposed it qualified as old. The upshot was Al would let it go for $15. We struck a bargain, but as I had only $12 on me, my father cheerfully fronted the payment, a loan.

For several years I had been fixing up old guns, and I took this one home to improve it as well.

One week later, Dad phoned. He came right to the point. "You got that old gun fixed up yet?"

"No, I replied, I've been kinda busy going to college."

"Well, hurry up and get it done, I just sold it to Junior Scroggie for $25."

You might well imagine I was pretty mad. Reluctantly I did redo the gun. I never even got to shoot it. Dad sold it to Junior for $25, and then Jr. told me he was offered $125 for it. He refused to sell.

Well, that was my dad, a character to be sure. He had a lot in common with the title character in Hugh Leonard's play, *DA*. I'm sure going to miss the old guy. To quote the play, *Da you will always be a wasp in my head.*

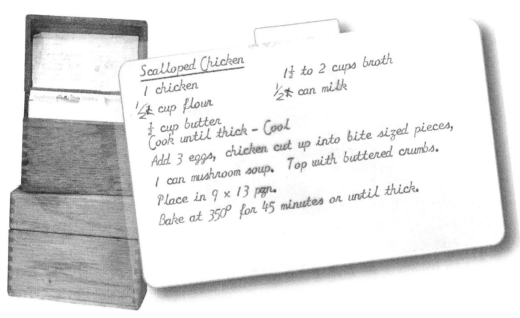

Scalloped Chicken   1½ to 2 cups broth
1 chicken   ½ can milk
¼ cup flour
½ cup butter
Cook until thick - Cool
Add 3 eggs, chicken cut up into bite sized pieces,
1 can mushroom soup. Top with buttered crumbs.
Place in 9 × 13 pgn.
Bake at 350° for 45 minutes or until thick.

The Measure of a Man

It was in the mid-1960s when the Fehring family moved to our small town. I don't recall the year, but I do remember that I was still playing Pee Wee baseball, so I was not yet in high school. Norb and Helen brought their own team of boys with them in the move. Jerry, the oldest was college-age (or perhaps beyond), Jack was four years older me, Matt a year ahead of me in school, and Pat a year behind. I recall that Pat and his two older brothers were very athletic, but Matt was the opposite of the term. The Fehrings were Catholic, and as there were so few of us Catholics in Lenox, they were a welcome addition to the school and parish.

The entire Fehring family was instantly popular. Nice parents, handsome, engaging kids. When Norb and Helen celebrated their 25th wedding anniversary, the parish threw them a big party. My father helped organize the event and nearly succeeded in having a keg of beer in the church basement. At the last minute, it was decided to move it to a discrete side yard of the church property.

Years went by, and Jack graduated, then Matt. Matt, it seemed, was not merely uncoordinated; he had a bad set of kidneys. I believe it was in '71 or '72 that he and Norb went to Iowa City Medical Center, for a then-experimental kidney transplant. Karen and I drove up to visit Matt and Norb. It is possible that the visit sealed our lasting relationship with Matt, Norb, and Helen. Matt survived and, for a few years, thrived. He ended up at Drake University with Karen and me, and we became that strange animal known as "family away from family."

Their kids all grown and away, Norb took a new job in central Iowa and relocated himself and Helen to Lake City, then a couple of years later they moved to Lakeview. It became a regular thing for Matt, Karen, and I to go up and visit on weekends. We'd have dinner and drinks at a local dinner club and then stay to watch the bands and to dance a bit. In fact, I distinctly remember one group named Still and the Bootleggers. They were so bad that we had to listen to the lyrics for a bit before we could decide what song they were playing. We unquestionably loved them.

Time moved on, and by then, Karen and I were coming to visit as a married couple. We were invited up for a long weekend in the summer, and I decided to pack a few of my favorite guns. I packed an 1824 muzzleloader and an 1865 cartridge rifle from the Indian Wars along with some other guns. It turns out Norb had a few of his own. He brought out a beautiful Winchester High Wall in .32-40 caliber and an original WWII German Lugar. You know—the famous one with the big toggle on the back and the slim menacing barrel.

Norb knew of a place to plink located in an old quarry with a bunch of dunes. We lay/sat on a low knoll and shot into another about 50 yards away. It made a perfect backdrop to keep things safe. We installed our makeshift targets and banged away. Loading an antique muzzleloader is slow, so we had plenty of time for some good conversation. I always enjoyed Norb's companionship, as, over the years, he and I had become friends too—the father of my dear friend Matt.

We shot and talked for the better part of two hours. I treasured the opportunity to handle some fine old weapons. Of course, I was jealous and offered to buy the Winchester, but Norb assured me all of his guns were going to his boys when he passed on. 'Nough said. When it came time to shoot the Lugar, I took a few shots. When I handed it back, I asked him how he came to own it?

Norb was tall and spare with a handsome hangdog face and expressive eyes that could take on the look of a bloodhound. Always quick to smile and tell a joke, but at this moment, his eyes grew hooded as his mind retreated

to another place and time. I could see it was not a pleasant memory. Nevertheless he soldiered on with his story.

"It was nearing the end of World War II, I was a Grunt, a foot soldier, and I had walked across a good chunk of Europe. We saw a whole lot of boys who never came home. By this time, most of the fighting was finished, and many of the Nazi troops were laying down their arms and giving up in droves. Regardless, we were still involved in shooting situations, and we took all precautions. It was raining, cold, and going on dark when we bivouacked. On orders, we got busy digging shallow foxholes where we would spend the night. At some point, the rain stopped, and I slept soundly. It was nearing morning, you know, that deep dark before the dawn when something woke me. I opened my eyes and reached out for my rifle. I froze when I saw, not three feet away, a young German soldier standing over me, pointing his pistol directly at my chest."

"What did you do?" I ask, asked wide-eyed.

"Well," Norb continued in his droll way. "We stared at each other for a long heartbeat, and to my everlasting happy surprise, he reversed his weapon and handed it to me in surrender. That German soldier wanted to trade the pistol for a cigarette, and I was more than happy to oblige. The gun? That's the gun you've been playing with this afternoon."

Listen, this is a man I had known from childhood through adulthood, a person with whom I shared tears, laughter, prayers, and life. We had a history. But until that very moment, I had never taken the true measure of the man. 🏠

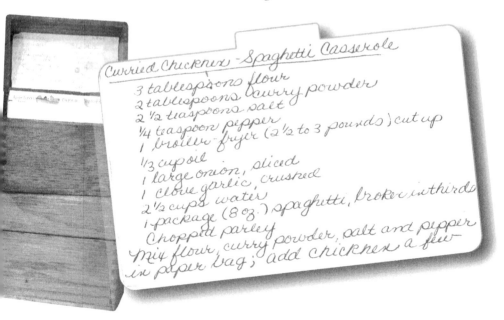

Curried Chicken – Spaghetti Casserole

3 tablespoons flour
2 tablespoons curry powder
2 1/2 teaspoons salt
1/4 teaspoon pepper
1 broiler-fryer (2 1/2 to 3 pounds) cut up
1/3 cup oil
1 large onion, sliced
1 clove garlic, crushed
2 1/2 cups water
1 package (8 oz.) spaghetti, broken in thirds
Chopped parsley
Mix flour, curry powder, salt and pepper
in paper bag; add chicken a few

Now That's a Truck!

In 1987 Karen and I were living in rural Kansas. In December of 1980, we'd relocated from Des Moines to a five-and-a-half-acre spread just outside of Lawrence. Since graduating from Drake in 1977, Karen had been working as a pharmaceutical rep and me as a graphic designer. The first year we were in Kansas, I opened a design shop in Lawrence. Initially, business was good, but when school let out, and the 28,000 students left town, so did my business. My initial foray into self-employment came to an ignominious end.

In early 1982, I was hired as Art Director for a publishing company in Kansas City. It was a 32-mile drive to work each day, but it took me through some beautiful country, and I did not mind the commute. When I moved to Kansas, I was driving a three-quarter-ton Dodge pickup that got around twelve miles to the gallon on a good day. With no air conditioning, it was not exactly suited for a suit and tie job. One of Karen's pharma friends arranged for me to purchase a sedan that was going out of their fleet. It had a lot of miles, but it was a pretty nice car. It was not, however, ideal for country life, so I went to a local dealer, and for a few hundred dollars, I purchased a little yellow Datsun pickup with a whole lot of miles on it.

For a few years, I drove that little truck on the weekends to cut wood and up to Iowa for my hunting excursions. Old Jake, my black lab, would snuggle up on the passenger floor and sleep the entire trip going and coming. If Karen went home to see the folks, Jake rode back in the bed of the truck in a dog box. Eventually, Jake got old and passed on to where all good bird dogs go. Our son, GK, was born in 1984, and both my car and truck gained more miles from my drives to the office and hunting trips. By then, the Datsun was used primarily for hauling wood, taking the garbage cans to the road, and limping to and from my jaunts to Iowa.

Over the years, Karen has participated in many training exercises designed to improve the pharma reps' abilities. Often, she would return home and try them on me. I have become the beneficiary of a lot of free training. I well remember one such exercise. The question from the moderator was simple: "When were you happiest in your life?" Now, that is a simple question, but also a fully loaded one. Any answer is automatically fraught with danger. *Were you happiest when you were five-years old? When you and your first spouse were married? Does that mean you are unhappy now?* Well, you see the problem.

I thought about that weighty question and then stated with certainty that while I am a happy person and have no regrets, that I was happiest in 1987 when I was 34 years old. Why, you may ask. It's a pretty easy question for me to answer, for that was the year that everything seemed to be just right in my life. The publishing company where I worked had grown to international proportions, and I was the Creative Director. I was thin, won a lot of design awards, dressed like Don Johnson (*Miami Vice*), and was in general pretty insufferable. I thought of myself as an ART Director, capital letters. Once a year, I was invited back to my alma mater at Drake to speak with young design students, and local colleges asked me to be a guest speaker on occasion. I was often requested to judge student portfolios. In addition to those reasons, Karen had just given birth to Bradley, our second. We both traveled extensively, and I was pretty darn sure that I was King of the World.

Well, by this time, both of my vehicles were on their last wheels. I located a Nissan dealer in Kansas City, and he made me a deal I could not refuse. If I could drive both car and truck into the dealership, he would sell me a brand-new Nissan King Cab truck for $11,000 and give me $5,000 for my old clunkers. Deal. I well remember the Saturday we drove the car and truck the 40 miles into KC. I prayed every mile of the way that both vehicles would arrive, motors running, and wheels turning. Thank goodness, they did.

The Nissan was a spiffy little truck. Silver paint with air, bucket front seats, five-speed on the floor, and good gas mileage. Two rear seats folded down in back, so now the boys, mom, dog, and luggage could travel comfortably to Iowa and back. GK was buckled in behind Mom, and baby Brad was behind me buckled into his car seat. That way, if he needed attention, Mom could just lean around and reach him, no problem. A year after faithful old Jake passed, I inherited Droopy, a Springer Spaniel, and he traveled like a prince in his dog box in the truck bed.

Fall of '87 came around, and Brad was nearing six months. Karen decided to ride to Iowa with me on my hunting excursion to spend the weekend with her folks. Accordingly, we packed clothes and gear for babies, parents, and hunting, and off we drove. The trip to our childhood home is a mere three-hour drive beginning in eastern Kansas, north through the western edge of Missouri, and culminating in southern Iowa a few miles north of the Missouri border. I have always loved the Midwest, and driving through familiar country in the fall of the year is one of my favorite things to do. During the drive, one can see the colors change, and the crops come out of the fields. It always makes me happy to know I am drawing closer to my boyhood home.

Saturday, I was up before the dawn and out on the farm, pursuing the beautiful ring-necked pheasant. I had a good day with Droopy, shot my limit, and headed back to town in the early afternoon. After I cleaned the birds, I got myself cleaned up and decided to see if any old friends were hanging out downtown. As luck would have it, my old buddy Dick was in the saloon nursing a beer, elbows holding down the well-worn bar. "Hey, Callahanski!" He shouted when I entered. An inside joke as we were both of the Irish persuasion, I smiled and returned his greeting with a hearty handshake and a "set 'em up" to the bartender. Jack placed our libations on the bar, and we proceeded to catch up on marriages, babies, work, crops, all the things old friends are wont to discuss.

Dick and I had grown up together, been on the same ball teams, the same church, our families knew each other. We spent an hour or so nursing beers and talking about our several siblings, farming, my job. It was a nice visit. "Well, I think Martha will have dinner on the table, so I better get back up the street."

"Yeah, I've some chores to do. I'll walk out with you," he said.

I parked my new truck in front of the tavern, and I could not resist the opportunity to show off.

"Hey, what do you think of my new truck?"

Dick eyeballed it for a minute and asked, "Where are the tools, old wire, dents, and scratches?" He gestured to the pickup parked next to mine.

It had some use on it I must agree. It had once been a 2-tone red and white. It was mostly faded orange, and what had been white was gray or rust covered. There were gashes, dents, and scratches. The bed was a riot of old fertilizer cans, tools, baling wires, and a few empty beer cans.

Looking at my brand-new Nissan, Dick lowered his eyes and, in a mournful voice, opined, "That's not a truck." Then a light came over his face, he straightened and smiled, placed his hand on the bed of his old beater and proudly exclaimed, "Now that's a truck!"

You know, he was right.

Ronnie Faulk's old truck, from my sketchbook.

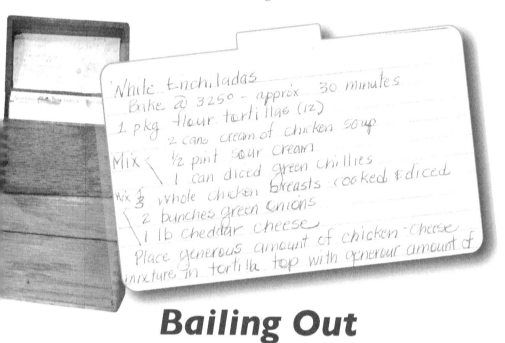

White Enchiladas
   Bake @ 325° - approx. 30 minutes
1. pkg flour tortillas (12)
     2 cans cream of chicken soup
Mix   ½ pint sour cream
     1 can diced green chillies
Mix   3 whole chicken breasts cooked & diced
     2 bunches green onions
     1 lb cheddar cheese
Place generous amount of chicken-cheese
mixture in tortilla. top with generour amount of

Bailing Out

I had just settled into my chair in the kitchen of the old farmhouse when our host reached over and grabbed an 8 x 10 framed photograph. "Have I ever shown you this?"

My friends, my son, and I were on our annual trek, hunting pheasants in Southwest Iowa. For several years we had been coming up to hunt the Robinson farm. Dewan is the father of a close friend and at that time was into his 80th year and beyond. Dewan still worked 500 of the 1,000 acres he owned. The rest was in five-foot tall switchgrass that was home to an enormous population of wild pheasant. While we always managed to bag a few, the pheasants clearly had the advantage over the hunters, even with our dogs and guns.

Dewan opened up his lands to anybody who wanted to hunt, but we were special guests. Our small payment was to break for a cup of coffee and day-old doughnuts, visit with him and Marge, share stories of our families and catch up on the year past.

I took the framed photo from his hand and looked at it carefully. It was their wedding photo taken shortly after WWII. Dewan was in uniform and Marge was just beautiful in a blazing white silk gown. Always an atractive-woman, she had a beauty that defied the ages. Even nearing 80 she remained lovely.

"That's a great picture," I replied handing it around the table. Dewan seemed to forget about the photo as soon as he'd handed it to me. "Did I ever tell you about my plane going down in Europe?"

"No, I don't believe you have. I think I would remember."

Dewan sat down and began rolling out a treasured memory as we all sat rapt at the table, our coffee growing cold. "We were on a flight over France, and I was a gunner on a Flying Fortress–the vaunted B-52. We were flying in formation when one of the planes above us just fell out of the sky. It was our bad luck that on the way down it sheared off one of our wings. There we were flying on one wing and going down. The plane turned sideways, and a call came from the pilot. *Bail! Bail! Bail!* was the order."

"Did you?" I gulped. The table was now at rapt attention. No one was eating or drinking, all eyes on our storyteller.

"Well, we tried to open the door, but it was now well above our heads, and the air pressure would not let it release. We were going down pretty fast at this point. We finally managed to force it open but the air rushing in was tremendous. I was ordered to get out, but when I would try to push myself through the door, the air pressure would push me back down."

"Oh my God," I gasped, "what did you do?"

I was trying to imagine what must go through a man's mind while rocketing towards the earth in a big tin can with the only escape route visible but unattainable.

Dewan continued, "I grabbed the frame and pushed up, then I felt a boot on my butt pushing me from behind. I managed to push out and away from the falling plane, opened my 'chute and floated down."

"What happened to your friend?"

"You know, I looked back and saw other 'chutes open. The plane fell away from me, but by some miracle, everyone else got out. We were picked up pretty quickly."

We all sat back in our chairs and breathed. Each of us reached for our coffee, not knowing just what to say to such an incredible story of survival.

Finally, "That's quite a story, Dewan."

Dewan smiled, reached across the table and plucked up the wedding photo. "See Marge's wedding dress? I had that dress made from the parachute I was wearing when I bailed out of the plane."

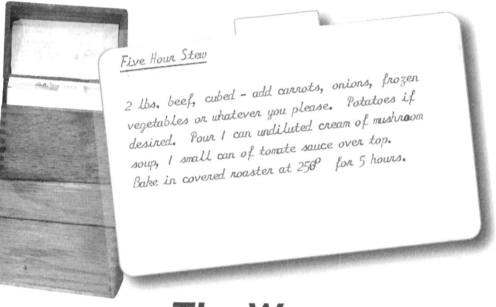

Five Hour Stew

2 lbs. beef, cubed – add carrots, onions, frozen vegetables or whatever you please. Potatoes if desired. Pour 1 can undiluted cream of mushroom soup, 1 small can of tomate sauce over top. Bake in covered roaster at 250° for 5 hours.

The Wave

I am told that the 1970s sporting phenomenon and group participation the *Wave*, is an example of metachronal rhythm. You know, forty-thousand people in a stadium standing and waving their arms progressively , like undulations of the ocean. I have not a clue as to what metachronal rhythm might be. But no, I'm not going to talk about that Wave. I'm referring to the good old-fashioned hold-up-your-hand, palm out, and move-your-arm-repeatedly-in-greeting, wave.

I consider myself fortunate to have been reared in a small rural community. As an extension of that good fortune, I have, over the years, been privileged to introduce people from all over the world into my hometown. When our journey brings us closer to home, my passengers invariably notice that we are being acknowledged in a most friendly fashion. People wave at us. I generally get questions like, "Do you know that person?" Sometimes I do, and as often as not I don't. That's when I get to explain The Wave. The local wave, that is.

Now, if you are reading this, and were also reared in a small community nearly anywhere in America, you'll most likely know where I'm heading with this tale. The writer Alice B. Toklas famously quoted, "A rose is a rose is a rose." But, as I gleefully get to explain to my visitors, a wave is not just a wave.

There are several different types of waves. Here are but a few.

The arm wave: as described above, the waver raises a hand, palm out and vigorously moves their arm in greeting. Often accompanied with a smile. A sub-group is merely raising a hand up then down, perhaps sharply, or languidly.

The one-finger wave: when you see a person driving with one, or both hands on the wheel, the one-finger is when the greeter merely raises one finger in silent greeting. This wave is not to be confused with the one-finger gesture that is most decidedly unfriendly. The sub-group here results when the salutation is achieved as all four fingers fly up, then return to the wheel.

The head nod: in my time I have often observed two locals on the road and seen both nod their heads in passing, virtually simultaneously. The variation is the Way Back: when the eyes and chin go up, and the head back into the shoulders. Also, loosely classed with the nods is the shoulder shrug. Self-explanatory.

It always makes me happy to explain to my guests that, yes, even if I don't personally know all the people who wave to me, their greeting is sincere. Friend, neighbor, or stranger are all alike in our little world. Years ago, during my freshman year in college, I quickly deduced who was small town and who was city. When I walked between classes, I would eagerly greet people with a smile, a wave, and a hello. Those from more populous environs would look a bit startled and then down and away from me. But those who were from rural Iowa would smile and greet me in return.

So, if you happen to see me driving down the road, gimme a wave. If you are partial to the one finger, I'll hope it is the better of two angels.

Grandma and Grandpa Gray on their 35th wedding anniversary with Great Grandma Wheatly, Grandma's mother. Grandma Wheatly had eleven children. I was fortunate to be able to know her and spend time at her home.

Goulash
1½ lbs beef stew meat or boneless chuck
2 Tbsp shortening
½ cup water
8 ounce can tomato sauce
2 onions, peeled & chopped
1 clove garlic, peeled & chopped
1 Tbsp paprika
2 Tsp salt
2 tsp instant beef bouillon crystals
1 tsp caraway seed

Old Man

It was late afternoon when I parked my truck in front of the barbershop. After many years of living away from the Midwest, Karen and I had, at last, moved back to a place that felt like home. We left the Kansas City area in 1990 and spent the next twenty years on a peripatetic journey across the United States and back again. First to Columbus, Ohio, then Philadelphia, across the continent to San Diego, and back across the continent to New Jersey just outside of New York City. We loved the adventure and all the different places we could now call home, but I missed the prairies and being close to both our families. When the opportunity presented to come home, we did not hesitate. In April of 2010, we moved into our home in Parkville, Missouri, just outside of Kansas City.

Kansas City greeted us with a cold, wet spring and a scorching summer. It had become my habit to travel with my hunting dog, Cromwell, whenever I ran errands. After so many trips together running errands and traveling across the continent and back again, Cromwell was a seasoned traveler, leaping into the truck and taking his place on an old rug in the front passenger seat. He curls up in a ball and, from time to time, lolls his head over for an ear scratch. As one might imagine, after so many thousands of miles driving along, just the two of us, I have gotten into the habit of talking to Cromwell.

I even have pet names for him. Sometimes I call him Slim, or Slim with a Saddle, after the cowboy characters, but more often than not, I just call him Old Man. As in, "How ya doin' Old Man?"

After our last trip from New Jersey to Kansas City, Cromwell spent so much time in the truck he thought it was his home. But when the temperatures in Missouri that spring climbed close to 100°, I hesitated to leave Crommie in the truck. In the end, I relented, and we were off to do some errands. Karen was traveling for a few days, so I was in no real hurry to get back home. We took our time. Since I was close to my barber, I thought, "Why not stop in for a haircut?" When I moved to Parkville, I'd found my local barbershop, which is staffed by three lovely talented ladies. I liked them, their work, and their prices.

I emerged from the shop newly shorn and opening the truck door; I said loudly to Cromwell, "How ya doin' Old Man?" At that very moment, a movement caught my eye. I looked over at the sidewalk right in front of my truck into the startled eyes of an energetic looking elderly gentleman. With a disconcerted look at me, he said, "Well, I'm okay, I guess, how about you?"

I was abject in my mortification. I turned bright red. I stammered and searched for a logical explanation to that which the elderly gentleman could not see, but plainly could hear.

"No, no–NO!" I stammered. "I was speaking to my dog." I gestured towards the sleeping mutt.

The old gentleman looked even more confused.

I furiously pursued my explanation. "You see, I talk to my dog, and I call him Old Man. Really. Seriously. He's right here." But of course, Cromwell stayed hidden, sound asleep and well out of the man's sight.

"Well…" he said with some suspicion still in his voice, "that's alright, I'm going down here for dinner. You have a nice evening." And off he went as baffled still as he was before.

I slumped in my seat, and rocked with laughter at the joke I had played on myself, reached over and scratched Crommie's ear. The "Old Man" and his silly master headed for home.

188

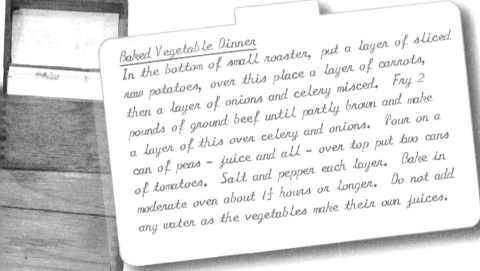

Baked Vegetable Dinner
In the bottom of small roaster, put a layer of sliced raw potatoes, over this place a layer of carrots, then a layer of onions and celery misced. Fry 2 pounds of ground beef until partly brown and make a layer of this over celery and onions. Pour on a can of peas - juice and all - over top put two cans of tomatoes. Salt and pepper each layer. Bake in moderate oven about 1½ hours or longer. Do not add any water as the vegetables make their own juices.

A Sheltering Place

It's here. It arrived early last week. The first chilly bite of fall crept in like a thief at a wedding. It is a bit early this year coming as it did before the end of September.

From year to year, our chilly visitor drops in anywhere from September to late in October. Here in the northern hemisphere, the grass is yet green and growing. But the leaves have taken their cue and begun to put on their gaudy makeup for the Harvest Fest soon to come. Some leaves have even started the steady drift to earth that signals our third season chore, raking. But for now, the change of season is merely a suggestion found in the early morning chill when I walk up the drive to fetch the newspaper.

The thing is, when I feel that first bite of fall my mind immediately turns to thoughts of the opening of pheasant hunting season in Iowa. At the end of October, it is still a good month and a half away, so I am somewhat previous in my planning. Although the opening weekend is only two and one-half days of actual hunting, it is the anticipation and the preparation that count for nearly as much as the actual hunt.

When the temperature drops below 70° during the day and 60° at night, every wife I know begins lobbying to turn on the furnace. Sweaters come out of closets, and my wife insists she is "freezing". When I calmly remind her she was a bio/physics major and freezing is yet 30° away, she just pouts, glares daggers at me, and turns on the furnace setting it at 68°. Myself, I am far too busy planning my trip to notice or care. To battle the heat I don a t-shirt and begin my preparations for the hunting trip.

Hunting clothes stuffed in bags after the final hunt of the previous year are pulled out and laid out in my gun room. Hunting pants are pulled on. Are they a bit snugger this year? Oh my, time to get out for a bit of exercise. Moving rocks, splitting wood, lifting my small weights to make sure my arms don't get exhausted from lugging a shotgun all day. Next, of course, shells are extracted from the hunting vest and placed back in their proper containers. There are categories and sub-categories. For example, .12-gauge shells are the ones slated for the Iowa trip, appropriate for the wild birds of the open prairie. Same with the .20-gauge shells in the larger shot size. But wait, I have a warm-up hunt at the game farm, so I need to make sure there are plenty of twenty-eights and four-tens. Each shell is sorted according to gauge and shot size, then placed in their specific containers. This exercise is so I don't pack the wrong rounds with the wrong guns for a hunt.

Of course, this annual excavation of antique sporting goods leads inevitably to my shotguns. Are they clean and functioning? Yes, but maybe I should take each one out and clean it again, just in case. Throw them to my shoulder, work the action, and ponder which ones will make the journey this year. Which to the game farm for warm-up? And which to carry in pursuit of the wild Iowa birds? I always take at least two shotguns, often three. If one gun fails, I don't want to risk being a thousand or even a hundred miles from a working shotgun. Without question, the first gun I pack will be my Remington semi-auto in twelve-gauge. It's not even a consideration as it is my best field gun, light and accurate, quick to the shoulder. Oh yeah, it goes to Iowa no doubt. But which second or third gun will go? Should I take the Fox classic double? The little Crescent Arms double in twenty? Or maybe the old break-top single-shot? With the nifty sleeves I have for it, I can shoot shells in either twelve or twenty. Decisions, decisions, this is fun.

OK, my clothes are sorted out and ready to go. Repacked neatly, probably for the first and last time this year. They find their way back into their travel bags and placed back in the gun closet. The guns are clean and functioning. Which will go is a choice that will be mulled over a thousand times before I leave for Iowa. Now it's time to pull everything out of the dog bag. Shooting glasses? Check. Cleaning supplies? Check. Orange raincoat, in case of rain? Check. Knives for cleaning the birds not yet shot? Here I must pause. I have a couple of dozen pocket knives, at least. Some of the knives are decorative, some antique, and some are all business. I separate the ones I think I might use on my hunt and begin to sharpen each one in its turn.

By now (according to my wife) I have wasted enough precious time playing with my toys. When the fall bite comes to visit her, her thoughts turn to putting away lawn furniture and digging up bulbs for winter storage. These activities are not on my agenda, but I will grudgingly participate. After all, she cannot remove the thoughts of dogs and birds and friends from my head, can she? I am happily a thousand miles away in my daydreams while I go about my husbandly duties.

The annual pheasant hunt has been a part of my life since I was old enough to walk. Back in the 1950s and through the 1960s our area held some of the

The road that runs by our farm. It has been paved for many years. Many of the roads that criss-cross the state are still gravel.

best pheasant hunting in the Midwest. As a little boy, I can recall the remote gravel roads of our county becoming a traffic jam for the first two weekends of the opening each year. I can't prove it, but I think I could have found license plates for cars in nearly every state of the union, with the exception of Hawaii and Alaska. Perhaps a bit of an exaggeration, but not by much. My father had many old friends, and they were always afforded land on which to hunt and a hearty welcome when they stopped by the house.

By the time I left home in 1971, the birds had begun to thin out. The farms were being cultivated right up to the roadways. Some farmers even took out their fences to get additional land for row crops, corn, and soybeans. So much cover was lost the birds did not have a proper place to nest and hide from predators and the elements. And when some severe winters and wet springs hit Iowa, the overall pheasant and quail population was severely impacted. By the 1980s no-till farming was being practiced, and the fences and waterways restored. Through the 90s we experienced a nice resurgence of the pheasant population. Unfortunately, the combination of weather and heavy pesticide usage has once again brought the pheasant population in southern Iowa to new lows.

In spite of the warp and woof of life, I always return to my home on the opening weekend of pheasant hunting and again at Thanksgiving or Christmas. It is a place I need to reach out and touch with all my senses, at least once each year. By late October the green grasses of the pastures and ditches take on their fall colors. After a couple of sharp frosts, the greens fade to a wheat-colored brown. The weeds and grasses turn red, yellow and orange hues intermixed with the green foliage that refuses to give up its color. Mother nature paints the countryside with a delicate palette of soft yellows and browns, punctuated with smears and strokes of bright primary colors. The heartland of America becomes an Amish patchwork quilt laid over the rolling hills and gentle valleys, stretching from the Ohio Valley to the eastern slope of the Rockies.

There are as many reasons I return to my hometown each year as there are stars in the vast prairie sky. Habit is one, but that hardly explains my clinging to the ritual like a cocklebur to my dog's tail. The simplest of the many answers is family and friends. A huge part of my identity comes from my upbringing on our little farm in rural Iowa. I have, in life, traveled many miles from the rolling Iowa hills of my youth, both in real miles and intellectually. I return each year because this is where I find my sheltering place. A

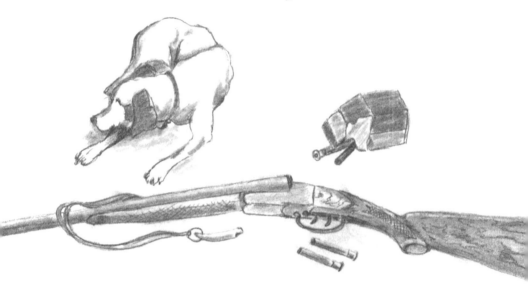

place where my family welcomes me, and my friends gather around me. For a couple of days each year, contrary to the musings of Thomas Wolfe, I do go home again.

Home. Again. I think the idea that we cannot find the home of our youth stems from the fact that so many who leave their homes in their youth do not return for a long time or for any length of time. I have watched, and even in my small way been a part of, the changes in our little community. I am never so far removed that I feel out of place when I return. Even so, as I am of that place, I am no longer there. It is a simple fact.

Friends, of course, have become a magnet for my return. Many, many years ago I would travel back, and as often as not I would hunt alone. Over the years, as we moved from city to city I found kindred souls who deigned to join me on the opening weekend of pheasant hunting. This tradition of friends goes back a long way. One friend, I have been privileged to know since my days in college. Hunting together once a year is the glue that cements our friendship. And, our friendship has stood the test of time.

I have hunted with friends much of my adult life. These men helped rear my son in the hunting field and taught him the basics of hunting and of being a man. I have been pleased to watch him grow from a little boy with a big shotgun, into a grown man interacting with my friends as an adult. We meet once a year and reacquaint ourselves with the rituals of the hunt: laughter, good food, drink, cigars, friendship, and most of all family. Over the years my family has become theirs and their families mine.

Family, of course, is the real reason for returning home each year. The birds are merely a convenient excuse. So very many years ago when I was searching for a way to leave, I was also discovering a way to stay. Season after season I return. Year in and year out I bring old friends and new. I, we, are welcomed, fed, and enormously entertained. There is a warmth about my in-law's home that if one could bottle it, the world would stay intoxicated forever. It is to this island of hospitality I come again. Where I always find my sheltering place.

My family on vacation, Thanksgiving 2016, Santa Fe, NM. Me, Grandpa Howland (Keigh), Karen, Brad, GK, and Grandma Howland (Martha).

Remembering the Round Bale

On a recent drive to our ancestral home passing from city to prairie
Our auto slides past miles of verdant fields of the Midwest breadbasket

Early August, the countryside persists as green as the Emerald Isle
An acknowledgment of plentiful rains and profuse sunshine

Our sojourn sails by a newly shorn field of clover, causing my mind to wander
Wander back to a memorable ritual of my youth

> Strong young men slide off moving trailers, keeping pace with rolling lowboys
> The object of the day, the "round bale," hundreds of them, loaded, stacked, then unloaded

> In this manner we earn our money for cars, clothes, and girls, a time-honored tradition of farm life
> The outfit of the day—t-shirts, jeans, and sneakers, topped by a ball cap with tractor logo

> Each teen totes his personal hay hook like an Old Western gunfighter coveted his guns
> Approach a bale, sink in the hook, lift, and then toss the bundle onto the lowboy

> One-by-one, on each side, the hay is stacked end-to-end until the conveyance will hold no more
> Hop on board for the short ride and try to catch a breeze in Summer's swelter

> Back in the yard, one unloads as the others repair to the hot, dusty barn
> Hay bales travel up the elevator single file and tumble inside, then each is hooked and stacked

> Load in, load out from early morning cool to the scorching heat of summer afternoons
> Lowboys burdened two deep and five high, repeat, repeat until the last bale is stowed

Today the small round bale is in the past, replaced by giant round bales
Huge bundles that weather in the field and no longer need strong young men to help store them

As we pass on through the beautiful blue-sky countryside, I am left to ponder
Today, how do strong young men earn money to spark their girls?
I have no idea

The Impossible Poem

I want to write the impossible poem
a poem whose descriptions match memories
to speak of a drive through rural lands of my youth
breadbasket of America where I dwell, still

It is not far distance-wise
but for those who have not sprung from its soil
it can be a challenge to visualize
one can be told, but until one sees, well…

Driving out of the city, traffic in the rear view
our journey passes from one state to another
today, the land shakes loose its mantel of summer
preparing for fall, once-green crops now sere, ready for harvest

Gliding over concrete paths as if on a magic carpet
casually observing rolling hills, rivers lined with leafy trees
houses, barns, crops hugging the soil, corn, soybeans
pastures populated with cattle, brown, black, white

Colors, myriad colors so challenging to sketch
the many shades of green, broken by weeds, red and brown,
dun crops, trees hinting at their annual transformation
then the sky, the vast beautiful, endless prairie sky

Atop a rise, a panoramic view extends for miles
clouds gather on the horizon casting shadows
portent of rain, then scuttle away replaced by sun
shadows running across the land, an ever-shifting panorama

If you were to travel through, view this for the first time
you might exclaim "how pretty" or even "boring." I have heard it said
but you can not see it from my eyes, the road I have trekked
uncountable times over decades, the journey to and from

These eyes have seen the land in all seasons, all weathers
the vision that is in my eyes is layered
layered with myriad overlays
each frame the same, yet different

Oh how, how can I explain to you that which I cannot?
the drives, the seasons, passing from one home to another
before children after children and now grown and gone
yet, here we are passing through the same land on the same journey

I don't just see buildings, livestock, hills, trees, crops, and colors
my vision is one of generations. Generations before me.
Generations grown and gone
structures fallen, then rebuilt, land finding a new purpose

If you can, come with me on my voyage
hopefully not just once, view the land not merely in your eyes
but see it in your soul look, look, look
then you may understand my search for the impossible poem

My painting of the one room school house that was on our farm. It has long since been
torn down. All that remains is a flat grassy spot, not yet given over to tillage. I attended a
one room school very much like this one for kindergarden and first grade.

About the Author

Photo courtesy B. Calla.

Kēvin (Keevin) Callahan is an award-winning painter, writer, photographer, poet, and sculptor. He works in acrylic, watercolor, wood, photography, fiction/non-fiction, and poetry. His award-winning artwork hangs in collections throughout the United States, and in Canada, Europe, and Israel. His writings include *ROAD MAP- Poems, Paintings & Stuff* (available through Flying Ketchup Press in print and E book), one self-published novel, *Morris' Code*, two anthologies of non-fiction short stories, *A Day Remembered*, stories of his years in the field pursuing upland game. His fictional *Chinese Checkers Run*, is an exciting adventure story of flight and pursuit. All available on Kindle. Kēvin earned a BFA from Drake University in Des Moines, IA, with post-grad work at San Francisco Art Institute, (Larry Abramson) and the Ox-Bow School, Art Institute Chicago, (Phil Hanson/Michelle Grabner). Kēvin currently works and resides with his wife in Parkville, MO and both of his sons are accomplished artists.

For more info contact the author at

kevin@bsfgadv.com

Other Story Collections from Flying Ketchup Press

Tales from the Goldilocks Zone

Tales from the Dream Zone

Tales from the Deep

Stay with Me, Wisconsin by JoAnneh Nagler

This New Job's Murder: The Melody Shore Mysteries by Carole Ann Jones

Pray Like a Woman by Polly Alice McCann

Night Forest: Folk Poetry, Art & Stories

FLYING KETCHUP PRESS ®
KANSAS CITY, MISSOURI

Flying Ketchup Press A Kansas City Publisher for the epic acceleration of great literature, poetry, children's books and fine arts materials. Our mission: to discover and develop diverse voices in poetry, drama, fiction and non-fiction with a special emphasis in new short stories. We are a publisher made by and for creatives with the spirit of the Heartland. Our dream is to salvage lost treasure troves of written and illustrated work- to create worlds of wonder and delight; to share stories. Maybe yours.

Made in the USA
Middletown, DE
01 September 2022

72565688R00117